SHADOW
of the PIPER

Best –
J.P. 16off

SHADOW
of the PIPER

A Novel By
L. P. Hoffman

www.hopespringsmedia.com

THE SHADOW OF THE PIPER
By L. P. Hoffman

www.ShadowOfThePiper.com
www.LPHoffman.com

Scripture taken from the New Living Translation
Copyright © 1996, 2004, 2007. Used by permission of Tyndale House Publishers. All rights reserved.

Published by Hope Springs Media
www.hopespringsmedia.com
P.O. Box 11, Prospect, Virginia 23960-0011
Toll-Free (866) 964-2031 Fax: (434) 574-2130

International Standard Book Number:
978-1-935375-02-9

Printed in the United States of America

Cover and book design by Hope Springs Media and Exodus Design

To the Light that shines in the darkness.

Into the street the Piper stept,
Smiling first a little smile,
As if he knew what magic slept
In his quiet pipe the while

And, like fowls in a farm-yard when barley is scattering,
Out came the children running.

The Mayor was dumb, and the Council stood
As if they were changed into blocks of wood

All the little boys and girls,
With rosy cheeks and flaxen curls,
And sparkling eyes and teeth like pearls,
Tripping and skipping, ran merrily after
The wonderful music with shouting and laughter.

When, lo! as they reached the mountain-side,
A wondrous portal opened wide,
As if a cavern was suddenly hollowed;
And the Piper advanced and the children followed,
And when all were in to the very last,
The door in the mountain-side shut fast. . . .

From THE PIED PIPER OF HAMELIN
by Robert Browning

PROLOGUE

The child hid in the darkness. Above him, the motionless belly of the train creaked and sighed as tons of steel settled in the cool night air. He heard the crunch of gravel. Slow, deliberate steps moved closer. Intuitively, the boy stifled a whimper and drew near the wheels of the train, which still radiated warmth from its long journey.

With his arms and legs drawn up in the fetal position, he tried to listen but could hear only the *thump thump thump* of his own heartbeat. He worried that the sound would give him away. Then, as he feared, a ragged pair of boots stopped beside him. The child's heart beat even faster. His eyes fixed upon feet that were so close he could have reached out and touched them. Suddenly, a cigar littered the ground, scattering embers like fireflies. A glowing coal lit on his knee, but he made no move to brush it off. The boy squeezed his eyes shut and fought the nausea rising in his stomach as a stream of sickening cigar smoke curled around his nose. Mercifully, the feet moved on.

The boy stayed where he was for a few moments, counting softly to ten. Then, like a frightened rabbit, he bolted, neither knowing where he was nor where he was going. Behind him, the thunderous sound of boots on pavement propelled him around a large building and into a black alley. The boy willed his legs to go faster, but his little limbs turned to molasses as the feet behind him closed in.

—◦◦◦—

"So much to be thankful for," Mavis Berry told herself as she lifted her lantern and looked about the cavernous room. Memories of another time lingered like ghosts. She could still imagine racks of colorful clothing, the glint of rhinestone jewelry, and the musky smell of the perfume counter. In the days before shopping malls, everybody in Pittsburgh had shopped at Mayfield Department Store.

On the high ceiling, a ladies' lingerie sign hung askew, an icon of the past. Now the walls were decorated with graffiti left by street-smart Zorros.

Mavis brushed broken glass from the tile floor, unrolled her sleeping bag, and settled down to pray. A gust of wind blew hard against the aged brick building. It whistled through a cracked window, sending a shiver down Mavis's spine. On the other side of the room near an old lunch counter, a rat rustled through a pile of trash. She pulled her rag wool sweater tight around her fleshy shoulders. Even though the prospect of spending the night in the old department store was a bit spooky, nothing could move her from this spot. Tonight was Mavis's first evening in the new home of the Pittsburgh Rescue Mission. Her brown eyes welled with grateful tears when she thought of what the Lord had done.

Earlier in the year, Mavis had gone to city hall to fight an eviction notice served on the building where she had previously cared for the homeless. It hadn't been much—just a warehouse shack on the shanty side of town—but to those who shuffled through life with heavy burdens, it had been a place to find a friendly face and a warm meal.

At city hall, she'd made her charge. "They're out there—folks just like us, except they had a bad turn of events. Some try to drown those feelings in a bottle, but I can see the pain in their eyes." Mavis's ebony hands folded on the podium as she searched for the right word. "Shame," she said. "They carry it with 'em everywhere. They don't even think they deserve to be loved." The room grew silent as all eyes fixed on Mavis. "Can you understand that kind o' despair? They don't believe anyone could love 'em. That's the message they get from this world. But it doesn't have to be that way. Please, you can't take away what little they got."

One of the city councilmen leaned back in his chair and pressed his fingertips together. "Ms. Berry," he said after a few moments, "it's not that we don't want to be charitable here. But the building you occupy is a firetrap. It poses a major safety threat, not only to the people you're trying to help but also to the surrounding buildings. I'm afraid it must be condemned." He straightened some papers on the table. "What's next on the agenda?"

The mayor glanced at the local news cameras, then rose from his seat and moved to Mavis's side. "I would like to say something on behalf of this saintly woman," he announced. "Ms. Berry, your tireless work with the homeless has not gone unnoticed in this community. Quite frankly, we need more fine people like you. I, for one, want to show the city's appreciation by donating a building for your humanitarian endeavors."

An excited rush of whispers passed among the councilmen. "Mayor, what did you have in mind?" a bald man asked, his face pinched in a disapproving scowl. He quickly composed himself as the news cameras shifted his way.

"Well," the mayor pondered, "what about that old Mayfield store? Haven't we been discussing what to do with it since its tax default and forfeiture? I can't think of a better use for that old place. After all, it is located in an area where we have a significant indigent population." He puffed a proud smile for the cameras. "As Mayor of Pittsburgh, I think it's time we let the heart of this city show." He placed his hand on Mavis's soft shoulder and gave her a reflective look. "Ms. Berry has spent her whole life giving to others, and I think it would be unconscionable to throw her out on the street."

After months of legal wrangling and processing permits, the key to the old Mayfield department store had finally been placed in Mavis's hand. It was an answer to prayer, nothing short of a miracle.

Now, in the quiet of the empty building, Mavis gave thanks to the One whose love compelled her. *Ah, Lord God, she thought, there is nothing too difficult for You!* With eyes full of faith, Mavis looked beyond water stains, graffiti, and broken glass and saw only blessings. "A little elbow grease and it'll be a palace."

Mavis dug out her thermos from her backpack. She filled its plastic lid with steaming coffee, raised it to her lips, and then lowered it as a faint whimpering sound met her ear.

Mavis cocked her head to listen. *Maybe a cat.* She heard the sound again, louder now and followed by a gravelly voice. Someone was in trouble! Mavis hoisted her large frame from the floor and said a quick prayer as she pushed open the swinging doors behind the lunch counter.

The cries were coming from outside. Mavis ran to the doorway that led to the alley, threw the bolt, and thrust it open. There, behind the dumpster, a man held a squirming child in one arm. His startled eyes shifted from Mavis to the boy. He pried his sweaty hand from the boy's mouth and snarled, "This ain't yer business, lady. Just a family matter 'tween my boy and me." The man rubbed the stubble on his chin with the shoulder of his shabby coat and shifted the boy in his arms.

Even from where Mavis stood, she could smell the pungent musk of body odor. "Now, you can't lie to me, mister. You just come off the rails, didn't ya?" Mavis approached. She stopped a few yards away and placed her hands on her rotund hips. "I don't believe that child is yours."

"I'm warnin' ya, lady." His voice was harsh and raspy.

Mavis held out her arms. "Give me the child."

With agile swiftness, the man pulled a knife from his boot and held the blade to the boy's throat.

Mavis froze in her tracks as the child dangled in his captor's arms. The boy, no older than five or six, looked at Mavis with wide, pleading eyes. She gave him a reassuring nod before turning her attention back to the man. "Now, why'd you wanna to hurt this little boy? Did somebody once hurt you?" Her tone was smooth and steady. "What you're doin' to this child won't make things any better, now, will it?"

He stood his ground, knife poised, but his bloodshot eyes blinked.

Mavis looked him square in the eye. "In Jesus's name, put that poor child down!"

Abruptly, as if the words sent a shockwave through his body, the man clamored backward and fell, dropping the boy and the knife.

Mavis scooped the child into her arms and kicked the knife away. "You get outta here," she ordered. The man scrambled to his feet and bolted into the darkness. "And don't you ever come back this way!"

Inside the building, Mavis locked the doors and carried the trembling child to her bedroll. She sank to the floor and cradled the boy in her ample arms as his little body quaked with sobs. "Little ones to Him belong; they are weak, but he is strong," Mavis sang softly. "Yes, Jesus loves me, yes, Jesus loves me, yes Jesus loves me, the Bible tells me so."

When the child calmed down some, Mavis offered him her tuna sandwich, and he devoured it like a hungry puppy. Full and warm, the boy yawned and studied Mavis with grateful eyes.

"What's your name, honey?" she asked.

He opened his mouth, but only a strange, guttural stammer escaped his lips.

That's when she noticed the marks on his neck and head. *This child's been beaten!* Mavis reached out to touch the purple markings on his neck, but the boy recoiled. "It's all right, baby," she soothed. "I'm not gonna let anyone hurt you."

In her arms, the child drifted off to sleep, and Mavis

tucked him into her sleeping bag. She sat beside him, listening to the wispy sounds of his breathing. His little fingers coiled snugly around hers and twitched and tightened with his restless dreams. A wellspring of love stirred deep within Mavis's heart. This felt different from her usual sense of compassion; it was much deeper.

Mavis kept vigil throughout the night, praying fervently for wisdom and guidance. *Could it be,* she pondered, *that God has sent one blessing so quickly upon another?*

By the time the first ray of morning light came streaming through the window, she felt a peace settle over her soul. Mavis had no idea what kind of hell this child had experienced in his short life, but she couldn't risk sending him back into that fire. *It'll be tough to bring up the boy myself,* she reasoned, *especially a white child.* Yet Mavis knew that was not a consideration in the Lord's eyes.

A patch of sunlight brushed across the child's face, and he began to stir. With a yawn and a stretch, he opened his sleepy eyes.

"Good morning, little one." She rested her chin in her hands. "You need a good, strong name." Mavis tapped her chin. After a moment, she clapped her hands together. "I know what I'll call you. Jesse! That's a perfect name for such a fine young man. It means 'God exists,' and, honey, you are living proof of that!"

TWENTY YEARS LATER...

CHAPTER 1

Pittsburgh

Cali ducked into the shadows of a brick building as the vagrant paused and looked over his shoulder. He turned in her direction with an expectant look. She stiffened, sure she'd been spotted. To her relief, the factory whistle bellowed, and the old man pulled a bottle from his dirty coat pocket and raised a toast.

"To the suites." He cackled and downed the dregs.

The teenager waited as the vagrant coaxed the last golden drop from the bottle. He tossed it in the dumpster and was on his way again.

Won't be long now, Cali thought as she followed from a distance. A gust of wind picked up a pile of gutter trash and dropped it in a clump at her feet. Bad weather was moving in.

The old man pulled up his collar around his leathery neck and picked up his pace. Once or twice, he stopped, rolled his shoulders beneath the spattering of rain, and glanced back; but Cali was swift and clever, always slipping out of view. Four city blocks later, the hobo reached his destination, the Pittsburgh Rescue Mission.

This has to be it, she told herself, noting the "Jesus Saves" artwork painted across the windows.

The rain came faster, flushing the street dwellers from their hovels. She held back as they scurried for shelter beneath a doorway with a plaque that read Come to Me, All You Who Are Heavy-Laden, And I Will Give You Rest.

Though she had not slept in days, the last thing on Cali's mind as she crossed the street was rest.

The smell of food, mingled with something akin to wet dog, assaulted Cali's senses as she stepped inside the spacious dining room. Dwarfed among the gathering and lost in the rumble of lively conversation, Cali searched the area, squinting under the florescent lights. She did not have to look far.

"Hey, Bruno, how ya doin'?" From the other side of a lunch counter, a young man wearing a wool knit skullcap grinned at the homeless man. "I was beginning to wonder if you'd make it in today. Say, when are you going to pose for one of my charcoal drawings?"

The vagrant shrugged his bony shoulders and flashed a grin, exposing the blackened skeletons of his few remaining teeth. He stepped up for his serving.

From beneath a ledge of black bangs, Cali studied the younger man's face for any resemblance to a photograph taken of him when he was a child. Chestnut hair spilled from beneath his knit cap and rested in unruly waves against his neck. His pale coloring was right but the jaw line had matured. There was a definite family resemblance that brought a chill to her soul. *It has to be him*, she thought. But then he glanced her way.

Cali quickly dropped her gaze. Those warm, gray eyes carried a kindness that matched his smile. It confused her.

When she looked again, the young man was busy filling plates with food.

Behind the counter, two aluminum doors burst open and a huge African-American woman emerged from the kitchen, her arms loaded with a large platter of turkey.

Cali grabbed a tray from a table and fell in behind a lady who was nervously twisting knots in her tattered handkerchiefs. Scarves of silk, satin, and chiffon covered the street urchin's head, the ends dangling like colorful streamers. More scarves were tucked into the waistband of her skirt—plaids, flowers, polka dots, even one with a Southwest pattern.

The line moved like rush-hour traffic, and Cali's fingers twitched in boredom. She reached out and lightly tugged on the woman's western scarf. With every step forward, Cali released it a little more. One last pull, and the scarf came loose. Feeling pleased with herself, Cali quickly shoved it deep into the pocket of her baggy jeans.

The scarf lady stiffened as though some internal alarm had sprung. She whirled around and shrieked, "You took my scarf!"

"I don't know what you're talking about." Cali casually studied the chipped black polish on her fingernails.

"Give it back!" The woman's eyes were wild with indignation.

Cali pointed to her layered turban. "You must need all those scarves to hold your brain in."

"I'll teach you to steal." Scarf lady grabbed Cali by the wrist.

The heavyset woman hurried across the room, waving her big arms in the air. "Now, JuJu, you let go of that child!" she yelled.

"But, Mavis, she took something that belongs to me." She attempted again to extricate the scarf from the teenager's pocket. Cali exploded, biting, clawing, and kicking.

"None of that, now." The large woman wedged her girth between the two and pushed them apart.

"I didn't steal anything!" Cali spat defiantly and took a step back. She felt hot. Adrenaline pumped through her veins like she was a cornered animal. She stood on shaking knees, nervously fiddling with the ring in her eyebrow. Cali's dark gaze darted from behind greasy bangs, looking for an escape.

"Calm down, honey. Ain't nothing that can't be worked out." The woman leaned forward with a smile. "I'm Mavis." Suddenly, her brow wrinkled. "Honey, those dark circles of yours tell me you could use some rest." She touched Cali's cheek. "Darlin', you're burning up with a fever!"

Cali slapped Mavis's hand away. "Don't touch me." She held a finger up in warning. "If you touch me again, you'll be sorry."

The room fell quiet, and all eyes turned her way. Cali felt weak, and her head was spinning. *It wasn't supposed to go like this*, she thought, but for the moment, another plan eluded her. Instinct told her to run. Cali yanked the scarf from her pocket, hurled it to the floor, and dashed from the building into the darkness and the pouring rain.

———

As the evening drew to a close, Jesse stood near the

door holding a box of black garbage bags. "They aren't raincoats, but they'll do in a pinch," he said, handing them out to those who were preparing to venture out into the deluge. Jesse imagined the throngs trudging through the muddy back lot to their makeshift dwellings by the river. Tin City, as it was known.

Mavis stood beside him offering hugs and prayers. She cast an empathetic look Jesse's way. "Remember when the rescue mission was open on cold nights to everyone who could find a space to lay their head?"

Jesse offered the last bag and sunk empty hands into the pockets of his faded jeans. "Fire code regulations," he said. "Back then it seemed the mission was warmed by body heat alone."

"At least the fire marshal still lets us take in a few," Mavis said with a heavy sigh.

After the last person left the building, Jesse helped clear leftovers. He stacked dirty trays onto a cart and rolled them into the kitchen. Mavis seemed unusually pensive. Jesse heard her praying quietly as he rinsed the dishes. "Something on your mind?"

She grabbed a stack of trays and slid them onto a shelf. "That pale girl with the black hair—the one who was fighting with Juju. You ever seen her before?"

Jesse rubbed his chin and thought about it. "Nope."

Mavis's expression fell, and she chewed the inside of her cheek. "That's one sick child, physically and spiritually." She unfastened her apron and hung it on a nail by the pantry.

"I'll ask around while I'm out doing my street ministry."

"You goin' out?" Mavis raised an eyebrow.

Jesse laughed. "I don't think many people will be out on a night like this." He put his arm around her shoulder and they listened to the rain as it steadily fell upon the roof.

Suddenly, Jesse walked to the back door and grabbed a raincoat from a hook.

"What are you doin'?"

"I'm going to go look for that girl." Before Mavis could protest, Jesse stepped out into the alley. The overflow from the swollen gutters ran between the buildings like a small river. Jesse lifted the raincoat's hood over his head, pulled the string tight around his face, and splashed up the alley toward the local teen hangout.

Business was slow at Dino's Pizzeria and Video Arcade. Except for two kids playing the machines, the place was empty.

The slick-haired manager eyed Jesse as he crossed the threshold, sloshing puddles from his tennis shoes. "I'm closing early," he barked.

"I won't be long." Jesse headed toward the kids on the other side of the room. The boy pounded furiously at the video game controls. A few seconds later, he yanked on his dreadlocks and slammed a fist on the Plexiglas. "I need fifty cents."

"I only got two dollars in change left," his girlfriend said, eyeing Jesse.

The boy snatched the coins and fed them into the machine. He threw his whole body into the game as the minutes passed. Finally, the score flashed on the screen and the boy pounded the side of the machine with his fist. "I almost had it this time!" His eyes lit on Jesse.

"Hey, you got a quarter?"

"Sorry."

The young man slung his arm over the girl's shoulder. "So, what's up, Jesse?"

"I'm looking for a girl, about fifteen, maybe sixteen, with longish jet-black hair and a pierced eyebrow. She's new around here."

"You mean that weird chick?" the girlfriend exclaimed. "I seen her around. What a spook."

"Do you know where she is now?" Jesse asked.

"I told her about the Place, but I don't know if she ever found it. I think she's strung out or somethin'. She kinda gave me the creeps."

With mop in hand, the manager mumbled something and flashed the lights to signal closing time.

Jesse stepped back out into the elements. The Place was a block from the railroad tracks in an area that was once largely residential. Now, due to the demand for warehouse space, most of the old apartment buildings stood in ruins, waiting for the wrecking ball. The rooms of one such building housed clusters of teenagers huddled together to ward off cold and loneliness. They were mostly runaways—or throwaways—who were trying to form a family where their own had failed them.

Jesse climbed the fire escape on the side of the building and entered through a broken window on the second floor. The old linoleum was slippery with mud from those who had gone before him. He lost his balance and fell.

From the corner of the dark room, a flashlight clicked

on, blinding Jesse. Before he could climb to his feet, a gun barrel pressed tightly against his cheek.

"One more step and I'll blow your teeth to Philadelphia."

"Hey, it's me, Jesse!" He slipped the hood from his head and wiped rain from his face.

A young man with red hair and freckles giggled nervously. "Sorry, I didn't recognize you."

"No harm done." Jesse picked himself up from the floor.

"It was my turn to stand guard tonight. Guess I fell asleep." The boy smiled sheepishly. "We can never be too careful. Last week a couple hobos from the tracks tried to crash the place. It took ten of us to run 'em out, 'cause Lenny was off somewhere with the iron." He leveled the .38 Special at Jesse.

"Hey, Billy, be careful with that thing," Jesse said as he ducked out of the way.

The young man leaned forward and whispered, "It don't got any bullets, but don't tell nobody." He grinned. "What ya doin' out tonight?"

"I'm looking for someone." Jesse described the girl. "I think she might be sick."

"Yeah, she's here. Up on the third floor in Veronica's room. You'll need a flashlight. I got an extra."

Jesse thanked him and walked down the corridor to the stairwell.

The communal third floor was the heart of the building. With a few old sofas and chairs, the hallway between the doors of the apartments had become a haven to the city's wounded children. Soft light from a few open rooms spilled out into the hallway and lit a path for Jesse. He passed two young boys who were sleeping upright on a small couch. The older boy, middle-school aged, had his arm protectively around a younger one, probably his little brother. Questions rolled through Jesse's mind, some deeply personal. Before moving on, he prayed these kids would find a refuge from whatever they were fleeing.

Near the end of the hallway, the door to Room 337 stood ajar.

Jesse could hear the sound of muffled voices. He knocked softly.

The door opened and a gangly young woman with a blunt, chin-length haircut smiled broadly. "Jesse!" She ushered him inside. "It's great to see you."

He lightly kissed her cheek, then followed her into the living room of the apartment. It was dark because the windows had been buffeted from prying eyes by cardboard boxes taped across the glass.

Veronica fiddled with a lantern, muttering something about low batteries. The room was homey despite the fact that it had been furnished mostly with items salvaged from dumpsters. Except for the artwork. A gallery of talent was displayed on Veronica's walls, including some of Jesse's earlier charcoal drawings. He remembered the name of every social refugee he'd ever drawn.

Veronica stood beside him. "Your pieces are some of my favorites. You always somehow manage to capture their haunted souls."

Jesse quickly changed the subject. "I came out tonight

to look for a teenage girl. She was at the mission earlier this evening and we think she's very sick."

Veronica nodded and gestured toward a closed door. "She's in there. I'm glad you came. I didn't know what to do, 'cause she's in pretty bad shape."

Jesse found the girl mumbling incoherently beneath mounds of blankets. He knelt beside her and put his hand on her forehead. It was almost hot enough to burn. Jesse threw back the covers and picked her up. The girl clenched her jaw and her arms twitched as if the cool air had slapped her. Jesse felt chills convulsing in waves through her body. "I've got to get her to a doctor."

Jesse sent Veronica ahead to call for a cab, then carried the sick girl to a convenience store around the corner. The rain revived her for a moment. She opened her eyes and stared at Jesse. "It's you."

Headlights penetrated the darkness. The cab sliced through the torrent and rolled to a stop. "Hey," the cabby said, looking the girl over. "The kid's not gonna get sick in my cab, is she?

"No," Jesse said, trying to sound reassuring. "But we need to get her to the clinic as soon as possible."

"Let me guess. The free clinic, right?" the cabby asked as he pulled away from the curb. "She better not have AIDS or anything like that." The man glared at Jesse in the rearview mirror. When Jesse didn't answer, he drove faster.

Ten minutes later, the cab pulled up to the curb outside a cinder-block building with windows made of glass brick. "Six bucks," he barked.

"I don't have any cash, but if you'll go to the Pittsburgh

Rescue Mission and tell Mavis Berry that Jesse sent you—"

The cabby let out a mouthful of obscenities. "You and Typhoid Mary get out of my car!"

Jesse apologized as he lifted the young woman out of the cab, but the driver just gestured obscenely and peeled away from the curb.

Inside, the waiting room was long and narrow, with empty rows of institutional chairs upholstered in red vinyl. At the far end of the room, a sleepy-eyed receptionist peeked through a small window. She took one look at the girl in Jesse's arms and called for help.

In a flash, a nurse appeared in the doorway and ushered them to a tiny examining room that smelled of boric acid and rubbing alcohol. Jesse gently laid the girl on an examining table.

The doctor, a short, boxy Asian gentleman in his early fifties, entered. As he gathered the girl's vital information, she drifted in and out of delirium.

The nurse gasped when she looked at the digital thermometer. "Doctor, her temperature is 105," she whispered.

"Prepare this young woman for a thorough exam." The doctor turned to Jesse. "Young man, you will have to leave."

In the waiting room, Jesse thumbed through the forms that the receptionist had given him to fill out. It occurred to him that he did not even know this girl's name. Everything had happened so fast. He had not thought to ask Veronica if she knew anything about her.

Jesse set the clipboard aside, rose to his feet, and paced under a flickering florescent light. Above the receptionist's station, a wall clock ticked yet never seemed to change. After what seemed like hours, the door leading to the examining rooms opened. The nurse motioned to Jesse. "Would you come this way, please?" She directed him to a tiny room at the end of the hallway and pointed to a chair wedged between a cluttered desk and an overloaded bookcase. "The doctor will be with you shortly."

Jesse looked at the diplomas and certificates that hung on the wall behind the desk until the doctor came in. The man sat at his desk and cleared his throat. A minute slipped by while the physician rubbed a spot on his temple. Finally, he leaned forward and looked solemnly at Jesse. "She has a very serious problem, a severe systemic infection."

"Is she going to be all right?"

The physician shrugged, then looked down at his small hands. "We are giving her a powerful intravenous antibiotic, but to be honest her prognosis does not look good. I called the hospital. They're sending an ambulance to transport her there."

"Could she die?" Jesse blinked and swallowed hard.

"I see this every day," the doctor snorted. "You young people think you're invincible." He stood and shook his finger at Jesse. "She should have seen a doctor months ago. She's had the worst postnatal care I've ever seen. A piece of the placenta was left in her uterus and it caused an infection. You could end up raising the baby alone!"

"Baby?" Jesse pushed himself up from the chair. "What are you talking about? This girl was sick and I brought her here, that's all. I don't even know her name."

The doctor sucked in a sharp breath and his eyes grew

wide. "I apologize. I assumed, since you brought her in. . . ." The doctor lowered his head and the room grew quiet. "All we can do is wait."

"And pray," Jesse added.

The physician looked tired. Disco uragement etched deep into his features.

"It couldn't hurt," he said, as the ambulance attendants arrived to take Cali away.

CHAPTER 2

Things moved fast in the hospital emergency room. A group of doctors and nurses swarmed around the teenage girl like bees while the receptionist asked Jesse questions he could not answer.

After determining that the girl was in critical condition, the doctors moved her to the intensive care unit.

Jesse made a quick call to Mavis to explain the situation. "She could die. Only immediate family are allowed in. The doctors got her name—Cali—but that's all I know about her."

Alone now in the waiting room, Jesse dropped into an uncomfortable chair, massaged a stubborn kink in his neck, and leaned back. He felt chilled from the damp and bone-tired but had made up his mind to stay until the mystery girl was out of danger. Jesse felt strangely protective of her. "Lord," he whispered, "You understand the situation better than anyone because there's nothing hidden from You. Please help Cali."

An hour passed slowly. Jesse felt himself getting sleepy and closed his eyes. Blood-red cliffs rose on either side of him, too steep to climb. He was desperate to escape. The shadow closed in.

"Wake up, baby."

Jesse lunged from his seat with a jerk. Blood was pumping hard through his veins.

Mavis was standing in front of him, her expression flooded with empathy. "It was that dream again? Wasn't it?"

Jesse wiped a mist of sweat from his forehead. "What are you doing here?"

"Thought you might need some dry clothes," Mavis said.

She waited respectfully as a hospital chaplain read to a distraught elderly woman. "Yea, though I walk through the valley of the shadow of death, I will fear no evil, for thou art with me."

"Besides, I also thought you could use some company," Mavis said. "How about some coffee?"

"If you're buying," Jesse said. "Oh, that reminds me— I owe the Yellow Cab Company some money."

"I'll take care of it." she assured him.

They walked together down the hallway to the coffee machine. Mavis handed Jesse a plastic grocery bag and directed him to a restroom. "Go change out of those wet things. When you come out, there'll be a nice hot cup of coffee waitin' for you."

As Jesse stepped into the restroom, he thanked God for Mavis and wondered what his life would have been like without her. She had told him of the fated night when she'd found him, but Jesse carried only one memory from that time: the sound of rails clacking beneath the boxcar. He had come on a train, but from where? The question raised others. . . .

Jesse pulled on a pair of clean, dry jeans and a t-shirt, then stuffed the wet clothes into the plastic bag and joined Mavis near the vending machines. She handed him a Styrofoam cup.

He took a seat beside Mavis and stared at the swirl of steam rising from the coffee. "I've been thinking about the night you found me. How come you didn't you notify the authorities?"

Mavis looked at Jesse with resolve. "That was a long time ago, baby. You sure you want to dredge this up again?"

He waited.

"I just followed my heart," Mavis sighed. "I got no regrets, 'cause my heart told me that you were running from something evil."

CHAPTER 3

From her bed in the ICU, Cali listened to the morning shift change at the nearby nurse's station.

"The coronary in Room 324 make it through the night?" the incoming nurse inquired without a hint of emotion.

"A stroke came in around 1:00 AM," the other nurse said flatly.

Cali heard the rustle of paper.

"What else?"

"Let's see, one automobile accident. Doesn't look good—head injury. We're also treating a uterine infection. That girl has serious issues."

Cali strained her ear, but the nurse dropped her voice to a whisper.

In the hallway, the breakfast cart squeaked to a stop. A kitchen worker read the order on the door, then entered the room with a tray of tasteless broth and cherry Jell-O.

"You expect me to eat this slop?"

The woman offered a lazy shrug. "I don't make the rules around here." She straightened her hairnet and sauntered away.

Cali opened the Jell-O cup, dumped it into her hand, and squeezed it through her fingers, stifling a giggle. She rubbed the red slush onto her pillowcase and laid her head beside it.

When a nurse entered the room, Cali gurgled, "Help me." Her eyes fluttered weakly.

The nurse gasped. "Oh, mercy!" She flew to Cali's side to assess the situation. Her face flushed with anger when the teenager burst into eerie staccato laughter.

"Young lady," the nurse barked, "we've got better things to do than put up with your shenanigans!"

Cali felt the muscles in her body tense. *She yelled at me.* Familiar rage tingled up her spine and pulsed through Cali's fingers. Her gaze locked on the woman like a missile.

The nurse took a cautious step backwards.

Without blinking, Cali reached for her broth and poured it on the floor.

"Oh, that's great." The high-pitched tone of the woman's voice betrayed her unease. "Now we need to clean up two messes."

Was that fear in her eyes? Cali felt a measure of satisfaction.

In the hallway, she heard hushed words and caught glimpses of other staff as they scurried past to sneak a peek. *Show time!*

She lobbed her catheter bag like a water balloon and ripped the IV from her arm. Blood trickled from her veins and she smeared it over her skin like lotion.

By the time security arrived, Cali was crouched in the corner, with psych ward reps circling her like buzzards.

A tall man in a white coat knelt beside her. "We're here to help you."

A precocious grin tugged the corners of Cali's mouth. "I've been bad," she said contritely, "but that nurse threatened me."

"I did no such thing!"

The psychiatrist silenced the nurse's protest with a motion and turned back to Cali. "Illness can sometimes cloud our thinking. You've already been through a lot. I promise nobody's going to hurt you. Do you understand?"

Cali nodded and milked out a couple of tears.

The psychiatrist stood. "Get our patient cleaned up and the IV going again," he ordered, then tossed a patronizing glance at Cali. "I'll be back in a little while to talk with you."

After some animated discussion in the hallway, a brave nurse volunteered to reinsert the IV and catheter. Through it all, Cali lay passively on the bed and stared out the window.

———

Cali looked around the hospital room, drab except for a bright orange stripe painted on the wall. An uncomfortable-looking chair faced a TV anchored in the corner near the ceiling. She watched the orderly preparing one of the beds for her. He was a black man, probably in his late sixties. He hummed an old blues tune as he fluffed the pillow.

"There ya go, little lady," the orderly said in a sandpaper voice. "It's all ready for ya. I'll just buzz the nurse." He smiled, but she could sense a tense reserve. No doubt, the staff had been talking.

"I am not getting back in that bed," she growled, low and ominous like a threatened cat. "I'm not staying in this place."

The old man leaned forward and offered to help her from the wheelchair. His hand shook slightly. "Now, I don't want any trouble. I'm just doin' my job."

Cali grabbed the orderly's outstretched hand and dug into his flesh with her fingernails. She laughed. "How do you like being forced?"

The orderly grimaced in pain. "Please! I ain't done nothin' to you."

An aide appeared in the doorway, then hurried off to summon help.

Cali released her grip from the old man's hand.

The orderly drew it to his chest and cradled it with his other hand as the doctor rushed in. "She made me bleed!"

The head nurse motioned toward the door and called to one of her underlings to clean and bandage the man's wound.

From beneath the fringe of her long black bangs, Cali watched with amusement.

———

When the doctor walked into the hospital room, Cali was sitting quietly in her wheelchair. "Now, what seems to be the problem?" He stopped a respectable distance from his patient.

Cali caught the look that he flicked to the nurse standing nearby. She loathed him for it, but her face remained stiff. "I'm sorry." She punctuated her apology with a sweet smile. The nurse frowned skeptically. "I'm feeling much better, so I don't see any reason to stay in the hospital."

"I think you should stay for at least another night. You had a surgical procedure called a D&C. You're recovering from one of the worst infections I have ever seen, and it is not to be taken lightly."

"I apologize for all the inconvenience I've caused and especially for getting so emotional this morning. But I really want to check out now. You can give me some pills to take. I promise I'll be a good girl and take them all."

The doctor's stringy eyebrows furrowed. "One more night," he said. "We'll decide tomorrow morning if you're ready to leave."

"You can't make me stay here!" Tremors of rage rumbled beneath Cali's flesh.

"Are you refusing treatment?"

"Yes."

The doctor studied her for a moment. "How old are you?"

"Twenty-one!" Cali jutted her chin forward in defiance.

The doctor pursed his lips. "Try again."

"Are you calling me a liar?" She bowed her neck. "This is your lucky day, Doc, because if I was underage my parents would sue you for treating me without their consent." Cali stood and leaned close to his face.

He leaned back. "Young lady, I suggest you get in that bed right now. If you cooperate, then I will consider your request. If you refuse, I'll have you transferred to the sixth floor for a psychiatric evaluation."

Cali climbed into the freshly made bed like a docile

kitten. She started to cry, just a little. "I'm so sorry. I never meant to treat you all so terribly," she whined. "I just want my baby. My baby."

The physician and nurses left the room.

Out in the hallway, Cali heard the doctor questioning a nurse. "What do you know about her infant?"

The response was terse. "My job is to see that the patient gets proper medical care. I'm not a social worker."

"I'm just trying to find a way to help this girl," the doctor said.

"This is the first time she's even mentioned a baby. All we know about this girl is what she chooses to tell us, for all that's worth."

"She needs counseling, but I don't think she's ill enough to be committed." There was a long pause, then Cali heard the physician sigh. "All right, get the patient ready to leave. I'll sign the release forms."

I won this round, Cali thought, but something told her that the games that lay ahead would not be so easy.

CHAPTER 4

Jesse stood beside Mavis at the nurse's station trying to make eye contact with a young nurse. He waved his hand to get her attention but she was busy filling little cups with pills.

Mavis loudly cleared her throat.

The young woman looked up. "I'm sorry. I didn't see you there." Then she added shyly, "Can I help you?"

"We'd like to visit the young woman who was moved up here an hour or so ago," Mavis said.

"I think her name is Cali," Jesse added.

The aide thumbed through some papers on the counter. "I don't see anyone by that name."

"Are you sure? Please check again," he urged.

The woman double-checked. "No," she said firmly, "she's not here."

Mavis patted Jesse's hand to calm him. "Maybe we got the girl's name wrong."

"There's a Cathy in Room 210."

"That could be her," Jesse said.

"Automobile accident?" the aide asked eagerly.

Jesse and Mavis both shook their heads.

"Do we have a problem here?" An older woman marched into the nurses' station. She dismissed the aide with a glance, then turned to Mavis and Jesse. "I'm the head nurse. Can I help?"

"We're looking for a girl," Jesse explained. "She was just transferred from the ICU. We think her name is Cali."

"She was released." The nurse snapped her wrist officiously and looked at her watch. "About twenty minutes ago."

"Do you know where she was going?" Jesse asked.

The nurse adjusted a comb in her silver hair. "You might check in the billing office. Your friend would have been asked to fill out papers for the state."

Jesse headed for the stairwell. "I'm going to look for her!" He blew out of the doors at the bottom of the stairs and bolted for the main lobby, skidding to a stop beside an orderly pushing an empty wheelchair. "Excuse me—did you just bring a young girl downstairs?" Jesse offered a brief description.

"Sure did—can't say I was sorry to see her go." The orderly grimaced, then sheepishly added, "Sorry, no offense intended if she's your kin."

"Where is she?"

"Out that door. That's all I know."

Jesse saw no sign of the teenager out front. Up the street to the right, he noticed a shaded bus stop, but the bench was empty except for a magazine fluttering open in the breeze. Across the street, Jesse saw a young man pushing a little boy in a wheelchair through the parking lot, two smaller kids giggling behind them and running to catch up.

Jesse searched for Cali's pallid face among the people ambling through the maze of cars. A strange, prickly sensation crawled across the back of his neck, and he spun around. There on a concrete bench beside the door sat Cali with her head bent back against the wall.

Cali studied him through half-closed eyelids. "What took you so long?" She ran her tongue over her teeth, revealing a silver stud.

"How do you feel?" Jesse sat next to girl. "You've been pretty sick. Are you sure you're doing the right thing checking yourself out?"

"What are you? My mother or something?"

After a clumsy silence, Jesse spoke. "What are you gonna do now?"

She shrugged. "I don't know. Maybe I'll jet over to the French Riviera and soak up some rays. Or check into a health spa. Oh, yeah." She rattled a bottle of pills in her hand. "I mustn't forget to take my pills three times a day like the good doc ordered."

"I'm serious, Cali."

She picked at a hole on the knee of her jeans. It ripped. Her eyes darkened. "I'll probably go back to the Place and do a little time with Mother Superior. Maybe I'll let her sermonize at me until I'm back on my feet."

"Child, you'll do no such thing," Mavis announced as she stepped through the entryway. "You're coming with us and I won't take no for an answer. We need to get some good food in you, girl, and build up your strength."

Cali drew her hands to the side of her face and spread her fingers. "Oh, yessa, masta," she mocked.

Mavis bent down and leaned close to Cali's face. "You listen to me, girl," she said firmly. "I have a few rules that we'd better get straight between us right now."

Cali seemed stunned by the formidable woman.

"At the mission, we do unto others as we want them to do unto us, and that includes respect. If you can't adjust your attitude enough to get along, well, then I guess you'll be on your own."

Cali's mouth fell open, but no words rolled out.

Mavis patted her hand. "I think we understand each other now. The door is open, honey. It's up to you."

"I'm ready to go." Cali stood, but her legs seemed unsteady.

As the three of them walked to the bus stop, Jesse watched Mavis. Her lips were tight, her face pointed down, and her steps were quick and pensive.

They didn't talk much on the ride to the mission. Cali rested her head against the cool glass of the bus window, her hands limp in her lap. Her unblinking eyes seemed fixed on some unseen object.

Jesse's heart ached with compassion. Was it sadness he saw in this girl's hardened features? Or desperation? He wondered if he'd ever find out.

———

At the mission, Jesse tried to make their new guest feel welcome. "Would you like something to drink? A Coke maybe?" Cali sunk her hands sunk deep into the pockets of her jeans and shrugged a stiff shoulder, then dropped into a soft chair.

"Child, you look as pale as a bucket of milk." Mavis turned to Jesse. "Why don't you show Cali where she'll be staying?" Mavis pushed up her sleeves. "If anyone's gonna eat dinner here tonight, I'd better take those big pots of soup outta the fridge."

Jesse led Cali through the dining room and up a flight of wide stairs, then down a long corridor. "These rooms were once offices, so they don't have restrooms. There's one just up the hall if you need it." He opened a door and waited for Cali to pass through. Two rollaway beds and three cots lined the room's bare walls. From a cloudy window, sunlight spilled upon worn linoleum.

"It's stuffy in here," the girl whined. "Does this thing open?"

Jesse tugged on the rusted window latch and got it open a couple of inches. "That's the best I can do."

"Thanks."

"This is your bed." He bent down and straightened the plain wool blanket on an old army cot. "I'm sorry we don't have a bed with a mattress for you. They're already spoken for. I hope you'll be comfortable anyway."

Cali shifted her weight from one foot to another. Jesse turned to walk out the door.

"What's the game here?" Cali snapped.

Jesse looked over his shoulder. "Excuse me?"

The teenager parked her hands on her hips and narrowed her eyes. "You don't fool me. You got some kinda racket goin' on here, right? I mean, it's gotta take money to run a place like this. So what's the catch? Prostitution, drugs, what?"

Jesse laughed. "You're joking, right?"

She stared at him. "If I've learned one lesson in this world, it's that nobody gives somethin' for nothin'."

Jesse felt a surge of pity for this girl, whose cynicism had ripened at an early age. "You're wrong. There's nothing illegal going on here. The mission operates through charitable contributions. It has never run at a profit—probably never will." His words came gently. He searched her face in earnest. "Cali, there are people who give, not because they want something in return, but because they care. They serve others out of love and compassion." Sadness and despair seemed to blanket the room. "Why is it so hard for you to believe that anyone would want to help you out of kindness?"

The girl raked her shirtsleeve across misty eyes and set her jaw stubbornly.

"We don't want anything from you, Cali. But we do hope you will come to realize how much God loves you."

"Yeah, right." She threw herself across the cot. "I'm so tired." Cali's words trailed off.

"Of course you are," Jesse said. "You get some rest." He backed out the door and quietly closed it behind him. He had seen many troubled kids, but, somehow, this one was different.

—◦◦◦—

Down in the kitchen, Jesse found Mavis chopping carrots for a big pot of stew. From the corner of the room, gospel music issued from a cheap boom box, but Mavis was not singing along as she usually did.

"Smells good," Jesse said, reaching over her shoulder to sneak a piece of carrot. "Where did we get all the fresh vegetables?"

"I arranged for donations from a local grocery chain. From now on, we'll get all the slightly old vegetables they used to throw away." Mavis slapped Jesse's hand as he reached for another carrot. "Are you here to work or eat?"

Jesse grabbed his apron and baseball cap from a hook and washed his hands. "I can't help myself." He took a spoon from the drawer and sampled the soup. "Mavis, you've done it again."

She waved him away. "Get outta here. But don't go empty-handed." Mavis pointed to the pot of soup. "I'll get the rolls out of the oven."

Jesse carried the huge pot into the dining room. Mavis trailed behind with a huge batch of oven-fresh rolls. Before she could even dip the ladle into the steaming kettle, a long line began to form.

Mavis offered a blessing. "Thank You, Father God, for all that you provide. Bless this food and each person here, and those who could not be with us tonight." She paused. "And one more thing. Help us to be mindful of you in our daily lives. Amen."

As Mavis dished up bowls of soup and passed them off to waiting hands, she leaned close to Jesse. "Why don't you take dinner to Cali?"

Jesse filled a bowl, set it on a tray with a glass of milk, and climbed up the stairs.

He rapped on the door, but there was no response. Balancing the tray in one hand, Jesse turned the knob and went inside.

Cali lay motionless on the cot. Her eyes were closed.

"You asleep?" A cacophony of city sounds spilled through the open window—an ambulance, a police car, a drunk yelling obscenities.

With tray in hand, he stepped closer. A floorboard groaned.

Cali opened her eyes.

"I thought you might be hungry." Jesse set the plate on an old coffee table next to the cot. "How are you feeling?"

"I'm thirsty."

"I brought milk." He handed it to her.

She took it reluctantly. "Not exactly what I had in mind, but it'll do." Cali slipped a bottle of pills from her pocket, popped one in her mouth, and sucked her milk down like a greedy child.

Jesse backed toward the door. "If there's anything we can do for you, just let us know."

"Please don't leave. I don't want to be alone right now."

"I'd like to stay, but Mavis needs my help downstairs." Jesse felt uneasy. "We'll both come back up after dinner to check on you."

Cali's features softened and she bit her lip.

"It shouldn't be too long," he reassured her.

Suddenly, the teenager spilled from her cot and sprawled on the floor at Jesse's feet. "Please don't leave." Cali grabbed his ankle and clung fiercely.

Jesse felt her fingernails digging into his ankle. "I'll stay for a few minutes—just let go."

"Promise?" Cali relaxed her grip.

"Yes."

She released him and sat cross-legged on the floor, her hands folded calmly on her lap.

Jesse sat next to her, trying to gather his thoughts. He'd counseled countless people over the years, but this girl was like an untethered balloon in a windstorm. Jesse was at a loss for words.

Cali fixed her gaze upon him. "You know, don't you?" Her eyes were so intense they seemed as if they had probed into his soul.

A tiny alarm sounded inside of Jesse, and he fought the urge to spring to his feet and hurry for the door.

"You're the only person who can help me."

"Lots of people can help you," Jesse said carefully. "You just need to give them a chance."

"Do you think it was an accident that I showed up here?" Cali's words sounded strange and throaty. "I came looking for you."

"But you don't even know me." Jesse's heart began to pound. "Do you?"

She picked at some loose skin on her cuticle. "My baby girl was stolen from me." Cali made her finger bleed and sucked on her wound. "They said she died. I know better." Cali hummed a vaguely familiar tune, drew her knees to her chest, and rocked rhythmically on the hard, cold floor.

You're in over your head, Jesse told himself. "Who took your baby? Cali?" But the girl had retreated to someplace within her mind.

CHAPTER 5

In the first morning light, Jesse awoke with a start. His blanket lay in a twisted heap next to the bed. Beads of sweat soaked his face—the dream again. Recollections floated past and vaporized like formless shadows.

He clenched his fist in frustration and turned toward the window. A faint glow of sunrise dusted his room. Jesse sat up and looked at his watch. The time was a quarter to six. He rose and dressed quickly in jeans and a flannel shirt. He raked a wide-toothed comb through his wavy hair, slipped on a wool cap, and then went downstairs to make a pot of coffee.

Jesse was startled to find Cali sprawled in a chair by the back door of the kitchen. Her hair was a tangled mess and she wore the same clothes she'd had on the day before.

"What are you doing down here so early?" Jesse asked.

She shrugged. "Same thing as you, I guess."

"How are you feeling this morning?"

Cali rose and walked over to him. There was a lilt in her step that seemed strangely incongruous with the sallow skin and purple circles under Cali's eyes. "I feel fantastic!" she said. "In fact, I feel good enough to travel."

Jesse raised an eyebrow.

"I'm leaving today. Why don't you come with me?"

"Where are you going?"

"That's for me to know and you to find out," she said in a singsong fashion.

"I don't want to play games, Cali."

The girl stepped closer to Jesse, her eyes wide and pleading. "You'll help me, won't you, Nathaniel?"

Jesse drew a sharp breath. He felt blood throbbing through his temples. "Why did you call me that?"

A Cheshire-cat smile spread across Cali's lips. Her eyes narrowed. "Come with me and you'll find out."

—⁓—

Jesse laid his hand on Mavis's arm. "We need to talk."

Mavis glanced at the duffel bag lying at Jesse's feet, then grabbed her apron, threw it over her head, and turned away. "Would you tie this for me? It seems I'm gettin' bigger around every day!"

Jesse fastened her apron, feeling the tension in her back. "Mavis, I have to leave," he said softly.

Her shoulders slumped.

Jesse put his arms around Mavis. "You know how much I appreciate everything you've done for me, but I'm leaving with Cali."

"You don't even know this girl. Why would you go with her?" Mavis wiped her eyes with the apron.

Jesse poured two cups of coffee and carried them to a little drop-leaf table by the coat rack.

"Cali said she came here looking for me. I think she knows something about my past."

"You believe that?" Mavis studied Jesse's face.

He struggled for the right words to make her understand. "I know it seems crazy, but I feel this incredible peace, like the Lord is leading me."

Mavis blew steam from her coffee. "You've never been impulsive. I've always known God had something special in mind for you, and yet . . . ."

"What?"

"Be careful who you trust." Mavis set her coffee cup on the table and touched Jesse's hand. "Especially that girl."

As if summoned, Cali poked her head through the door. "What's takin' so long?"

Mavis struggled to her feet and walked over to Cali. "Where are you going with Jesse?"

"Why, down the Yellow Brick Road, of course."

"Child, that smart mouth of yours is gonna land you in trouble some day if it hasn't already." Mavis looked back at Jesse as if imploring him to stay.

"I'll call you soon," he reassured. "I promise."

Mavis faced Cali again. "Just how do you plan to get where you are going?"

"I've got a car," she chirped. "It's at the industrial plant parking lot down the street." Cali threw her arms up in exasperation. "Jesse, you coming with me or not?"

"Wait!" Mavis raised her arm like a crossing guard and moved across the kitchen to rustle through a cluttered drawer. A few moments later, Mavis found what she was seeking. She hurried back to Jesse with a folder in her hand. "I want you to have this."

Jesse opened the folder and thumbed through its contents. "I can't believe you saved all these," he said.

"Every drawing you ever did," she said with a nod. "Had to fish some of them out the trash can."

"But why?" Jesse pulled a childish drawing from the collection and laughed. "Most of these don't deserve a second look."

"I wouldn't be too sure." Mavis locked eyes with Jesse. "Some of the things you drew as a little guy were pretty interesting. Like this one." She put her finger on a piece of wide-rule notebook paper and slid it from the stack. It was a rough pencil drawing of a brick building with an unusual jagged roofline. "There's no building like this around here. Think about it."

"This is very touching," Cali said in a mocking tone, "but can we be dismissed from kindergarten class?" She crossed her arms and tapped her foot on the floor.

Jesse kissed Mavis's cheek and turned to go, but she stopped him once more, this time to press some money into his hand. Her firm look cautioned Jesse not to protest.

"Call me," Mavis said as he slipped out the door with Cali.

Beneath the cloudless autumn sky, the pair walked toward the factory parking lot without exchanging a word. It wasn't hard to spot Cali's car, which looked like an abandoned junker. She hurried to her Subaru wagon and brushed her hand over spots of gray primer as if it were a pony. Cali stooped to reach inside the wheel well. She retrieved a key and tossed it to Jesse. After noting the

Montana license plate, he unlocked the trunk and, brushing aside logic, threw the duffel bag inside.

CHAPTER 6

Hamlin, Montana

"I hope the highway to Kingston isn't slick. My tires are bald," Roxanne Volcovich said, pushing open the rusty iron gate.

April trailed behind as they approached Mrs. Crabtree's old Victorian house. "Why did it have to snow today of all days?"

Roxanne sensed her best friend's apprehension. "Relax," she said, brushing powdery flakes from her jacket. "It's only the first snow of the season. I'm sure the road will be fine."

"Why couldn't we live in Florida or Southern California?"

Roxanne cast a playful look over her shoulder. "Somebody's got to live here."

April stopped in her tracks and motioned toward the bay window. Through the leaded glass window they watched an old lady dancing. The woman twirled about as if she were waltzing with an invisible partner waving her hands in the air. April flipped her blonde hair over her shoulder and scowled disapprovingly. "She looks like she's pretending to be a tree or something."

Roxanne giggled. "That's just Mrs. Crabtree. She's cool."

"I've heard stories about her. Like once, when J. C. Penney was having a white sale, she started dancing right in the middle of the store."

"It must have been a great sale!"

"You're impossible, Roxie."

"Yeah, but you're still my friend, right?"

"Well, somebody has to be," April teased.

Roxanne hurried up the weathered wooden steps. "You coming?"

"I'll stay here," April said from the base of the porch.

Roxanne knocked on the door, trying to decide whether the house was dirty white or beige. It had been so long since the place had seen a coat of paint that it was hard to tell.

The door swung open and Mrs. Crabtree stepped onto the porch to collect some hugs.

"Oh, how I needed that!" The old woman put her hands on Roxanne's shoulders and studied the girl's face. "Something's wrong. What is it, honey? Is it your papa?"

Roxanne forced a smile and shifted her weight to the other foot. "Nothing's the matter, Mrs. Crabtree. Really." She felt a sting and was certain the old woman knew.

"I bought some Red Zinger tea. Come on in and have a cup." Mrs. Crabtree spotted April, who was loitering at the gate. "You're welcome, too, young lady."

Roxanne cleared her throat and held up her hand. "Actually, I just came by to tell you I can't clean house for you today. Something came up. May I do it tomorrow instead?"

A compassionate smile folded across the old woman's wrinkled face. She took Roxanne's hand and patted it. "Of course, dear. Come whenever you're able. I'll pray for your safe travels." Her faded blue eyes turned to April. "God's will be done."

"Thank you, Mrs. Crabtree," Roxanne called. "I'll see you tomorrow after school."

The girls waved goodbye, then hurried over to their little green Volkswagen.

"What did she mean, 'I'll pray for your safe travels'?" April asked.

Roxanne shrugged. "I don't know." She crossed her heart. "I swear, I never told anyone we were driving to Kingston."

April wrinkled her nose. "Is Mrs. Crabtree psychic or something?"

Roxanne jumped behind the wheel of the Volkswagen and turned the key. "I don't think so. She doesn't believe in that kind of stuff." She dropped it in gear and pulled away from the curb. "Theda Mae says God uses her to pray for people, and sometimes He tells her what to pray."

"God talks to her?" April searched for the classic rock station on the car's radio. "I think the woman's wacko!"

Roxanne grabbed her sunglasses from the dashboard and slipped them on. "How about a Coke and some fries for the road?" she asked, steering her car into a McDonald's drive-through.

Roxanne placed her order. When the food came, she

handed April a drink. April was slumped in the passenger seat looking pale and defeated. "It'll all be over soon."

April grew quiet as they turned down the highway toward Kingston. "Roxie, stop the car. I'm gonna be sick!"

Roxanne slammed on the brakes and pulled onto the shoulder. April opened the door and nearly fell onto the gravel.

When she finished heaving, April closed the car door and laid her head back against the seat.

Roxanne handed her a wad of Kleenex. "April, if this is what it's like to be pregnant, it's a wonder anyone is ever born."

April began to sob.

"I'm sorry," Roxanne said, pushing back her own swell of tears. "I didn't mean to upset you."

"I'm all right." April flipped the visor down and looked in the mirror. "Let's just go." She blotted her mascara with the tissue.

They traveled without exchanging a word. April turned the radio volume up and rolled her window down.

Roxanne gripped the wheel. *It'll take more than loud music to chase these troubles away,* she thought.

Beneath a light flurry of snow, Ozmand Wright and his friend Rudy sauntered across the brittle, dormant grass of the city park to the log shelter. On warm summer evenings, its structure housed town meetings, charity bake sales, or old folks swaying to the Elks Club band; when the cool northern air arrived and the days grew shorter, though, the city park changed hands.

The usual group of teenage boys was sprawled beneath the shelter. Despite slight variations in hair and clothing, they all exhibited the same restless spirit.

"Look who's here," someone said. "It's Rudy and Oz!"

Rob Hall looked like a dragon as he blew streams of smoke through his big nostrils. He launched his smoldering cigarette butt in the air. "Where were you guys today?" He spun the wheels of his beat-up skateboard with dirty fingers.

Rudy lit a cigarette of his own. He flipped his straight, dark hair from his face and blew a smoke ring.

Beside him, Ozmand tugged down the bill of his painter's cap, trying to conceal a grim outbreak of acne.

"Rob wants to know where we were today," Rudy snickered.

"Weren't we at school?" Ozmand said with feigned innocence.

Rudy watched over the top of his mirrored sunglasses as a smoke ring landed on his finger. "Did you guys see that?" All heads nodded.

"I'm serious," Rob continued. "This morning when Tina was in the principal's office she saw your names on the truant list. And she heard the principal say there's not going to be a next time."

Rudy put the back of his hand to his forehead and gasped. "I think I'm going to faint!" His eyes rolled back with a flutter and he sprawled on the cement floor, waiting for the laughter. None came.

In the doorway of the log shelter, Cyrus stood, a look of

disgust upon his face.

Ozmand wondered how long Cyrus had been there. He cast an uneasy look toward Rudy, silently imploring his childhood friend to behave himself.

Cyrus flipped his skateboard onto the shelter's slab and steadied it with his street shoes. As he launched out on his wheels, a swath of bleached white hair floated like a feather on the side of his buzzed head. Cyrus did a 360 flip as though it was easy, working his usual magic.

Cyrus had arrived in town nearly two years earlier, yet no one had ever had the nerve to ask him where he'd come from or why he had chosen Hamlin to park his skateboard. Maybe it was the appeal of the hilly, winding roads of this old mining town. Cyrus's past, like his age, was a mystery. Still, there was no denying that this maverick was a skateboard master.

Ozmand's respect for Cyrus ran deep, just as the others' did—with the exception of Rudy.

Cyrus capped his exhibition with a combination of an ollie and a spinning maneuver. In midair, he wrapped the board around his back foot, then caught the board with his other foot and performed a perfect landing.

"An Ollie Impossible!" The crowd thundered their approval.

Cyrus basked in the adulation before selecting one of his dutiful subjects, a scrawny, wide-eyed kid called Spider. "Here, hold this." Cyrus tilted his board and shot it out from under his feet, sending it flying through the air.

Spider caught the projectile in the stomach.

Rudy clapped, slow and loud. "The great Cyrus is out

among the little people. To what do we owe the honor of your distinguished presence?"

"Shut up, Rudy," Spider snapped.

Cyrus pulled a joint from his pocket and lit it, then glared at Rudy through small, squinting eyes. He inhaled deeply and then picked a piece of marijuana from his tongue. Cyrus stubbed the joint out on the picnic table and slipped the butt into his shirt pocket.

"Show us some more of your moves, Cy," another boy cried.

"Yeah, show us," the others chimed in.

Cyrus retrieved the skateboard with a snap of his fingers, then smirked at Rudy. "Say hi to your sister Roxanne for me."

"You touch her and I'll make mincemeat out of your face!"

Cyrus laughed and swaggered out of the park's shelter with his board slung over his shoulder.

"Way to go, Rudy," someone in the crowd heckled. "You can be such a jerk!"

A few of the boys hurried after their idol vacating the park's log shelter.

Ozmand folded his arms across his chest. "I don't know what you've got against Cy."

Rudy shrugged. "I just don't like him, that's all."

"I'm hungry." Ozmand drummed on his stomach. "Let's go over to your house and see if your mom baked anything today."

They walked to the old company part of town and ambled past rows of cookie-cutter houses. Rudy's house was the second from the last on a winding cobblestone street.

"You gonna work the mines like your dad some day?" Ozmand asked.

"You kidding?" Rudy snorted.

Ozmand followed his friend through the front door. "It was just a question."

The smell of fresh-baked cinnamon rolls drew the boys into the kitchen.

"Can I move in with you?" Ozmand asked.

"Hey, Ma, I'm home." Rudy peeled off his sweatshirt and draped it over the back of a kitchen chair. "It's always so hot in this house," he complained.

"You know your father gets chilled." Mrs. Volkovich dried her hands on a dishtowel and brushed a strand of dull brown hair from her brow.

Ozmand hovered near the pan of rolls cooling on the counter.

"Help yourselves to the cinnamon rolls, but be careful," she said. "I just took them out of the oven."

"Would you be my mom, Mrs. V?" Ozmand asked. He retrieved a fork and plate and returned.

"You're here all the time as it is!" Rudy chided, stuffing a roll into his mouth.

Ozmand settled down at the kitchen table, turned his cap backward, and devoured a roll. Rudy reached for another, but his mother grabbed his hand.

"Rudolph," she said sternly, shaking her finger, "your school called this morning. What am I going to do with you?"

Rudy flashed a sheepish grin. "I don't know, Ma. It's probably just a phase." He scooped her tiny frame in one arm and lifted her from the ground.

"Put me down!" Back on her feet, she mumbled something under her breath. "Seriously, son, if you don't want to end up working in the mines, you have to study. You're a smart boy and there are scholarships available. You have to try harder."

"Can we talk about this later, Ma?"

She placed the tray of cinnamon rolls down beside Ozmand and peered out the window with tired eyes.

"Where's Papa?" Rudy asked.

"He's taking a nap." She rubbed a spot on her back. "Is that cigarette smoke I smell on you?"

Rudy dodged the question like a pro. "You didn't try to lift Papa again today, did you?"

"Well, I helped him into bed, and yes, I do have a little muscle twinge, but it will go away." She grabbed the sponge next to the sink and wiped some crumbs off the counter. "Your father's having a rough day."

"He's getting worse isn't he, Ma?"

Mrs. V's shoulders slumped forward, and suddenly Ozmand wished he was anywhere but there.

She set the sponge down and clutched the edge of the white porcelain sink. "He will get better, son." She mustered a smile. "You boys want a soda pop? There's some in the fridge."

"I'm gonna start coming home for lunch and right after school, so if there's any lifting to be done, it can wait until then. Okay, Ma?"

Mrs. Volkovich nodded, then picked up a basket of laundry by the basement door. "I'll be downstairs if you need me. Clean up any messes you make," she said, then stumped down the stairs.

Rudy opened the refrigerator and grabbed two Cokes. "Hey, Oz, catch!" He tossed him a can, but it landed on the floor and rolled to his feet.

"Thanks a lot, Rudy." Ozmand chased him around the room with his finger on the can's tab.

"If you open that you'll have to clean up the mess!" Rudy returned to the table and stuffed a huge hunk of cinnamon roll into his mouth.

"What's wrong with your ol' man, anyway?" Ozmand asked.

Rudy chugged some Coke. "Don't know for sure. He's losing feeling from his waist down."

"From what?"

"Ma thinks it's a miner's disease. From breathing in lead and other stuff." Rudy wrinkled his nose. "You'll never catch me in one of those mines."

"Man, that's rough." Ozmand said softly. He stared at a drop of condensation on top of his soda can. There was nothing more to say.

Roxanne maneuvered her Volkswagen into the only parking space at the Kingston Women's Clinic.

"What time is it?" April asked.

"Five minutes later than the last time you asked." Roxanne smiled at April, who drew her knee up to her chest and hugged it. "We have to go in now or you'll be late for the appointment," she gently coaxed.

"I'm scared, Roxie." Her eyes were glassy and fearful.

Roxanne hurt for her best friend, yet she was not sure how to help her.

"Tell me what to do," April whispered, her voice tight.

"I can't tell you what to do." Roxanne tried to think of how she would handle the situation, but her thoughts came up empty. "Maybe you should talk to your boyfriend."

April began to sob. "Logan can't help me now." She raised her other knee and buried her face.

Roxanne touched her friend's head as her own eyes filled with tears. "Listen, April, maybe you should think about this. Could be this isn't right for you." Roxanne sniffled. "There are other options."

"Like what?" April snapped. "Marriage? I'm only sixteen. Logan wants to go to college, and I do too. What will happen if I have a kid?"

"There's always adoption," Roxanne reasoned. "I have a cousin who's adopted. Mom always said the birth mother gave the most precious gift a person could give."

"Everybody would know I was pregnant." April stretched out her legs and lightly touched her stomach.

"Well, it's up to you," Roxanne said, looking at her watch, "but you need to decide right now if you want to get an abortion or not."

"I can't, Roxie. I mean, it's so final." April took a deep breath.

Roxanne opened the car door. "I'll go in and tell them you changed your mind."

April grabbed Roxanne's wrist. "No. Let's just go. I just

want to leave right now and forget about being pregnant for a while. Okay?"

"You're the boss." Roxanne closed the door and started the car. "Let's go to the mall and get some pizza."

"Great idea."

Hordes of high school kids loitered around the fast food alley at the mall. Roxanne and April bought a cheese pizza and some drinks, then went to search for a table where they could talk privately.

Roxanne took a bite of her slice. "What are you going to do?"

April pulled a piece of paper from her pocket. "I got this number from some bulletin board." She handed it to her best friend.

"'Pregnant? We can help. . . .'" Roxanne read aloud. "You're not serious!"

April snatched the paper and shoved it back into her pocket. She stared at her plate. Her blonde hair spilled across her cheeks.

Roxanne leaned on the table. "You've got to tell Logan."

"I can't," April whispered in a voice so tiny it could barely be heard.

"Why not?"

"He's applying for scholarships. He thinks he might have a shot at MIT." April's lip quivered, and her eyes brimmed with tears.

Roxanne looked away. She feared the worst—telling April's parents—was yet to come.

"I'm not hungry anymore." April shoved the plate of pizza across the table.

"You should eat something," Roxanne said, aware that she sounded more like a mother than a friend. Roxanne folded a napkin around the leftover pizza. "We can take it with us." She wished that a warm meal was all that her best friend needed.

CHAPTER 7

"Thank You, Lord," Jesse said, as he steered the car off the highway toward the only rest stop he had seen for miles. He stopped the Subaru and released the hood latch. Steam spewed from the radiator. He gave Cali a sideways glance. "We have to cool it down."

"What do you want me to do?" She folded her arms across her chest.

"Would you get an empty cup and fill it with some water, please? We need to try to lower the temperature before we can take off the radiator cap."

Cali skipped over to a dumpster, riffled through the trash, and then held up a discarded water bottle like a trophy. "What's your preference?" she called. "Sink or sewer water?"

Jesse smiled weakly and watched her disappear into the women's restroom. "Hope she's kidding," he muttered.

Cali came back with a full jug, which she poured on the radiator. "Now what?"

Jesse raised his shoulders and let them drop. "Let's give it some time."

"I can't believe this!" Cali's lips formed into a pout.

"We're only about an hour away from Hamlin." She sulked over to her old car and kicked the fender.

"Hey, while you're over there, would you reach in and get my jacket?"

Cali grabbed his denim coat, threw it at Jesse's feet, and stomped back to the ladies' room.

It had been a strange trip. Traveling with Cali was like grappling with a spoiled two-year-old, maybe worse. She refused his offers to buy her a decent meal, eating nothing but soda crackers and smoked oysters, which made sitting in the same car a challenge. Then there was her temper. Cali liberally used words that would make a stand-up comedian blush. Earlier in the day, she'd even picked a fight with a gas station attendant, which quickly escalated from a screaming match to a physical attack. Jesse had had to pull Cali from the poor man's back and pry her fingers from his hair.

Later that day, as they drove in silence, Jesse wondered about his decision to go with this girl. And yet a sense of peace encompassed him, even in the midst of all this insanity. He also felt compassion for this strange teenager who vacillated between belligerence and retreat.

Jesse sat on a little patch of grass and pulled a map from the pocket of his coat. He figured they were about fifty miles from Hamlin. On the second day of traveling, Cali had finally told Jesse where they were going, but she'd made it clear that was all the information he was going to get until they arrived. After three days in a car with Cali, he knew it was fruitless to press her for answers. Sometimes he thought he was beginning to understand her, glimpsing visions of her pain like slivers of glimmering glass. Her mood would shift as quickly as the wind, and her eyes would cloud over as she clenched her jaw in rage.

Jesse knew she could hurt him if she wanted to. It was nothing personal. Cali would strike out at anyone if she felt threatened.

When the radiator cooled, Jesse filled it with water and started the car. He honked the horn and waited for Cali. She sauntered out of the restroom with her hair and t-shirt dripping.

"What did you do?" Jesse teased. "Fall in?"

Cali sneered and rolled her eyes. "Funny ha-ha!" She opened the car door on the driver's side. "Move over. It's my turn to drive."

"It's your car," Jesse said, "I'm just along for the ride." *Maybe the ride of my life*, he thought.

Cali put the car in gear and backed out of the parking space. "Would it be terribly rude of me if I asked you to shut up?" She smiled and batted her eyes at him.

Jesse smiled back, welcoming the silence. "That suits me." He looked out the window, impressed by Montana's beauty. A herd of antelope grazed among the sagebrush, and an occasional eagle soared just below the clouds. They drove for a while beside a freight train and Jesse counted railroad cars.

Cali turned off the freeway and started up a two-lane road toward a small, rust-colored mountain. Even in the late afternoon sky, the scars and pits of mines were visible on its surface.

Jesse felt his muscles tense as they loped over the rolling hills toward their destination. Just over the rise, a sign came into view: Welcome to Hamlin, Population 8,287.

Cali rounded a sharp curve and the town appeared below them. Houses sprang from the edges of rocky crags, gullies, and hillsides like patches of tenacious weeds. Jesse saw one home built around a huge rock. Each construction project must have been a challenge and, ultimately, a source of pride. The streets seemed almost an afterthought, cut into the hillsides and winding haphazardly through the town below. Some were nothing more than stone-covered pathways leading to the mines. Above it all, perched atop an impressive red cliff, stood a majestic structure built of native stone. It was striking yet cold.

Jesse looked up, studying the building's arched gothic windows, which reflected the fiery colors of the setting sun. "What is that?"

"That's the Ellington ' place." Cali dodged a pothole on the primitive blacktop road. "They own the mines. They practically own the town."

Main Street circled around a large gray building with a mural of a buxom cowgirl holding a brown bottle. The mural read Hamlin Beer—A Taste of the West. Cali parked next to it.

Jesse got out and stretched, peering at the boarded-up windows. "So this is a brewery?"

"Used to be," Cali said, locking her car. She looked around, then leaned forward and whispered, "Once you drop into this valley, you will never get out alive." She threw her head back and let out a hideous laugh.

"Cut it out, Cali." Jesse looked at his watch. It was 6:30. "Come on, I'll buy you dinner."

"Well, all right, if you insist! There's a coffee shop just around the block. They always have a kettle of soup going."

They crossed the road and headed down a side street. Jesse and Cali passed a bookstore, some novelty shops, and a couple of bars that seemed only natural for a street called Brewery Lane.

Cali cut through a vacant lot that was used for horseshoe tournaments, then down an alley and around the back of a building faced with river rock. Jesse hadn't realized how hungry he was until the smell of steak and cottage fries filled his nostrils. He watched a man with a dingy apron empty a bucket of grease into a container near the dumpster.

"What about this place? Maybe we could eat here," Jesse said.

She shook her head. "This is the Hamlin Hotel and Restaurant. It's way too expensive."

Around the corner, next to a second-hand store, a rustic wooden sign hanging from heavy chains read Mountain Coffee and Herb Shop.

Cali pushed her way through the swinging doors and led Jesse across a plywood floor painted with assorted artwork. They took a seat at a corner table with mismatched chairs. The only other customer, a woman with a tangle of gray hair, sat in the back playing Solitaire.

A man clad in army fatigues handed them a flat piece of driftwood with the espresso and tea list burned into it.

"What kind of soup do you have today?" Jesse asked, laying the piece of wood on the table.

Without a word, the man motioned to a blackboard on the wall. Today's Special—Corn Chowder was scribbled in blue chalk.

"It's good," Cali assured Jesse.

"I'm sure it is. We'll have two bowls." Jesse handed back the menu.

"And what to drink?" The man's eyes blinked behind thick lenses.

"I'll have some chamomile and mint tea," Cali said.

"Just water for me."

The man peered over the rims of his glasses. "You're obviously not from around here."

"It shows?" Jesse grinned.

"No one drinks the water here," Cali explained. "Cause of the chemicals they used for leaching—it's in the soil."

"We use bottled water in everything," the waiter said.

"That's fine with me."

When Cali and Jesse were alone again, he pressed her for some answers. "You said you'd tell me everything when we got to Hamlin. Well, we're here."

Cali shifted in her chair. "Can't we eat first? I'm starving."

"Quit stalling."

"Okay, okay." She threw her hands in the air. "But I need to visit the little girl's room first." She rose from her chair just as the soup arrived in little cast-iron pots.

"The tea needs to steep," the man said flatly. He placed a basket of whole-wheat crackers on the table.

Cali slipped through the bead curtains near the back of the shop. Behind the veil, Jesse could make out her form in the shadows. She spoke into the wall phone, waving manically. She turned and looked back at the table.

"Here's the tea." The man appeared with a mug and set it down hard.

"Thanks." When Jesse looked back, Cali was no longer in the hallway.

The soup grew cold as Jesse waited. Finally, he went to investigate. He knocked on the ladies' room door and called Cali's name. There was no answer.

He poked his head back through the beaded curtains. "Excuse me, ma'am?"

The woman playing cards looked up and her eyebrows rose. "You talking to me?"

"I'm sorry to bother you, but my friend hasn't come out of the restroom and I'm beginning to get worried."

"I'll go check on her," the woman offered. She went into the restroom and returned with a shrug. "No one's in there."

Jesse's spirit sank.

"I can tell you why that girl left and maybe even where she went." The woman ushered Jesse to her table. "Does ten dollars sound like a fair price for that information?" She pulled a deck of tarot cards from her pocket and held them out to Jesse. "You'll need to cut the deck."

Jesse tried not to cringe. "No, thanks."

"What's wrong?" the woman cooed with a raised eyebrow. "Don't you believe in the spirit world?"

"Yes, definitely, but I don't trust the spirit behind those cards."

"Oh?" she said tersely. "And what spirit is that?"

"Satan," he said softly. "The Bible says he is the father of lies, so he's the last one I would ever seek advice from."

The woman stood and gathered her cards, mumbling something hostile under her breath. She scurried from the teashop, leaving Jesse alone with his thoughts and two bowls of cold soup.

CHAPTER 8

April watched the dusky scenery pass in a blur. It felt good not to think. No tears, no joy, no future. . . . She bit her quivering lip. Beside her, Roxanne was busy driving her car down the road that snaked toward Hamlin.

"Do you see how the lights from the town are glowing in the sky?" Roxanne asked. "It looks kinda eerie, doesn't it?"

Dark clouds churned low over the village, casting muted patterns of light. "Uh-huh," April whispered, wishing she could fly away and take refuge in their misty folds. "Roxanne, I'm sorry I haven't been very good company."

"That's okay."

"Do you ever wish you had the power to change things?" April sat up straight. "Sort of like that old show, *Bewitched*. When I was little I used to wish I was just like Samantha."

Roxanne laughed. "Reruns are so lame, but I was into *Gilligan's Island* when I was a kid. Do you suppose that means I'm destined to be shipwrecked?"

April grabbed her nose and wiggled it. "There, I turned you into a doofus." She looked at Roxanne with wide-eyed surprise. "It works!"

The girls roared with laughter as they drove through the gulch.

"Hey, did you see that?" Roxanne pointed.

April looked on, picking up the shadowy outline of some old buildings. "See what?"

"I thought I saw a light on in the brewery."

"Of course you did, Roxie. It's the ghost of Brewery Gulch."

"Have you ever seen a light on there before?" Roxanne asked.

"No," April said. "It can only be seen by a certain type of person."

"What kind of person?"

Roxanne turned up Main Street and drove toward the better part of town. "Why, a doofus, of course!"

"You jerk!"

Her friend's infectious giggle made April smile, but it quickly faded when Roxanne pulled into the driveway of a brick, ranch-style house that sat between two manicured evergreen shrubs. A light shone in the window.

"Want me to go in with you?"

April stepped out of the car. "No, thanks. I'll see you tomorrow at school." She mustered a brave smile and walked inside.

The living room, as usual, smelled of lemon oil. Everything was in its place. The coffee table books were set just right and the furniture looked as if it was sitting in a showroom.

April took off her shoes so she wouldn't track any dirt

onto the spotless white rug. She could still see the tracks left from the vacuum cleaner. "Mom?" she called softly. There was no answer. April padded across the room in her stocking feet and peeked into her parents' bedroom. No one was there. Down the hall, the door to her brother's bedroom stood ajar. The room was dark except for a haze of moonlight that fell through the window. April could just make out her mother's silhouette in the chair by the window.

"Mama?" she said as her eyes adjusted to the darkness. "Sorry I'm late."

April noticed the framed photograph of her brother laying in her mother's lap. She hurried to her mom's side and knelt on the floor beside her. "Mama, please. This won't bring Benny back." She took her mother's hand, but the woman pulled from her grasp and looked away. Mrs. Gilbert sat silent for a few moments, and then a long, arid sigh trickled through her thin lips.

"Please, Mama. I'm here."

Her mother turned mechanically and stared at her daughter. "Are you?"

April clutched the arm of the chair. Resting her head against the hard wood, she began to weep. "I'm sorry I'm late and that I didn't call." Her sense of shame was almost more than she could bear. April wished it had been her instead of her brother who'd died. Down deep, she believed her parents felt the same.

Suddenly, April felt a hand on her shoulder swing her around. Her father stood before her. Leland Gilbert was a stern, joyless man with sharp features and a receding hairline.

"Do you know where I've been all evening?"

April opened her mouth, but no words escaped.

"Out looking for you." His breath smelled of alcohol. "You are a sorry excuse for a daughter."

Mr. Gilbert grabbed April by the chin and turned her face toward her mother. "Take a look at what you've done to this woman." He held her face so tight it hurt. "You disgust me." He transferred his grip to her arm, nearly lifting her body off the ground, and then tugged her down the hallway.

Mr. Gilbert shoved April through her bedroom door. She stumbled backward and fell onto her pink shag carpet. April lay there looking up at her father. He stood over her like a giant. Disdain spread across his face.

April wanted to hide. *I've let them down again.* "I'm sorry, Daddy."

Her father turned and walked away.

April climbed to her feet and switched on the bedroom light. Everything looked perfect in her world. Her white canopy bed had a ruffled Priscilla ensemble of pink gingham. Rows of white, scalloped shelves held an assortment of delicate porcelain dolls. April reached for a tattered Raggedy Ann doll on her bed and clutched it to her breast.

"What am I going to do, Annie? I've really made a mess of things." She glanced in the mirror, wondering how long it would be before others noticed her changing shape.

April slipped on her nightgown, turned off the lights, and climbed into bed. She pulled the covers up around her face and lay in the darkness, waiting for sleep's sweet escape.

The temperature dropped rapidly after the sun went down. Cali had taken the car and Jesse didn't have enough money left for a motel room. His thoughts turned to survival. Jesse found two large cardboard boxes and put one inside the other, a trick he'd gleaned from the street people in Pittsburgh. He spent a miserable, sleepless night in the makeshift shelter, shivering until his muscles ached.

The streets of Hamlin were still quiet as the early morning sun fell warm upon the cardboard wall. Jesse felt himself getting sleepy.

"Did you hear me, son?"

Startled from his sleep, Jesse raised his hand and blinked against the light. A large figure towered over the cardboard box.

The man scratched his bushy beard. "Hey, Emma!" his deep voice rumbled. "You'll never believe what I found!"

"Whatever it is, leave it," a woman's voice returned. "We're already feeding half the cats in the neighborhood. The last thing we need is another stray."

The stranger lifted a finger to his lips and winked at Jesse. "You'll want to see this one."

"Oh, for crying out loud, Lars, you're an impossible softie, but I'm putting my foot—" The woman peered inside the box and her jaw dropped.

The man bellowed with laughter. "Sorry, Mama, I couldn't resist."

"Are you all right? What's your name, young man?" The woman cautiously reached inside and offered her hand.

"Jesse," he said, stretching his stiff legs. "I'm fine—just a little embarrassed to be discovered like this."

The big man pumped Jesse's hand. "I'm Lars Willis, and this is my beautiful bride, Emma."

The woman, probably in her fifties, brushed a runaway strand of silver hair from her forehead. "You spent the night out here in the cold?"

"It wasn't so bad, really."

Lars scratched his bald scalp. "I still can't believe you fit in that box," he chuckled, "but they say good things come in small packages."

"The boy is probably not in the mood for clichés." Emma turned to Jesse. "I'm just grateful we found you."

"Remember this the next time I want to go dumpster diving," Lars said with a wink.

Jesse felt the pocket of his coat for his small, leather-bound Bible. "Wait!" He found it on the bottom of the box.

"Are you a Christian?" Lars asked.

"Sure am."

"Well, praise the Lord!" Lars boomed and slapped Jesse on the back. "A blood-bought, born-again brother in Christ?"

"Come on," Emma said. "We're going to buy you a warm meal." She hopped behind the wheel of the old pickup truck parked at the curb. "We just need to make a quick stop at the Christian Outreach first."

Lars squeezed next to his wife and waited while Jesse fished for his seatbelt. "You must have driven with Emma before," Lars chuckled when she jammed the truck in gear and squealed onto the road. "See what I mean?"

"I believe that we were meant to find this boy." Emma pulled up to a wedge-shaped building that stood at the intersection.

"Wouldn't doubt it, Mama," Lars agreed as the trio assembled on the sidewalk in front of a door decorated with a crude cross.

Lars lifted a crate marked "Bibles" from the bed of the truck as Emma slipped the key into the door.

"Are you pastors?"

"In a sense," Emma said. "More like street evangelists who run a Christian outreach."

Lars set the box just inside the door. "What we'd really like to do is find a way to reach our local youth."

"Yeah?" Jesse said. "I did something along those lines in Pittsburgh."

"Interesting," the couple echoed simultaneously as they piled back into the truck.

They drove through the heart of town. The buildings, mostly made of brick or quarried stone, looked to be in good shape. On closer inspection, Jesse noticed that the wood around the windows and doors hung crumbling from dry rot, evidence of years of neglect in the harsh Montana climate.

Lars waved at a ghostly shadow of a woman who watched them from the window of her second-story apartment. She raised her hand and pressed it against the glass.

"Mama, we need to remember to pray for our neighbors."

Emma looked at Jesse. "There's a lot of suffering in this town—alcoholism, domestic abuse, teen suicides."

"Yes, sir, the Devil is alive and well in Hamlin," Lars said as they parked.

The Roundup Café was busy. A few people sat at the

counter sipping coffee and reading the local paper. Lars, Emma, and Jesse sat in a booth. An old woman, her gray hair plastered down with a hairnet, pushed open the kitchen door and looked around. She seemed surprised when she spotted the new customers. She disappeared momentarily, then emerged with three sets of silverware and some mugs.

"How are those bunions today?" Lars asked.

"Can't complain. At least I can walk." The waitress readied her pen. "What can I get for you?"

"Three wrangler's specials, and heap a little extra on this young man's plate," Emma said.

"And coffee," Lars added, turning his cup over.

"Goes without saying." The old woman slipped the pen behind her ear and went to fetch the pot.

"You really don't have to do this." Jesse reached into his jacket and fished out some change.

Emma patted Jesse's hand. "Nonsense. You keep your money."

"How did you wind up in Hamlin, son?" Lars asked as the waitress poured coffee into their mugs.

Jesse told them everything. He explained how he'd shown up in Pittsburgh as a child with no memory and how Mavis Berry took him in and raised him to know and serve the Lord. He told them about Cali back at the mission, begging for help while giving him only broken pieces of information that hinted of his past.

The waitress set a plate of scrambled eggs and sausage in front of each of them.

Jesse and Emma bowed their heads as Lars offered a blessing.

"What did you do in Pittsburgh? Ministry-wise, I mean?" Emma poked at her scrambled eggs.

"I helped serve food to the homeless, and I worked with youth. Mostly street kids."

"So you're the one!" Lars hollered.

Jesse almost choked on his coffee. "Excuse me?"

Emma leaned forward and spoke discreetly. "What my husband is trying to say is that we asked God to send someone to help."

"But we didn't expect Him to ship you parcel post!" Lars interjected. Laughter rippled around the table and faded.

The couple's faces turned serious as Lars spoke. "We could use your help here, son."

Emma nodded. "The children of Hamlin are in danger."

"How?" Jesse asked.

"It seems they are being drawn into something sinister." Emma set her fork down. "Why don't you come home with us. We have plenty of room."

Jesse mulled everything over as he finished his breakfast, but one thing resonated in his spirit: God, for whatever reason, had led him to Hamlin.

CHAPTER 9

April leaned through the door of the English Lit room, but the only sign of life was the teacher scratching out an assignment on the whiteboard. *It's still early,* she reasoned, and returned to the hallway to wait for her boyfriend. April felt nauseated as she scanned the faces coming through the door at the end of the hall. Logan was not among them. *How can I tell him?* April wondered, feeling alone among the morning throng of students.

Logan burst through the doors flanked by a half-dozen of his football teammates. They were laughing and shoving one another, fully absorbed in their raucous play.

April checked her watch—just a few more minutes until the bell. She watched with mounting irritation as Logan sauntered to his locker, shoved his coat inside, and retrieved a book. Then, as if it were an afterthought, he looked around. Logan's eyes brightened when they lit upon his girlfriend. "April!" He hurried toward her.

She turned away in sudden anger.

Logan grabbed April's arm and turned her around. "Are you ignoring me?"

Suddenly, Logan was the last person she wanted to see. After all, he was equally to blame for her troubles. "I didn't hear you."

"Maybe you should get your hearing checked." Logan put his arms on either side of her head, pinning her against a locker. "Where were you yesterday? I looked for you after school." Logan leaned close to April's ear. "I missed you," he said, and kissed her neck.

"Stop it, Logan!"

He let his arms drop to his side and stepped back. "What's your problem?"

April stared at him. "All you ever think about is one thing," she shrieked. The noise level in the hallway dropped sharply as attention turned to the young couple.

Logan looked around self-consciously, then studied April with an expression that was a mixture of anger and bewilderment. "Who needs this?" he snapped and strode away.

"Yeah, well who needs you?" she screamed and fled to the restroom.

———

April's mother, Darlene, threw herself into her housework. It didn't matter that everything was already spotless. She needed to go through the motions anyway. It helped her to forget. By 9:00 AM, she had cleaned out the inside of the dishwasher with ammonia and scrubbed the edges of the kitchen sink with an old toothbrush. When that was finished, she polished the family silver, which was reserved for special occasions. *Odd,* she thought as she rubbed, *that a special occasion has never come up.* Darlene's mind wandered over all the occasions in the past that now, in retrospect, seemed deserving of such an honor.

By 9:30 AM, there was nothing left to do. Darlene stood amidst the smell of Brasso and ammonia with a sense of panic rising in her heart. Her mind wandered through her immaculate home, doing a mental check of cupboards and drawers and closets. Everything was in its place, neat and orderly, except the one room she had left untouched.

Darlene walked down the hall to her son's bedroom and pushed the door open. Benny's photo, taken his junior year of high school, lay in the chair where she'd sat the night before. She ran her finger over the frame, skipping a blind eye over the defiant sneer on her son's face. Darlene envisioned Benny standing there, challenging his mother. "This is my room. Stay out of my stuff!" The ghost reared upon her, threatening to undo her.

Darlene shuddered, set the picture on the dresser, and tried to think of sweeter times. Benny sitting at the dinner table, raving about his mother's cooking; Benny positioned on first base in little league; Benny giving her a homemade valentine. Darlene had stitched these patches of time together like a quilt and pulled them close for comfort. She guarded her memories like a sentinel, always ready to chase away the truth when it threatened to intrude.

Darlene knew the pain she was causing her family. She could see it on her husband's face late at night when he nursed a bottle of whiskey. She could see it in April's eyes when she skirted silently around her mother. Darlene couldn't help herself. She had encapsulated Benny in a saintly shrine, ignoring the fact that he had been a tormented young man, defying his parents with violent outbursts and flouting drugs in their faces. In Darlene's mind, Benny was the perfect son, and her heart still ached like it had on that fateful afternoon. The memory of that summer day was as raw as if it had happened yesterday.

She recalled the hazy smoke of a distant forest fire hanging over the valley. Darlene had just settled in the den to fold a load of laundry and watch her favorite soap opera when a fire truck drove by, followed by a police car. Irritated by the distraction, she had turned up the volume on her program.

A friend from her bridge club called. "I just heard on the scanner. There's been a terrible wreck near the rims."

"Who's involved?" Darlene asked as a tiny alarm sounded inside her.

"I don't know, but they're calling for extrication equipment."

"Let me know if you find out more."

Darlene went outside. Off in the distance she saw black smoke curling upward beneath the rocky red cliffs. She knew April was teaching swimming lessons at the outdoor pool, but she didn't know where Benny was.

Darlene was still standing on her front lawn when her husband drove up. Surprised that Leland would be home at this time of day, she searched his face for an explanation. The sadness in his eyes made her want to run, but she couldn't move.

"Is it Benny?" she shrieked.

Her husband nodded. "He drove his car off the rims.

He's gone, Darlene."

Leland tried to hold his wife, but she pushed him away. "Liar!" She couldn't stop screaming. "It's not true! It can't be true!" But it was true.

A year and a half had passed since Benny died. The psychiatrist said she was coping well. *Stupid man.*

Darlene put the photograph of Benny back in its place and opened her son's closet. She knelt in front of a mound of dirty clothes and smelly gym shoes.

"Well, Benny, I guess it's finally time to clean your mess." The idea brought another wave of grief. Darlene threw herself into the task, maniacally digging through the pile of wrinkled clothing and shoes. She tossed a stack of well-worn pornographic magazines into a large black garbage bag. Darlene's eyes lingered on the gym bag Benny used before he quit the basketball team. She pulled it from the closet and opened it. His smell, entombed within the vinyl, floated through her senses. Darlene tenderly lifted her son's jersey from the bag and cradled it.

A familiar sound drifted into Darlene's consciousness. April must have left her cell phone on the charger. Annoyance turned to mild panic. What if it was another emergency? Darlene climbed to her feet and tossed Benny's shirt onto the pile of dirty clothes. As it landed, a small, red book fell out of the jersey. Darlene reached for it but decided instead to race for the phone.

In April's room, Darlene answered, trying to sound calm. "Hello?"

"April Gilbert?" a professional-sounding woman inquired.

"Who's calling?"

"April, this is Marla from the Kingston Women's Clinic."

Darlene tried to process the information. "Yes?" she said weakly.

"April, I noticed you missed your appointment yesterday, and I wanted to know if you'd care to reschedule."

"I'm not sure. . . ." Darlene felt the blood drain from her face.

"Dr. McNight has an opening on Monday morning at 10:45." There was a pause. "April, you're nearing your second trimester. You need to decide soon if you still want to terminate your pregnancy." There was a pause. "April? Are you there?"

Panic crawled up Darlene's neck. "I'll get back to you." With trembling fingers, she disconnected and dropped the receiver as if it burned. Mascara-stained tears dropped onto the white carpet at Darlene's feet, and a guttural wail erupted from her core.

"I'm a failure!"

Suddenly, her sobbing halted, and an unearthly calm settled over Darlene. She drifted like a sleepwalker through the house, stopping at the medicine cabinet in the master bath. Darlene gazed into the mirror at empty eyes; and then, in resignation, she spoke one word.

"Failure."

Ozmand kept an eye on the high school principal as he

addressed the attendance officer. "Rudolph Volkovich and Ozmand Wright are to receive zeroes in all their classes today. They will not be allowed to do any make-up work."

The attendance officer scribbled a note as the principal cast a somber look at Rudy and Oz. "Young men, it's about time you accepted the consequences for your actions. I hope you know this will damage your grade point average."

Ozmand tried to ignore Rudy, who was snickering beside him.

Principal Albright's face reddened. "This may not mean much to you now, but some day when you can't even land a decent job, you'll only have yourselves to blame!" He returned to his office and shut the door.

The lunch bell rang. Ozmand and Rudy spilled from the office and fell in with the other kids as they filtered out of the building. A gust of chilly wind met them at the front door and they burst into simultaneous laughter.

"What an idiot!' Rudy mocked the principal's stern mannerisms.

Ozmand raised his hands in protest. "Oh, no, Principal Albright, anything but the grade point average!"

As they reveled in the moment, the other students scattered. Ozmand pulled the collar of his jacket up around his neck. "Wanna go to the video arcade?"

"Can't," Rudy said. "I promised my ma I'd go home for lunch to help out with my dad."

The wind scooped a pile of dry leaves and swirled them in a mini-twister. "Catch ya later," Ozmand called as his friend lumbered down the street. He shoved his right hand into his pocket and pulled out a fistful of quarters, enough for an hour of games and a candy bar.

"Hey, man. Where's your board?"

Ozmand looked over his shoulder, startled to see Cyrus leaning against the brick wall.

"I left it at home."

"Too bad." Cyrus mounted his skateboard and did a few circles around Ozmand. "Care to try mine?"

"Sure," Ozmand blurted, staring at Cy's skateboard. It was top of the line, made of the finest hardwood and sporting a painted snake that crawled through the eyes of a skull.

"Got any money?" Cyrus asked.

"Yeah."

"Tell ya what," Cyrus stepped off his skateboard. "Buy me a burger and I'll show you how to do a trick or two." He draped his arm over Ozmand's shoulder like they were old friends.

"That's cool."

"Let's go. I'm hungry." Cy started up the sidewalk, leaving his skateboard behind. "Are you coming?"

Ozmand hopped on the skateboard and rolled after his mentor. He paused for a quick flip-kick and a perfect ollie. It was almost like the board had power. As Ozmand weaved a serpentine path with liquid ease, he felt as though he was the center of the universe.

"Wow, Cy, this board is sick! I'd give anything for one just like it."

Cyrus smirked. "It's custom-made. Besides, you can't buy my kinda style."

When they got to the Dairy Queen, Ozmand bought Cyrus a double cheeseburger and had enough money left over for a small order of fries. They sat at a picnic table sheltered by a green fiberglass awning.

Cyrus ate his burger in three bites, shoving the last mouthful in before the first was gone. A dollop of ketchup oozed down his chin. He leaned back, flipped a patch of bleached white hair from his eyes, and belched.

A group of girls at a nearby table leaned over, whispered to each other, and giggled. Their adoring faces all turned in Cyrus's direction.

"Why do you hang out with losers?"

Ozmand swallowed a French fry. "What are you talking about?"

"I'm talking about Rudy—he's a loser."

"Hey, he's my friend. You got a problem with that?"

"Whoa!" Cyrus raised his hand in feigned surrender. "No offense. I like you, kid. You're okay. I just don't care much for your buddy."

"Well, Rudy thinks you're a jerk, too."

Cyrus's lip stiffened. "Yeah, well, that don't hurt my feelings," he said as they left the table.

On the sidewalk, Cyrus mounted his skateboard and trailed behind Ozmand as he walked. "A few of the guys are gathering at my place later." Cyrus lingered near the front steps of the high school. "Seven o'clock. Wanna come?"

Ozmand couldn't believe it. Cyrus was actually inviting him to his house. "Sure!" he called, as he watched the coolest guy in town roll away on his skateboard.

CHAPTER 10

At the Christian Outreach, Lars showed Jesse how to operate the publishing software and printer and handed him a prototype of a gospel tract titled God So Loved the World. Jesse recognized it as John 3:16 and the salvation scripture on the inside as Romans 10:9.

"These are good," he said, rolling up his sleeves. It didn't take long for Jesse to figure out the process. He printed, Lars cut paper, and Emma folded the tracts into booklets.

When the job was done, Jesse glanced at a wall calendar and blurted, "I forgot to call Mavis! She's probably worried."

"You can use my cell phone." Lars dug it from the pocket of his jeans and tossed it to Jesse, but it fell into a heap of old coats, hats, and gloves.

"One of these days, you're gonna break that thing!" Emma scolded.

"Sorry about that." Lars grinned as Jesse rooted through the pile looking for the phone. "Every year we have a Good Samaritan drive and we go door-to-door collecting warm clothes."

"There's not too many homeless in Hamlin, though,"

Emma interjected, "so we haul most of these things to a shelter in Kingston."

"I found it!" Jesse dialed the number for the Pittsburgh Rescue Mission and listened to it ring. "Hi, it's me!" he said when Mavis answered.

"Jesse, where are you?"

"I'm in Montana. A town called Hamlin. Cali ditched me right after we got here, but God is providing."

"I've asked the Lord to set his angels around you and keep you safe. " Mavis's voice wavered.

"Don't worry," Jesse assured her. "I've been invited to stay with a wonderful couple. Emma and Lars Willis." He gave her the number.

"God bless them," Mavis said. "Tell them that they've eased an old woman's mind."

"I'll do that." Jesse glanced out the window just in time to see Cali's car drive past. "I've got to run, but I'll talk to you soon." He hung up and pointed out the window.

"There goes the girl I told you about." Jesse leaped over the back of an old, overstuffed chair and bolted out the door.

Jesse spotted Cali's car parked next to the brewery and caught a glimpse of her slight frame hurrying into the bookstore. He sprinted up the sidewalk and followed her inside. Jesse looked around, but there was no sign of Cali.

The proprietor, a matronly woman with bifocals perched on the end of her nose, sat behind a long oak counter. She looked up from the book she was reading.

"Can I help you find something?"

"I'm looking for a girl."

The woman laughed and her double chin shook. "The

best I can do is recommend a good romance novel."

"She just came in here," Jesse explained. "Black hair, long bangs, around sixteen years old."

"Doesn't ring a bell. Sorry." The woman licked her finger and turned a page of her book.

"But she was just here a few seconds ago," Jesse pressed.

The proprietor gazed over the top of her reading glasses. "You must be mistaken, young man. We're the only ones here." She motioned to a man standing a few yards away. "Owen, did you see anyone come in the store?"

A bearded man with an unlit pipe dangling from his mouth stood in front of a bookshelf browsing the titles. "Nope," he replied without looking up.

"Mind if I look around?" Jesse asked.

"Suit yourself." The woman shifted her weight and the stool beneath her creaked.

Jesse walked to the rear of the store, where he discovered a small room with a sign over the doorway that read Used Books. He poked his head inside. The area smelled damp and musty, like the inside of a cave. He also detected a rather putrid odor that he couldn't place.

In the back of the store, the windows were boarded shut. Jesse's gaze fanned over flimsy shelves weighed down with hundreds of paperback novels. The only way out of the store was through the front, and yet there was no sign of Cali.

As Jesse turned to go, he caught his foot on the corner of an old Oriental rug and fell.

"Oh, my goodness!" The owner launched herself from her perch and bustled over to Jesse. "Are you hurt?"

"I'm fine." Jesse felt his face flush, embarrassed by the spectacle he had made. "I'm okay."

"Are you sure?" She bent over to straighten the rug. "I need to get this thing nailed down. We can't afford any lawsuits." She held out her hand to help Jesse to his feet.

The man with the unlit pipe stood expressionless, watching through eyes the color of slate.

"Thanks." Jesse smiled sheepishly. "I guess now that I've made a complete fool of myself, I'll be on my way."

Outside, Jesse closed the door behind him. He stood on the sidewalk feeling perplexed. Cali's car was still parked against the curb. He glanced up and down the street, but saw no sign of her.

Where could she have gone? Jesse looked back and was startled to see the bearded man watching him through the bookstore window.

———

Under the Oriental rug, beneath a trap door, Cali stood on an old ladder, her heart still thundering in her chest from the commotion above. She strained to listen while threads of light streamed through cracks in the floorboards overhead.

When Cali heard Jesse's voice, she didn't dare take another step. The ancient ladder's rungs creaked under her feet. Five minutes passed. Swathed in darkness beneath her was a catacomb of old mining tunnels that ran under the town—a path she had reluctantly traveled before.

On the floor above her, all was quiet now. Something skittered across her hand in the dark. She slapped at it, nearly losing her balance.

Above, footsteps drew closer. Cali strained again to hear.

Bang! Bang! Bang! Someone stomped on the trap door. The sound bounced off the tunnel walls and exploded in Cali's ears.

"You still there?" asked Irene, the book lady.

"Yeah!"

"If you're ever that careless again, you stupid little moron, I'll have you run out of town!"

"When does the next train leave?" Cali descended the ladder, leaving behind a few choice obscenities.

At the bottom of the ladder, Cali ran her hand over the rugged earth and found an old cloth sack right where she had left it. She rummaged through the bag until she found a flashlight and some unopened packages of C-cell batteries. With haste, Cali replaced the old ones and turned on the flashlight. She waited until her eyes adjusted before making her way down the passageway.

As Cali moved deeper into the shaft, it narrowed so much that she had to crouch down and then crawl. She crept through a small opening that expanded into a cavern large enough for her to stand. This was the part she hated the most. Murky water came up to her ankles, deeper in some spots, and foul-smelling liquid dripped continually from the rocks above her head. The stench seemed worse than the last time she'd been here. Cali suspected a sewer leak but didn't really want to know. She moved on, climbing a tiny flight of stairs into a larger cavern.

Intuitively, the teenager knew she was not alone; she

could feel his sickening presence. Cali fanned the beam of light, casting shadows like ghouls across the rocky walls. She aimed the light into a dark crevice and caught a silhouette.

"Don't shine that light on me," he warned.

She pointed the flashlight to the ground, but she had seen him. His arms were folded smugly across his chest. A cruel king seated upon on a crate throne. His proximity repulsed Cali, filling her with hatred. She wanted to spit in his face and run from eyes she knew were pinned on her, but defiance was useless. Cali was bound by invisible chains.

"I hate you!"

He laughed, though there were no pleasant notes in the sound.

"If you don't give my baby back, I'll. . . ."

"You'll what?" He gave each nostril a blast of nasal spray and sniffed hard.

"I could go to the police."

"Could you?"

No, she thought. *They are everywhere—even in the police department*. Cali began to cry.

"Now, now," he said, "don't whimper. You shall hold your infant, provided you do what I tell you."

"You're a liar," Cali screamed, covering her ears with her hands. "Why should I listen to you? I've already done what you asked. You're never going to give her back, are you?"

The man rose up from the crate. The beam of Cali's flashlight nailed him and she wished it was a bullet.

He snarled. "I told you not to point that thing at me." Behind him, his shadow loomed like a giant. The man took a deliberate step forward.

Fear flashed like a stab of lightning, and Cali wondered if she'd gone too far. "I'm sorry, I'll do what you ask. Please."

"These tantrums of yours are very disturbing to me. I find myself questioning your competence."

"I won't mess up. I promise."

"I'm counting on that—your baby's life depends on it." He tossed a manila envelope at her feet. "Read this, then burn it." He turned to go. "And remember, people are watching you."

―〰―

This can't be happening, April thought, standing in the hallway just outside the hospital waiting room. She leaned against the soda machine and closed her eyes. The gentle hum of the motor made her feel a little better. She felt sick to her stomach and her hands shook slightly. She heard a doctor being paged over the hospital's intercom system and heard the squeaky wheel of an orderly's magazine cart as it rolled by. April kept her eyes closed, wishing she could somehow make the world disappear.

Seconds seemed like minutes. April checked her wristwatch. Just two hours ago, in the middle of math class, she'd been called to the school office. When April arrived, she saw a barrel-chested police officer standing beside the principal.

He had looked at April with pity as she approached. "I've come to take you to the hospital," he said. "There's been an incident. Your mother. . . ."

On the way to the hospital, April had pelted the officer with questions. "What kind of incident? Is my mother okay? Why didn't Dad come?" Her queries were all met with silence.

April heard a clicking noise, then a *kerthunk*! Her eyes shot open see a nurse retrieving a can of soda from the machine.

"I didn't mean to startle you." The woman popped the tab and took a sip.

April could see her father through the open door of the waiting room. Leland Gilbert had been sitting in the same statuesque position since she'd arrived.

April slipped into the waiting room and sat beside him. "Dad," she said, touching his back. His blank expression didn't change.

The double doors swung open, and the family physician entered, with the hospital chaplain trailing behind. April's heart flopped in her chest. She hoped these messengers were bound for someone else.

"Leland," the doctor came to a stop in front of them. "I'm sorry. We did everything we could. But Darlene ingested nearly a whole bottle of sedatives." The doctor cast a look at the chaplain. "Too much time passed before she got here. I'm afraid that there was nothing we could do for her."

April tried to put her arms around her dad, but he pulled away to face the hospital's chaplain. "Reverend," he cried, "I've lost everything. There's nothing left for me to live for."

The words cut April's heart. She rose from her chair, backed from the waiting room, and bolted down the corridor. All she could think to do was run as far as her legs would take her.

Once outside, April stumbled down the road, her eyes blinded by tears, her sobbing so violent that spasms racked her ribs. *Breathe through your nose and call Roxanne.* She fumbled in her backpack for her cell phone and remembered that it was back in her bedroom on the charger.

April spotted a convenience store with a payphone out front. She scratched up some loose change and dialed. The call went to Roxanne's voice mail.

April slammed the receiver onto the cradle and stared at it as though it had betrayed her. *What am I going to do now?* She sank her hands into her pockets, and her fingers touched a piece of paper. It was the telephone number she'd pulled from a bulletin board.

April dialed and tried to compose herself as the phone rang.

"Hello." The voice was pleasant and singsong.

April's throat constricted. She struggled to force words from her mouth. "I'm in trouble," she whispered. "I was told that you could help."

CHAPTER 11

"It was so weird." Jesse sank into the lumpy sofa at the Christian Outreach. "I was sure I saw Cali go into that place. I felt like such an idiot."

Emma handed Jesse a mug of coffee and he thanked her.

"Is that the bookstore the local churches got all fired up about a while back?" Lars asked his wife.

"Yes. They were selling pornographic books and videos, and the high school kids were getting hold of them." Emma settled on the couch next to Jesse.

"The owner raised quite a ruckus over the whole deal," Lars reflected. "Freedom of expression and so on. But, in the end, she did get rid of the offensive stuff."

"That woman despises Christians," Emma recalled. "She organized a group that meets every Friday night in the basement of Ellington Hall. They call themselves SAFE."

"What does that stand for?" Jesse asked.

"Sanity Against Fundamentalism's Effects."

Lars moved to a makeshift cinder-block bookshelf. He pulled out a large, red dictionary and thumbed through the pages.

"What are you doing?" Emma asked.

"I'm looking up the word 'fundamentalist.' Here it is. 'One who believes in the literal inspiration and inerrancy of the Bible.'" Lars rubbed his beard. "Guess that makes me a fundamentalist!"

"Count me in," Emma winked playfully.

Jesse's mind wandered. He swirled the coffee in his cup and chewed his lip. "Hamlin has a lot of problems for a town this size," he said. "Maybe it's time to step up the prayer."

"It couldn't hurt," Emma agreed. "We attend a weekly Bible study at Theda Mae Crabtree's house. I'm sure she won't mind if we shift the focus to prayer."

Lars laughed out loud. "You kidding? Theda Mae is an old-time prayer warrior!"

"How soon can I meet her?" Jesse asked.

Roxanne dumped a pail of dirty water down the sink in Mrs. Crabtree's kitchen. On the stove a few feet away, a teakettle began to whistle. Roxanne set the pale down and dropped the damp mop inside. "Theda Mae, the tea water is ready!"

The old woman bustled into the kitchen. She rifled through a cupboard, produced an old transfer-ware teapot, and dropped a couple of teabags inside. "Will you join me, dear?"

"Sure." Elbows on the counter, Roxanne cradled her head in her hands and watched her elderly friend pour the steaming water into the teapot. "Theda Mae, you believe that

God listens to you, right?"

"Of course. He listens to everyone who reaches out to Him."

Roxanne scratched at a crusty spot she'd missed while cleaning the countertop. "How do you reach out to God when you can't even see Him?"

"With your spirit." Theda Mae opened an ornate tin of cookies. "Would you set this on the table, dear?"

The old woman opened a cupboard and retrieved two saucers and cups. "Have a seat," she said, setting the table.

Roxanne settled down at the drop-leaf table and selected a chocolate chip cookie from the tin. "Don't you have to go see a fortune teller or a medium to be in touch with your spirit?"

Theda Mae's eyes widened in surprise. "Heavens, no!" The old woman poured the tea and joined Roxanne at the table. "God's Word strictly forbids dabbling in anything of an occult nature. It's like picking a violet that is growing up through the jaws of a steal trap. He doesn't want us to get hurt."

Roxanne nibbled at her cookie as she considered the old woman's words. "What do you mean by 'spirit'?"

"It is the part of us created in God's likeness." Theda Mae's brow furrowed. "There are so many hungry souls."

"Not in this country," Roxanne interjected. "I mean, it's not like we're a Third World nation. Even poor people can get food stamps if they're hungry."

Theda Mae patted Roxanne's hand. "I'm speaking of a different kind of hunger. Let me see, how can I explain this?" She rubbed her chin and looked at the ceiling. "Ah!" She clasped her hands together. "What would happen if we filled our bodies with junk food?"

"We wouldn't be very healthy."

"That's right. Like our bodies, our spirits can also be abused and neglected. We must be very careful what we allow into our spirits."

"But how do we know what to put into our spirits?"

"That's easy," Theda Mae said, pointing to her Bible. "We've got the care and instruction manual right here!" She dropped a lump of sugar into her cup and stirred vigorously.

Roxanne rested her chin in her hands. "I'd love to have your faith."

Theda Mae brushed crumbs from her gnarly fingers. "You can, dear. I was about your age when I asked Jesus into my heart—best decision I ever made. I can't imagine living in this fallen world without God's strength and protection. Would you like to pray?"

Roxanne's heart stirred. *Why not?* she thought, and bowed her head. When it was over, no harps from heaven or peals of thunder were audible to her ears, and yet Roxanne knew something special had just taken place. Something very, very important.

Ozmand found nothing in the refrigerator at home but a doggie bag containing a half-eaten club sandwich. He sniffed it, curled his nose at the sour smell, and tossed it in the trashcan under the sink. He was starving. The small order of fries he'd had for lunch had not carried him very far.

In the freezer, Ozmand rummaged around until he located a turkey-pot pie. He popped it in the microwave and sat at the kitchen counter to wait. The house was quiet except for the tick-tock of the Felix-the-Cat clock that hung on the kitchen wall. It was 7:30 PM. His mom was working late again. It had been that way for as long as he could remember. When Ozmand was in second grade, his mother had enrolled in a correspondence course to become a legal secretary. After two failed attempts, she'd earned her certificate of graduation. Now, eight years later, the yellowed piece of paper was still displayed on the living room wall. She'd landed a good job working for the county attorney, who also happened to be the most eligible bachelor in town.

Ozmand wished his mother didn't have to work so hard. He rolled his eyes at the thought of his mother's words: "Everything I do is for you."

"Yeah, right!" He made a spitball from a napkin and threw it at the noisy kitchen clock. He couldn't help wondering if his mother's life would have been easier without him. She flew her burdens like a banner for all to see, oblivious to the fact that behind her back everyone called her "Poor Nan."

Ozmand Thomas Wright had arrived in the world after putting his long-suffering mother through thirty-two hours of the most awful labor a woman could experience. Three weeks later, his father ran off with a female drummer from a local nightclub band and was never heard from again.

Inside Ozmand, a dark seed of hostility grew.

The microwave beeped. He slid his pot pie onto a plate and devoured it, but the hungry feeling remained. Ozmand slipped on his jacket, retrieved his skateboard from the bedroom, and left the house without leaving a note.

The moon was beginning to rise above the rock rims, and a fall wind was blowing, carrying with it the frosty chill of winter. He turned the collar of his jacket and rolled up the road toward a cluster of old tract homes haphazardly constructed upon the hillside.

Ozmand stopped at the base of a primitive stone stairway that branched off in two directions. Both ways eventually led to Cyrus's place. He shrugged, took the path to the left, and shuffled past a row of old buildings, all of which were in a sad state of repair. The windows of one tiny house were broken and covered with cardboard and electrical tape. It hardly seemed sufficient to keep cold weather out, but the man who lived there was eccentric. Everyone knew him as Old Man Pratt. He had no family and few friends; in fact, his only contact with the outside world seemed to be his weekly visits from the local county health nurse and the volunteer from Meals on Wheels.

Ozmand wagged his head as he walked by. "Creepy," he mumbled.

Suddenly, a figure rose from the shadows of the sagging porch.

An ancient man shuffled toward the boy. As he moved, moonlight spilled across thinning wisps of white hair and jaundiced eyes. Mr. Pratt stopped when his shotgun was fully visible in the silvery light. With trembling limbs, he raised the weapon and shouted, "You get out of here!"

"Hey, man!" Oz held one hand in the air and his skateboard out in front of him like a shield. "I didn't mean anything."

"I'll shoot if you come near me." Old Man Pratt's mouth moved in a spastic motion. "I know what you kids are up to. God will punish you!"

Crazy old spook, Ozmand thought as he bolted down the street.

He soon reached Cyrus's house at the far end of the circle, built around an impressive rock outcropping. On the porch, Ozmand paused to compose himself. *The man should be locked away!* His pounding heart was lost in the pulsing rhythm of the stereo that thundered through the thin walls and vibrated underfoot.

Ozmand knocked and detected movement behind the pull-down shades.

The door opened. "Come on in." Cyrus slapped his back. "Hey, boys, look who's here!"

A half-dozen guys and a couple of girls were crowded into the small house. The smell of marijuana curled around his nose and hung at eye level like a haze of pollution.

Ozmand recognized most of the kids from school—the usual skateboarders, a few goths, and Kenny the Buff, who'd led last year's football team all the way to the state championship. Then there was Big Leon, the biker, who took up over half the sofa with his girlfriend, Dixie Dawn, nuzzling his hairy neck. Leon was the self-appointed leader of a local motorcycle gang called The Reapers. They took themselves very seriously, having no clue that their group was the butt of local jokes.

"Make yourself at home."

"Thanks." Ozmand sat on a large pillow on the floor.

The faint smell of Lysol mingled with vomit wafted up from the shag rug. The place was filthy, littered with overflowing ashtrays, beer cans, and drug paraphernalia—including a crack pipe.

"Want a brew?" Cyrus popped the top on a can. He watched the foam spill over the edge and dribble onto the floor.

"Sure." Oz took the beer and chugged half of it. No one seemed particularly impressed.

"I almost forgot to show you guys! Look what I got the other day." Cyrus pulled out a box from behind a chair, threw open the top, and lifted out a brand new pair of rollerblades.

"Hey, Cy, all right!" One of the boys sprang up and ran his hands over the boots. "Have they been road tested?"

"I've been workin' 'em over." He leaned against the wall and folded his arms across his chest. "They're cool."

"I bet you're good!"

Cyrus smiled smugly. "Let's just say my skateboard's got some stiff competition." He watched with pleasure as his newest purchase was passed around and admired.

"I'm gonna get some blades too," someone blurted with obvious envy.

"Me, too," echoed another.

Everyone except Leon and Dixie Dawn coveted the new wheels. "Come on, woman," Leon said, "let's blow off some dust." He heaved his huge torso from the sofa. A gray undershirt thinly covered the mounds of blubber that hung from his waist. "Let me know when you kids get your driver's licenses. I'll show you what the big boys ride." Leon laughed and followed his girlfriend as she sauntered out the door.

"Big boys, huh?" Cyrus sneered. "I hope we don't have to get as big as Leon!"

"Did you see the guy when he laughs?" one of the boys exclaimed. "He looks like Santa Claus."

"In a way, he is," Cyrus said. "The only reason I give that idiot the time of day is because he supplies my weed." He picked up a plastic bag from the coffee table and rolled a joint.

Outside, Leon fired up his Harley, and they listened as he roared away.

Cyrus handed the joint and a lighter to Ozmand. "You do the honors."

"Sure," Oz said, not letting on that he'd never been high. He fired up the marijuana cigarette and inhaled. His lungs felt as if they were going to explode. He tried to hand it to a girl with long, mousy brown hair, but she just gave him a vacuous look.

"Ignore her," Cyrus said, intercepting the weed. "She's visiting Little Nemo."

"Who is she?" Ozmand asked, keeping an eye on the girl. She sat in the corner with her back against the wall, her legs drawn close to her body. The stereo's headphones covered her ears but the jack hadn't been plugging into the sound system.

Cyrus cranked up the volume just to annoy Cali, but she stared straight ahead with unblinking eyes, her chin resting softly on her knees.

Cyrus shrugged. "Just an X chromosome I know. She's staying here for a while."

"I didn't know you had a girl."

"I don't," Cyrus snapped. He took another hit off the joint. "I could do a lot better than that." He blew ribbons of smoke through his nostrils.

Cyrus yanked one of the headphones from her ear. "Did you hear what I said, Cali?"

The girl glared at him. "Shut up," she hissed, then buried her face in her arms.

"What'd I tell ya?" Cyrus laughed. He stretched out his arm and flicked ashes on her head.

Ozmand wished he'd never asked. He felt bad for the girl but said nothing.

Cali launched to her feet and stomped into the next room, slamming the door behind her.

"It suddenly smells better in here, don't you think?" Cyrus crinkled his nose. A few of the boys snickered.

"If you don't like her, why is she here?" Ozmand asked.

Cyrus slapped his hand to his chest. "Because nice guys like me take in a stray dog every now and then." He took another pull and exhaled putrid air from his lungs. "But this one bites, and I don't think she's had her shots yet!"

A knock sounded at the front door, and Cyrus stubbed his joint in an ashtray. "See who's here, would ya?"

Ozmand rose and peered through the small, rectangular window. On the porch stood a man wearing a black cowboy hat and the unmistakable blue uniform of the Hamlin Police Department. "Cops!" he whispered with rising panic.

Cyrus appeared behind him. "Well, don't be rude. Let him in."

"But the place smells like weed!" Ozmand protested. "We'll be busted for sure."

"There's no need to get paranoid." Cyrus pushed Ozmand aside to open the door. "What can I do for you tonight, officer?" he asked.

"I have a complaint from one of your neighbors."

"Let me guess—the nice gentleman next door, perhaps?" Cyrus raised his eyebrows in mock concern.

"Just turn down the music."

"Certainly, Officer Scott." Cyrus flashed him a toothy grin. "Would someone turn the ear candy down a few notches?"

Satisfied, the lawman ambled back to his squad car and drove away.

Cyrus closed the door and slapped a hand on his forehead. "I try to be a good neighbor, but that's just never enough for some people!" The smile on his face faded and his mood darkened. "That ol' buzzard next door should be taught a lesson."

"Yeah, he's crazy," Ozmand agreed. "Pulled a gun on me tonight when I was walking up the sidewalk."

"You don't say." Cyrus's eyes brightened with interest. "That's a good sign."

"You're kidding, right?" Ozmand looked around the room for a response.

"Party's over!" Cyrus announced. "Time to leave."

The group exchanged glances, mumbled their protests, and then left in obedience.

What did I say? Ozmand wondered as he headed for the door.

Cyrus grabbed his arm. "Stay," he said in a hushed voice. "I want to talk to you." He closed the door and turned off the stereo.

Ozmand dropped to the couch, his knee jostling nervously. The house became suddenly quiet. Those who remained eyeballed Ozmand as if sizing him up. Oz wished he'd been dismissed with the others.

"Well?" he asked, fidgeting with the bill of his ball cap. "What did you want to talk to me about?"

"Mr. Pratt is a good judge of character."

Ozmand waited for the punch line, but his host's face was serious.

"That geezer is uncanny—always seems to recognize greatness."

"I don't know what you're talking about. He's just a crazy old man who pulled a gun on me."

"Yeah? He threw a Coke bottle at me," one of the remaining young men announced.

Ozmand listened as the others recounted stories of assault at the hands of the elderly man.

Cyrus rolled up his sleeve and exposed an ugly red scar. "He nicked me with an ax once."

"He should be locked up!" Ozmand gasped. "How come you didn't turn him in?"

Cyrus shrugged. "Maybe I just like tormenting the ol' boy with my presence!"

"So, what is this—the Mr. Pratt Hit List Club?" Ozmand punctuated the question with a spattering of nervous laughter.

Cyrus stared with an intensity that made Ozmand squirm. "Before I tell you anything, you gotta swear that you will never breathe a word of this to anyone."

"Sure, Cy." Ozmand's curiosity was piqued. "I swear."

"There's a club in town, a very exclusive group."

"If Old Man Pratt is a member, then I'm not interested," Oz quipped, and the group laughed.

"Let's just call him the first step of our initiation." Cyrus's lips curled into a wry smile. "It just so happens that we've got room for a new recruit." He placed a hand on Oz's shoulder. "There's no guarantee you'll be accepted, but I have a gut feeling. Are you interested?"

"Sure. Sounds cool to me." Ozmand felt flattered.

"Great." Cy walked to the window shade and picked at a frayed end. "There's just one thing. If you whisper a word of this to anyone—and I mean *anyone*—well, let's just say you might experience a run of bad luck."

"Hey, no problem." Ozmand held up his hand. "Not a soul."

"That's what I wanted to hear. Tomorrow night, meet me at the Brewery Lane horseshoe pits."

"What time?"

"Meet me there at 8:30. And wear something dark." Cyrus escorted Ozmand to the door.

"Later, man." Ozmand tried not to show his excitement.

Cyrus stepped forward and blocked the exit. "Remember what I said. Not a word to anyone."

CHAPTER 12

April awakened to blue flower wallpaper on a slanted ceiling. It took her a few seconds to remember that she was at a farmhouse somewhere outside of town. She peeled back the heavy quilt and slid out from under its warmth. The room, cluttered with memorabilia, was inviting and cozy, though a bit chilly. At the window, lace curtains hung softly across the quilted cushion of an old-fashioned window seat. April felt drawn to that spot. She curled up there, rested her chin upon her knees, and gazed at the world outside. Below was a small apple orchard with trees so burdened by fruit it looked as if the branches would snap. An early frost had nipped the leaves, turning them brown. Some had fallen at the feet of a family of concrete rabbits.

"Mama," April whispered, pressing her cheek against the cool glass and staring blankly at the countryside. Her unfocused eyes saw no beauty there, no beauty anywhere. *Mama, why did you do it? Why did you kill yourself?*

There was a brief knock on the door and it opened. The woman who had picked her up at the Quick Mart the night before stepped inside. She wore tight polyester leggings under an oversized pin-striped shirt.

"Call me Sylvia. All the girls do." That was all April could recall of the endless sea of small talk that had poured from the woman's mouth during the thirty-minute drive to the farmhouse. The whole night had been lost in the haze of shock.

"Oh, baby doll, are those tears?" Sylvia moved across the room with quick, tiny steps, her pink pumps clicking on the wood floor. She held out her arms and lifted April from the window seat, then pressed the girl's head to her massive bosom. "There, there, hon. Go ahead and cry, get it all out." Sylvia stroked April's long blonde hair and swayed her body like a mother rocking her infant.

It was too much. April's knees buckled and a wail rose from her core.

The woman's arms gripped her tight.

April pushed herself away from Sylvia's embrace and searched for sincerity in the stranger's face.

"Somebody's hurt you real bad, haven't they, doll?" Sylvia put her hands on her hips. "Well, don't you worry, 'cause Syl's in control now." Moon-and-star earrings danced as she leaned close to April's face. The smell of gel wafted from short, spiked hair.

"You get dressed and come downstairs whenever you feel up to it. Remember, doll, if you need to talk, I'm right here." Sylvia smiled, showing coffee-stained teeth. "You may not feel like eating, but you've got to keep up your strength." She reached out and patted April's stomach.

April tugged on her t-shirt. "I don't have any clean clothes."

Sylvia sashayed to the closet door and yanked it open. "Help yourself," she said, motioning to its contents. "Underwear is in the dresser. But, hey, what you're wearing is fine for now. I insist you eat a little something."

Sylvia curled her long acrylic nails around April's arm and led the teenager downstairs to the kitchen.

A tall, skinny man in his thirties stood near the stove. He poured a cup of coffee and handed it to Sylvia, then poured another one for himself. Over the rim of his cup, he took a long gander at their newest houseguest.

April sat quietly at the Formica table, trying to still her unease.

"I'm Wallace." The man ran bony fingers through stringy ash-brown hair.

She looked down, fixing her gaze on Sylvia's painted toenails.

"This is April," Sylvia said, settling onto a chair. Her eyes met Wallace's and she added, "Our new guest needs to keep up her strength."

"Oh, right!" Wallace shoveled oatmeal and bacon onto a plate and delivered it to April.

"Where's Melanie?" Sylvia inquired.

"I sent her out to the barn to look for eggs." Wallace grabbed the tongs and flipped the bacon.

Sylvia stretched her short, sturdy legs out in front of her as April took a bite of oatmeal. It tasted bland and heavy. She swallowed hard and laid her fork down.

The old wooden screen door swung open, and a very pregnant young woman carried a basket inside and set it in front of Wallace.

He peeked inside and counted silently. "Eight eggs? Is this the best you could do?"

Melanie rolled her eyes and rubbed her back. "It's still morning and I'm already tired."

"Your pregnancy is in the home stretch, doll baby," Sylvia cooed as the young woman settled into a chair at the table.

"I've been thinking about keeping my baby." Melanie rested her hand on her stomach. "If I got a good job and found someone to baby sit, I think I could manage."

Wallace stared at the young woman.

April moved and her chair squeaked, breaking the silence.

"Whatever you think doll." Sylvia's cool gaze shifted to Melanie and she flashed a clenched smile. "This is April, the little gal I told you about. I'm sure you'll make her feel welcome."

Wallace set breakfast in front of Melanie.

"I can't eat all this!" The girl stared at the eggs, bacon, and hash browns heaped on the plate and pushed the food away.

"Remember, doll baby, you're eating for two now. At least take a prenatal vitamin." Sylvia bustled over to the cabinet above the sink and tossed Melanie a bottle of pills.

Wallace lingered behind April, casting a shadow on the table. He reached over her shoulder and poured a glass of orange juice. *He smells of lard,* she thought, noticing the black grit embedded under his nails.

"Maybe I should see an obstetrician," Melanie said. "I've been so tired. . . ."

"That's normal." Sylvia patted the girl's hand. "I can assure you that everything will be just fine."

"Yeah, Sylvia's delivered lots of babies," Wallace interjected. "She's had medical training."

"Really? What kind?" Melanie inquired.

"I was a preemie nurse." Sylvia picked at her teeth with a long acrylic fingernail. "There's no crisis I haven't seen."

The girl seemed to relax. She washed down her vitamin and stared at the pulp on the bottom of her glass.

April noticed a hair swimming in a pool of bacon grease on her plate. She laid down her fork and quickly excused herself from the table.

———

Jesse stood in the doorway of the tiny studio apartment behind the Willis' home.

"As you can see, we've been using this space as a storage shed." Lars pushed a lawnmower aside and ducked under a cobweb.

"This gives me a good excuse to throw this junk away," Emma said. She lifted a stack of old magazines from the dresser and brushed the dust away. "Just needs a good cleaning."

Jesse rolled up his sleeves. "Give me a bottle of ammonia, and I'll take care of the rest."

"I wouldn't dream of letting a guest do the cleaning!"

"Consider it a down payment on rent, which I'll pay just as soon as I find a job." Jesse locked eyes with Emma. "I don't intend to take advantage of your kindness."

She opened her mouth in protest, but Lars draped his arm over her shoulder and gave her a gentle squeeze. "We don't expect rent, son, but I understand how you feel."

Emma sighed. "I may be outnumbered on that, but as far as the cleaning goes, how about a compromise? We can all pitch in." She rattled through a closet and emerged with an old mop bucket. "Daylight's burning!"

Before the afternoon was over, the men had moved the lawnmower and several tools to a grassy area between the buildings and tossed a tarp over them. Inside, Emma cleaned surfaces and mopped the floor.

Lars and Jesse carried in an old braided rug and a few extra pieces of furniture from the main house, and the studio apartment was soon transformed.

Emma arrived with the finishing touch, a vase of silk flowers, which she placed upon the tiny kitchenette table. "I thought this apartment could use a woman's touch."

"Do you have any spare cooking utensils?" Jesse chewed his lip. "I mean, ones you don't use."

"Absolutely not!" Emma put her hands on her hips and looked sternly at Jesse. "You won't need any pots and pans because you'll be eating with us." She held up her hand to halt Jesse's protest. "And I won't take no for an answer."

Jesse gave her a hug. "I appreciate everything."

"Oh, I almost forgot to tell you," Emma said as she adjusted the flowers. "The prayer meeting is tonight. We can count on you to come, right?"

Jesse nodded.

Emma turned to her husband. "Guess who's coming?"

"Jesus?" Lars said.

"Peter and Caroline Mathews are driving up from Kingston." She looked at Jesse. "Peter is the pastor of a church we go to whenever we're up in that neck of the woods."

Emma glanced at her watch. "The roast needs checking. I hope it'll be ready in time."

"Oh, Mama, you spoil us all." Lars winked at Jesse. "She just loves feeding people."

"How long have you two been married?"

"Thirty-three years this January," Emma said.

"No kidding!" Jesse was genuinely surprised. "You act like a couple of honeymooners."

"Oh, we've had our share of rough times," Lars volunteered.

"That's right," Emma said. "I don't think a marriage exists that doesn't come with its baggage. Ours did, but we stuck it out, and that's what counts."

"Down through the years, we've lightened our load by dropping a lot of garbage at the foot of the cross." Lars played with his beard. "You might say the Lord hauled our junk to His celestial dump."

"Come on, metaphor man," Emma said with a big grin. She hooked her arm through his. "Let's let the boy get ready."

"I won't be long."

After they left, Jesse picked up his Bible from the twin bed and opened it to the book of Matthew. "For I was hungry, and you fed me, I was thirsty and you gave a drink, I was a stranger and you invited me into your home." *Such a fitting verse for Lars and Emma,* he thought.

Jesse closed his eyes in gratitude. "Thank you, Lord."

CHAPTER 13

Cali skipped through the old part of town like a kid without a care. She ripped out a handful of weeds growing from a crack in the crumbling sidewalk and pretended they were a gift from a loved one. *Must be sweet to have a loved one,* she thought. Humming a tune, she jaunted happily down the street but stopped abruptly when she sensed that someone was watching her. Cali slowly turned around.

An older man with thinning hair eyeballed her from the doorway of his shabby apartment. He took the last gulp of his beer, crushed the can in his hand, and tossed it over his shoulder. His filthy jeans hung so low that Cali thought it a wonder they stayed on; it didn't matter. She imagined him as a rippling Adonis waiting there for her.

"Here," Cali said, offering him the bouquet of weeds. "These are for you, 'cause you're so cute!"

The man belched loudly. She blew him a kiss and danced off down the road.

On the outskirts of town, Cali threw a rock at the second-story window of the old granary, laughing as glass shards flew through the air and splintered on the ground around her.

Cali had no particular place to go—at least, not yet. The sun was sinking lower on the horizon, and her stomach told her it was dinnertime. She imagined all the moms hard at work serving heaping portions to their adoring families. When she was a little girl, she liked to pretend that she had one of those moms. The reality was that she was born into the arms of a sadist, a woman who loved to watch little things squirm. Cali never called her Mother and wasted no time grieving when she died. In fact, she would have spit on the woman's grave right then if she knew where it was. Cali's mood darkened momentarily, but she chased her murky thoughts back into the shadows.

She trailed along the railroad track, balancing on one rail and then the other. Below her feet, she felt the vibrations of the evening train some distance away. An abandoned mine stood about a quarter of a mile ahead. Cali bet herself that she could make it there before the train.

As she ran toward it, she tried to imagine the Ellington mine back when the train stopped there every day to haul away ore.

Cali jogged faster. She heard the train approaching behind her. It was skirting the town now and picking up speed for the climb out of the valley. *It will be close,* she thought. The idea excited her.

The engineer blew the whistle, but Cali only laughed and continued up the middle of the tracks. The horn blasted again. She glanced over her shoulder. The huge mass of iron was hurtling closer, so near that Cali could see the engineer's horrified face. Laughter bubbled from within. The engineer blasted the horn again and waived his arm wildly.

Cali stopped, turned, and faced the oncoming train, then laid herself across the track with her neck resting on the railing. She giggled like a little child watching a cartoon. The shrill sound of metal on metal shrieked through the air as the train's wheels locked and ground across the rails.

Cali yawned and rolled her body from the track as casually as if she were rolling off a chaise lounge. A split second later, and her life would have been ended.

Reveling in the darkness of her humor, she stood, brushed the dirt from her clothes, and watched the train slide to a stop.

The engineer leaned his ashen face from the window of the train. "Are you crazy? You got a death wish or something?"

Cali took a bow, blew him kisses, and strolled toward the mine with a light-hearted lilt in her step.

She reached the mine just in time to sit on an old, rusty ore cart and watch the train chug away.

She glanced around. Little, if anything, was familiar to her now. The old Ellington mine, once the bread and butter of the community, was now nothing more than another preservation cause for the aging women of the Montana Historical Society. The mine was boarded up with wood that was gray and weathered from harsh winters. DANGER was still legible in faded, red letters beside a black skull and crossbones, intended to scare away potential intruders.

The sun was sinking fast, casting alpenglow. Cali traced the grain of the wood with her finger and marveled at the colors. She drew her hand back and stared at a splinter that had pierced her thumb. *How can something that isn't human bring such pain?* Cali pulled the tiny piece of wood from her skin and watched as a droplet of blood formed in its place.

Anger began to rise. It grew until it could not be contained. Cali picked up a piece of iron. Rage took control, and she swung, unleashing her frustrations on the two-by-four braces in a frenzy. When the dust settled, half the mine's barrier was either ripped away or lay cracked and broken on the ground.

Cali took a deep, cleansing breath, stepped through the opening, and paused in front of the mineshaft. An old elevator platform and heavy steel cable lay in a heap behind the dark, gaping hole. She sat on the edge of the shaft, imagining the workers who'd once descended into the belly of the earth. She dropped the piece of iron into the hole and listened for its end. *Going, going, going, gone.* Thud. Like the brassy sound of an object landing in hell. Cali smiled.

As the light grew dimmer, Cali slipped a folded manila envelope from her pocket. She held the contents up to a beam of evening light that spilled into the mine. She read the letter twice, absorbing its implications. She doubted the veiled promises to give her baby back, but it was all she had. Most of all, Cali knew that if she didn't do as instructed, there would be hell to pay. She glanced back at Hamlin. In the distance, the town's streetlights flickered on.

I have no choice.

Cali slipped a lighter from her pocket and put the flame to the paper. She watched the typewritten words curl and brown before fluttering downward, temporarily invading the darkness of the pit.

Ozmand paused outside the door marked County Attorney. He shoved it open and found his mother seated behind her desk, just as he knew she would be.

Nan, telephone pressed against her ear, held up a finger to her son. "I'm sorry, Mr. Hardwig, but the court date has not been set. We'll let you know the minute we hear." She hung up and gave Ozmand a quizzical look.

"I need some money," he said loudly. "There's nothing at our house to eat." Ozmand leaned his lanky frame against his mother's desk.

"Keep it down," Nan whispered, looking back toward her boss's office. "Mr. Ellington is on a telephone conference." She pressed her lips together. "You know I don't like it when you come here."

"If you bought me a cell phone, I wouldn't have to," Ozmand said. "I'm hungry—just give me five bucks and I'll grab a hot dog at the Quick Mart."

His mother straightened a stack of papers on her desk. "I'm almost finished here. Then we'll swing by the grocery store and pick up a roasted chicken."

Ozmand sat on a straight-backed chair and watched as his mom dabbed a spot of rubber cement on her nylons. *Why can't she be normal?* he wondered.

She leaned back in her chair and stared at the light on the phone. "Mr. Ellington is finished with his call." She smoothed her hair, sat up straight, and busied herself with the papers on her desk, keeping an expectant eye on the boss's door.

When Brock Ellington emerged, Ozmand thought he heard his mother's breathe catch.

"Mr. Ellington ," Nan said, seeming to levitate from her seat, "I've finished the documents. Is there anything else?"

Pathetic. Ozmand wished he could crawl under his mother's desk.

"No, I think we can call it a day." Brock looked up from his smart phone. "Hello, Oz. Wow, I think you've grown a foot since the last time I laid eyes on you. Did your mother tell you she got a raise today?"

Ozmand shrugged and made no attempt to stifle a yawn.

"Son, Mr. Ellington is talking to you," Nan snapped.

Brock slipped his phone into his pocket. "That's okay. I remember being seventeen." He paused at the door and looked back. "Your boy is growing up fast. Remember what I said."

Alone in the office, Nan turned back to her son, her face crimson. "I can't believe your behavior. I didn't raise you to be rude."

Ozmand picked up an office magazine and flipped through the pages.

Nan let out an exasperated sigh. "I give up. Anyway, I'm not going to let anything spoil my evening." She paused. "Hey, you want to go out to dinner? You know—to celebrate my raise?"

"Beats rubber chicken," he said as he followed his mother to her Volvo sedan.

Ozmand raised an eyebrow when his mother steered her car into a parking space at the Hamlin Hotel. "Must be a good raise." When they came to a stop, he hopped out and opened the car door for his mother.

Nan's jaw dropped. "Are you Ozmand or an impostor?" She held her arm out for her son to escort her.

He looked around to see if any of his peers just happened to be cruising by. "Sorry, but I only do doors."

His mother smiled. "Yes, you're the real thing, all right." She tweaked his cheek.

"Cut it out!" he scowled. It was borderline bad to be seen in public with your mother but downright geeky to let her touch you. "Come on, let's go eat. I'm starved."

The place had imported French wallpaper and softly lit chandeliers. Tasteful piano music drifted from the lounge.

Ozmand recognized a few local faces, but most of the patrons were unfamiliar—probably out-of-towners.

"I should have put on my black dress," Nan whispered. "And you could use a tie and a jacket."

"It's okay, Mom, we're fine."

Nan scurried to their table behind the maître d' and snapped open the menu. "I've never seen so many pearls and furs."

"These people aren't paying any attention to you."

"You're probably right," Nan said. She leaned over and held her hand next to her mouth. "How many of these men, do you suppose, are wearing overly starched boxer shorts?"

Ozmand snorted. A woman at a nearby table turned and pressed her lips in terse disapproval.

The teenager cocked his eyebrow in the patron's direction. "Heavy on the starch."

His mother got the giggles, slipped a tissue from her

purse, and dabbed the corner of her eye.

The waiter arrived and took their order, then hurried away.

Nan reached across the table and touched her son's hand. "This is great, Oz. It seems like it was just yesterday that I could hold you on my lap and rock you to sleep. Now I never even see you."

Ozmand selected a black olive from the relish tray and shoved it in his mouth. "If you didn't have to work so much. . . ."

"Now, Oz, we've been over this before. You know it's a sacrifice that I have to make right now. And you know I'm doing it for you."

"Yeah, yeah, I know." He rolled his eyes.

When their meals arrived, Ozmand ate as if he hadn't seen food in weeks. "Hey, your paycheck just walked in." He pointed his steak knife in the direction of the door.

Brock Ellington stood chatting with the maître d'.

Nan set her fork on her plate, dabbed at her mouth with her napkin, and tried to catch her boss's attention by waving to him.

Near the hatcheck station, an attractive strawberry blonde slid a cashmere cape from her shoulders, revealing a strapless cocktail dress, and joined Mr. Ellington .

Brock turned from the attendant, placed his hand on his date's bare back, and escorted her to their seat.

"What a babe," Ozmand exclaimed, and stuffed another bite of steak into his mouth.

His mother's face paled. She seemed to be hyperventilating.

"Mom, you okay?"

"I don't feel well, honey. I think I might be getting a migraine." Her eyes filled with tears. "I'm sorry. I wanted this to be special."

Ozmand looked around, but no one was paying any attention. "It's okay, Mom."

She summoned the waiter and handed him her credit card.

"Can I get a doggie bag?" Ozmand asked.

"Of course, sir. I'll have the kitchen wrap it up." The waiter snatched the plate away.

Nan's eyes were on her boss, who had stopped to visit with a client. She grabbed her purse and whispered, "I'll be in the car," then headed for the exit.

Alone at the table, Oz feigned interest in the wine list until the waiter returned with his leftovers and the check. He signed his mother's name.

"Ozmand, what a surprise." Brock Ellington paused beside the table. "Are you here by yourself?"

"I came with my mother. She's not feeling too well, so she's waiting for me outside."

"What a shame, especially after Nan took my advice and did something special with you."

Oz stared at Brock. "You told Mom to take me out to dinner?"

"Well, it was just a suggestion. I know how fast you kids grow up." Brock brushed a piece of lint off the boy's shoulder. "You're becoming a fine young man. Nan should be proud. Tell her I hope she feels better soon."

Outside the restaurant, Ozmand slammed the bag of

SHADOW *of the* PIPER

leftovers against the building and made his way to the parking lot. He jerked open the door on the driver's side. "I'll drive."

His mother didn't protest. She walked around to the passenger seat of her Volvo and slumped into a passive pout. Nan didn't even complain when Ozmand floored it and burned rubber on the pavement.

She probably wouldn't notice if I drove straight to hell, he thought.

CHAPTER 14

Jesse liked Theda Mae Crabtree from the moment he met her. She was agile for a woman in her eighties, and her sharp eyes sparkled with life.

She ushered her guests through the door of her old Victorian house and hung their coats on a vintage hat tree. "Hugs!" Theda Mae opened her arms wide. Jesse was the first recipient. With hands still resting warmly on his arms, the old woman tilted her head back and peered at him through bifocals. "So, you're the young man Lars and Emma have told me so much about." Theda Mae gazed intently into his eyes. A few seconds later, a smile blossomed on her lips. "Yes," she said cryptically. "I am so blessed to meet you."

Mrs. Crabtree directed everyone to a sunny sitting room filled with an eclectic mix of relics. Delicate French furnishings sat on a richly hued Oriental rug, accented by tasseled lampshades and paisley curtains. An outrageous collection of Neo-impressionist art hung among autographed photos of vaudeville notables.

Theda Mae held out a tray of goodies. "These oatmeal cookies are a favorite of mine—an old recipe of my mother's." She seemed pleased when Jesse took two.

Lars approached a thirty-something couple. The man, tall and thin, looked like a daddy longlegs on the delicate settee that he shared with his petite wife. "Peter and Caroline! I'm glad to see you made it." Lars tossed a glance in Jesse's direction. "Come on over and say hello to our friends who pastor a church over in Kingston."

"Pleasure to meet you," the couple said in unison.

They engaged in a spattering of pleasant conversation while their elderly hostess bustled about making everyone feel welcome.

"We've known Mrs. Crabtree for about seven years now," Caroline said.

"What a blessing," Peter added, lacing his long fingers behind his head. "I don't know what I'd do without her. She's a real prayer warrior."

"That's an understatement," Caroline interjected. "Whenever my husband has a serious request, he calls on Mrs. Crabtree."

"Enough of this nonsense," Theda Mae scowled. "If we're going to talk about someone, I'd rather talk about the Lord."

Jesse lifted an old tintype photo from the coffee table. It depicted a man and a woman in theatrical poses and dressed in Victorian-style costumes. "Who is this?"

"Those are my grandparents," the old woman said proudly. "They were vaudevillians. I guess you could say I was, too, in a way. They sometimes took me with them when they traveled the circuit—they even used me in a few of their acts."

"Wow," Jesse exclaimed. "That sounds like an interesting childhood."

"I have no complaints. I got to see this big country, and I met some wonderful people along the way."

"How did you wind up in Hamlin?" Jesse asked.

"Love." She gazed at a silver-framed wedding photo that hung above a velvet crescent couch. "Augustus Crabtree was the love of my life," she said, smiling wistfully. "We had forty-nine beautiful years together, and I still thank the Lord for that."

"How is your daughter?" Caroline said quietly. Her gaze sunk to the coffee cup in her hand. She took a sip.

The elderly woman lifted a photo of a young woman in a business suit. "Betsy took a position with Nextel-Sprint and is living on the East Coast. We don't see each other as much as I'd like, but she's happy, that's the important thing."

Theda Mae looked quizzically at the younger woman. "Honey, I can sense your heart is troubled, but you mustn't worry. God has heard your prayers—just as he heard Hannah, Rebecca, and Rachel. If the good Lord could make them mothers, he can do the same for you."

"How did you know?" the young woman asked.

"Sometimes the good Lord tells me how to pray." Theda Mae turned to the group and rubbed her hands together. "Speaking of prayer, let's all get down to business."

"Good idea," Peter Mathews said. "I was fasting a few weeks ago and felt a strong witness for this town. Actually, a deep sorrow."

"Well then," Theda Mae said, smiling and joining hands with the group, "let's ask the Lord to train our hands for battle!"

Roxanne rang the doorbell and waited. Behind the white lace curtains of the Gilberts' living room, nothing moved, but that in itself was not unusual. Roxanne had never seen anyone actually use the room. It was always in picture-perfect order, with throw pillows perfectly fluffed, accents placed just so, and a blanket of snow-white carpet. April used to laugh about it, saying, "Mom would have a meltdown if she ever walked into the chaotic clutter of the Volcovich's home." There was always something wistful about the way April emphasized the word "home."

Roxanne punched the doorbell again, then opened the screen and wrapped her knuckles on the door. An orange leaf fell from a wreath that was fastened there and fluttered to the porch. Roxanne kicked it in frustration and was just about to give up when she heard footsteps.

The door opened just enough to frame Mr. Gilbert's disheveled face. He rubbed a hand across a rough crop of whiskers.

Roxanne struggled for words. "I'm sorry about Mrs. Gilbert," she blurted. "I mean, I can't believe. . . ."

He just stared at her with stony silence. Stale air moved through the crack in the door, carrying the distinct odor of gin. "What do you want?"

"I've been trying to get a hold of April." Roxanne sunk her hands into the back pockets of her jeans. "Is she here?"

"Her cell phone is in her bedroom." After a brief but awkward pause, April's father motioned the visitor inside. He wore a suit that looked as though it had been slept in. "I thought April was with you."

Roxanne followed him across the room and watched him plop down on a sofa. The rest of the house was a mess of newspapers, food wrappers, and empty bottles. The void left by Mrs. Gilbert's death was more than noticeable—it was profound.

The man slumped forward, holding his face in trembling hands. "Where could April be?"

"I'm sure she'll turn up." Roxanne tried not to sound too worried, yet her best friend wasn't even posting anything on her Facepage! Roxanne ran down a mental list of acquaintances and promised to make a few calls. Still, it seemed unlikely that April would have gone to anyone else.

Mr. Gilbert's eyes widened. "Do you think she'd hurt herself?"

The question raised apprehension. *April's pregnancy and now her mother's suicide.* "Mr. Gilbert," Roxanne said, "maybe you should call the police."

—⁓—

Police Chief Art Patterson's ulcer had been acting up again. He popped a couple of Mylanta tablets in his mouth and chewed them slowly. Art rubbed his chest and waited for the antacid to kick in.

His thoughts drifted to his impending retirement. By next spring, he hoped to be fishing on the Madison River; he'd always dreamed of taking a father-son fishing trip. Soon, if all went well, it would be a reality. He had arranged in advance, and his son, a junior partner at a prestigious law firm in Denver, seemed excited about the prospect.

It's a good thing they're putting me out to pasture, he thought. The truth was, Patterson's heart just wasn't in the job anymore.

"Excuse me, Chief." A short woman in uniform knocked lightly on the door frame. "There's a Leland Gilbert here. He wants to see you."

"Gilbert?" Patterson knew Leland from the Kiwanis Club. He was a quiet man with a tendency to drink too much, but generally a likable fellow. "Poor guy. He's had more than his share. . . ." Patterson trailed off, remembering his own personal loss. "Did he say what he wants to talk to me about?"

"He's here to file a missing persons report. I told him I could take the information, but he insists on talking to you."

"Send him in."

When Leland walked in, the chief motioned toward a chair and waited for him to sit. "I'm sorry for you loss," Art said gently. "I know how it feels to lose a wife."

Leland's shoulders slumped. He averted his eyes, a sign of guilt that Patterson had come to recognize through his years in law enforcement. Art could only imagine the feelings of guilt that accompanied a loved one's suicide.

Mr. Gilbert's lip trembled.

Chief Patterson pretended not to notice. He straightened a stack of papers on his desk. "What can I do for you, Leland?"

"I came to talk to you about my little girl." Mr. Gilbert stared at his hands. "April didn't come home last night. Actually, it's been two nights, and I. . . ." His voice broke.

"Well," the chief ventured, "It's probably nothing to worry about. After all, she just lost her mother. Maybe she needs a little time before she can face your grief, too. She's probably staying at a friend's house."

"I've already checked with her friends." Mr. Gilbert's voice was taut. "Nobody knows where she is!"

Chief Patterson picked up a pen and tapped it on the desk as his mind turned. April Gilbert must be a young lady by now, but the last time he'd laid eyes on her she was a skinny little towheaded thing. "I'll need a recent photo, cell phone number, Facepage account sign-in, and a list of any friends who might be able to help."

"She didn't take her phone with her," Mr. Gilbert said, "but I'll do my best to get you the rest of the information." The worried father gazed across the chief's desk. "Just find my little girl. She's all I have left."

CHAPTER 15

Ozmand rolled over in his disheveled bed and stared at his digital clock. It was almost noon; though his mother usually found some excuse to work on Saturdays, he could hear her banging around in the kitchen. *Probably scraping together some slop to eat,* he thought. Cooking had never been one of his mother's skills; to make matters worse, she wore a look of self-sacrifice upon her face whenever she attempted anything domestic.

Anger rose within him. He covered his head with his pillow. *She doesn't know me. She has no idea what makes me tick.*

Lately, his mother had been thrusting herself uninvited into his world, trying to talk when she'd previously shown no interest. As far as Ozmand was concerned, it was too late.

He grabbed his iPod and earbuds, cranked up the volume, then laid back to mouth the lyrics of Ram's Fire's latest release. He closed his eyes, allowing himself to drift along with the primal beat. Finally, with a yawn and a stretch, he rolled out of bed and dug through the dirty clothes hamper for his favorite American Eagle t-shirt and a pair of jeans.

When Ozmand emerged from his room, the house was quiet. He felt a strange mixture of relief and disappointment. "Alone, as usual," Oz murmured to himself, plucking a note from the refrigerator along with a five-dollar bill.

"Honey, I wanted to make you a nice lunch but ran out of ingredients and gave up. I decided to get my hair permed instead. Grab a burger. Love, Mom."

Ozmand curled his fist around the money, shoved it in his pocket, and picked up the phone. "Mrs. V, is Rudy there?"

"He's out back with his father," she said cheerfully. "They're working on his car. Want me to have him call you?"

"That's all right. I'm going out. I'll talk to him later." Oz hung up, grabbed his skateboard, and went outside.

The air was cool and dry and carried the frosty chill of winter. Ozmand felt goose bumps rise on his arms as he flew down the hill on his skateboard. He jumped the curb at the bottom and rolled slowly up the sidewalk, balancing on two wheels. Nearing the Burger Grill, he showed off with a couple of special maneuvers in case anyone was watching. He rolled to a stop at the order window. "Large cheeseburger and a chocolate shake."

A couple minutes later, Ozmand carried his tray of food to a picnic table beneath a canvas awning, where he practically inhaled his food. He gulped his milkshake so fast his head hurt. He glanced around at the sprinkling of middle-aged faces. *Where is everybody?* Oz wondered. The only people out were old people or mothers with snot-nosed toddlers. He left the garbage from his meal on the table and left.

Ozmand mounted his skateboard and serpentined toward the heart of town looking for anything to kill his boredom.

He found Cyrus practicing his rollerblade moves on Brewery Lane and marveled at how quickly Cy had mastered them. There was no denying his extraordinary athletic ability.

Ozmand pushed his skateboard to the side of a building and joined a row of fans. They all watched in awe as Cyrus seemed to defy gravity, exuding power and importance with every move.

Master of his craft, Ozmand thought. *Sweet.*

Cyrus made eye contact with Ozmand and gave him the thumbs-up sign. To Oz's surprise, a clique of cheerleaders from school smiled at him. Popular girls had never given him the time of day. He tilted his head and nodded in their direction.

Cyrus cut a sharp turn and slid to a stop in front of Ozmand. "Okay," he said, clapping his hands, "show's over!" He draped his arm over Oz's shoulder. "I have some business to discuss with my friend here, so why don't you all just take a little stroll?"

Ozmand waited while the group broke up and ambled off in different directions. One of the girls looked over her shoulder as she walked away. She smiled and coyly flipped her hair. The attention made him weak in the knees.

"You going to make it tonight?" Cyrus stooped to adjust a rollerblade.

"I wouldn't miss it." Oz grabbed a handful of gravel from the gutter and tossed it into the street. "You really think I've got a shot at being accepted into the club?"

Cyrus leaned his elbows back on the sidewalk and smirked. "Listen, kid, if I say you're in, you're in." He stood, caught his reflection in a store window, and ran a hand across a swath of bleached hair. "Meet me at the horseshoe pits at 7:30 and I'll take you on a little tour," he said, before skating down the street.

Ozmand whistled a tune as he strolled toward home. *Somehow, the sky looks brighter than it did yesterday*, he thought.

The chief of police sat at the counter of the Roundup Café and ate his chicken-fried steak in silence. Evenings were always the hardest time of day for Art Patterson. Five years had gone by since his wife's passing, and yet sorrow was still there to greet him at the end of each day.

Patterson dreaded going home to his empty house. *But tonight at least I'll have something other than the television to help pass the time.* He thought about the cardboard box sitting in the front seat of the cruiser, stacked full of files that had been warehoused in the backroom file cabinets. *It's a start,* he thought. Some of these unsolved cases had been filed away so long they had been forgotten; it was time to get his house in order. Maybe sifting through the past might help the next chief of police get a bearing on the small Montana town, but tonight Art was hoping it might bring a clue as to the whereabouts of April Gilbert. It was a long shot at best.

"More coffee, Chief?" The waitress, an attractive woman in her late forties, held out a pot of decaf.

He smiled. "Got any of the real stuff?"

"Coming right up." She grabbed a pot of regular and poured. "You planning to stay up past your bedtime?"

Patterson warmed his hands on the mug. "I have a date with a stack of papers."

She leaned against the counter. "It's a shame you have to work so much, Art."

Patterson knew the woman was flirting with him. He felt his cheeks blush. "Well, somebody's gotta keep the town free of crime for good folks like you."

"Order's up!" came a voice from the kitchen, and the waitress hurried off.

Art left a half-full cup of coffee and a decent tip on the counter and made his exit. He climbed into his Crown Victoria and steered the old boat through the neighborhood.

The town was quiet as he drove home. The usual dinner-hour lull. Art imagined the citizens of Hamlin sitting around their tables, eating home-cooked meals and sharing the day's events. It gave him a vicarious pleasure to think about that. He gently lulled his memory to a time when he'd shared that sense of family belonging. It was odd, but those little things he took for granted back then were the very things he missed the most now.

His house was a classic piece of Americana. Its cedar siding was painted pink, Bea's favorite color. A white picket fence bordered the small yard. The only thing missing was the beautiful daisy garden, which had withered and died from a lack of TLC.

Art parked in the carport and gathered his things. Inside, he placed the box of files on the kitchen table and walked through the house to turn on a few lights.

The red message indicator was flashing on his answering machine. Art pressed the playback button.

"Dad, give me a call when you get in."

Art punched a series of numbers into the telephone.

"Hi, son. I got your message. I was going to call you anyway. I found a great fishing vest up in Kingston. It has more pockets and a bigger pouch for the catch. I hope you don't mind, but I took the liberty of buying two of them."

"Listen, Dad, about that fishing trip. I ran into a bit of a conflict. One of our senior partners gave his two-week notice. Major changes around here—changes that could work into a promotion. I just don't think it would be in my best interest to go on vacation right now."

"I understand, son. You're a businessman." Art did his best not to betray his deep disappointment.

"Thanks, Dad. I'm sorry. I was really looking forward to wetting a line with you. Maybe next year, huh?"

"Sure, son. Give Judy and my grandbabies a hug. Take care." Art hung up and stood for a moment, staring at a family photo on the table next to the phone. The Pattersons at Disneyland, standing next to Snow White, their only child beaming in the foreground. Art smiled when he thought about that trip, back when Disneyland was young. At the time, they couldn't really afford it on his patrol officer's salary, but Bea had insisted.

"Don't look at the cost," she'd said. "It's a memory-maker, and you can't put a price on happy memories."

"You were right," Art whispered. He kissed his finger and softly touched the image of his rosy-cheeked wife.

He went back into the kitchen, where he pulled a Sara Lee cheesecake out of the fridge and cut himself a big slice.

So what if the doctor said he had a bad ticker and he was supposed to watch his diet? The way Art saw it, he didn't have much to lose anyway.

CHAPTER 16

Ozmand was sprawled across the living room floor watching a survival show on TV when Nan came home from the beauty parlor. He took one look at her curly perm and burst out laughing. "Didn't those go out with Starsky and Hutch?" he asked.

Nan's face turned red, and she snapped, "I don't need your opinion."

"It'll probably grow on ya," Ozmand smirked. "Get it?"

"I don't see the humor in this," his mother shrieked. She fled into the bathroom and slammed the door.

"I gotta go, Mom," Oz called. "I won't be back 'til late, so don't wait up." *If she did, it would be the first time,* Ozmand thought cynically. He grabbed his black canvas jacket and walked out the door.

He found Cyrus leaning against the old brewery near the horseshoe pits. The sun was just beginning to set, but black, roiling clouds blanketed the streets in darkness. The first significant winter storm of the year had descended upon the town of Hamlin, leaving the October air frigid. According to the weather forecast, temperatures were expected to drop below freezing.

Ozmand moved casually toward his new friend.

"You're a couple minutes late," Cyrus said. He pulled a joint from his pocket and put it between his lips, then flicked a lighter and cupped his hand around the flame. He inhaled slowly, allowing smoke to escape through his teeth.

Ozmand's eyes darted around, and he felt a rush of fear. "Right here? We could get busted!"

Cyrus finished exhaling, blowing stale, foul-smelling air in Oz's face. "I defy anyone to touch me," he sneered. "Listen, you're with me now, and that buys you a certain amount of privilege in this town." He studied Ozmand as if challenging him. "If you're not up to hanging out, then maybe you should skip on home to your mommy."

Yeah, right, Ozmand thought. He snatched the joint, took a pull from it, and waited for the buzz.

Finally, Cyrus tossed the spent weed on the sidewalk and let it smolder. "C'mon."

Ozmand followed Cyrus around the side of the building, stopping behind the Buckhorn Bar and Grill. There was a staircase leading to a basement. Fall leaves had gathered in the stairwell, giving the impression that few had entered there recently.

Cyrus fished a key from his pocket and slid it into the lock.

They entered a spacious room furnished with rich mahogany paneling and expensive-looking leather furniture. The floors were laid with stone tiles, and the bar was carved from dark wood.

On the back wall hung a large, gold-framed portrait of

a man. Ozmand studied the subject of the painting, whose slate-gray eyes seemed to follow his movements. It was creepy. Ozmand shuddered and looked away.

"What do ya think?" Cyrus asked.

"This place is awesome." Ozmand stood alone as his new friend moved over to the bar and grabbed a couple bottles of beer.

Cyrus tossed one to Ozmand, who settled into a soft chair, took a sip, and thought, *I could get used to this.*

"Normally, I don't let a guy know he's being evaluated for membership," Cyrus said, plopping down on a nearby couch. He took a swig of beer and belched. "But in your case I had a gut feeling that you're what we're looking for. So let's just say I pulled a few strings to get you here." Cyrus set his beer on the table and leaned forward. "Don't let me down." He enunciated each word deliberately.

"H-Hey, it's cool," Ozmand stammered.

The room began to fill until there were several dozen men. Ozmand had met some of them at Cyrus's house; others were people he knew from growing up in Hamlin, like Mr. Maxwell from the butcher shop. Oz spotted his dentist and the mailman who had once dated his mother. Ozmand recalled the repulsion he had once felt for the man; though many years had passed, his feelings hadn't changed.

Suddenly, Ozmand felt very out of place among the growing crowd of older men. "I can't believe it," he whispered to Cyrus. "There's my old middle-school principal over there at the end of the bar." He was visiting with a member of the school board. Ozmand watched as more people trickled in, older business types mingling easily with young goths.

Just then, a group of young people blew through the door, injecting their energy into the room. One of the kids went behind the bar, slipped a retro CD into the player, and cranked up the volume.

The music intensified with the steady beat of drums. "Judas Priest!" shrieked a young man. "All right! Classic!" He slapped another kid's palm, closed his eyes, threw back his head, and played air guitar with a passion. Half of the kid's scalp was shaved and had a snake tattoo on it. The other half was a matted gnarl.

"I've never seen him before," Ozmand whispered.

"He came down from Kingston."

"Who is he?"

"Never mind. Names aren't important here."

Near the bar, a goth fired up a resin-stained meerschaum pipe. The smell of marijuana curled around the room like incense. To Oz's surprise, the older folks seemed undaunted. Some even joined in.

Ozmand leaned toward Cyrus. "This is all right!"

The mood changed when a man wearing a red and gold hooded robe walked into the room. Someone dimmed the lights.

The man's features were obscured in the shadows of his deep cowl. However, there was no mistaking the obvious. *This is somebody important,* Ozmand thought.

"Our high priest." Cyrus confirmed with a whisper as the music stopped.

A hush fell over place. All those who were standing took a seat.

Ozmand noticed a gangly guy sitting in the corner. He was slumped forward, holding his face in his hands. He did not move or look up.

The man in the colorful robe raised his arms like wings.

Ozmand strained to hear the words that rumbled from the man's throat. He couldn't quite understand them.

The room was silent, the mood thick with tension. The robed figure turned toward the cornered man, whose eyes were wide with terror.

"We will cast our vote now." The hooded figure announced. On an ornate table to his right rested two items: a simple silver chalice and a black satin bag. A member hurried to the table as though silently summoned. With the bag in one hand and the goblet in the other, he carried the items about the room.

One at a time, the members reached into the bag and pulled out a smooth white stone, which they dropped into the chalice.

"Am I supposed to do that, too?" Ozmand whispered.

"No, you haven't been initiated."

When his turn arrived, Cyrus placed the white stone into the chalice and watched as the ritual was repeated.

"Nothing like a rigged vote," Oz quipped as the ritual repeated.

"Shut up!" Cyrus hissed.

The items were returned to the table where the high priest lingered speaking in low, guttural phrases. Suddenly, smoke billowed from the chalice, and the room filled with the putrid smell of burning sulfur. Fire engulfed the cup.

Ozmand looked around. All the others were saying

something, chanting a word he'd never heard before. The feeling was intoxicating, yet at the same time, terrifying.

In the corner, the accused began to moan as the flames died down.

Abruptly, the high priest spilled the goblet's contents onto the table. The stones had turned to black.

Faces snarled with rage at the condemned man. "Guilty—guilty—guilty—guilty." The crowd pounced like a mob and dragged him pleading from the room.

Oz's skin began to crawl. "What's going to happen to him?" he asked Cyrus.

Suddenly, the hooded figure pointed his finger toward Ozmand. He could feel those eyes upon him, and it raised the hair on the back of neck.

Cyrus jumped to his feet. "Brother Raven, let me explain." He placed a hand on his guest's shoulder. "This is the gifted recruit I was telling you about. I think his talents can be harnessed and. . . ."

The high priest's finger silenced Cyrus with a gesture. He turned abruptly and seemed to vanish into the shadows.

Oz felt a rush of relief when the lights came on. "Wow. This was a lot to take in." The teenager struggled for the words. "Don't get me wrong bro—I mean, it's all cool, but I don't really think the Piper's Guild is my kind of thing."

Cyrus took Ozmand by the elbow and ushered him down a hallway and into a windowless room filled with clothing racks. He grabbed a brown robe and snarled. "Put this on!"

After doing as he was told, Ozmand was escorted to a tiny cubicle about the size of a large closet. The space was empty except for a flickering black candle and a small red book sitting on a Persian rug.

"Wait here until they come for you." Cyrus paused in the threshold before closing the door. "As far as the Piper's Guild is concerned, you have passed the point of no return."

Alone in the room, Oz's breathing came shallow and quick. His heart thumped behind his ribs as he lifted the book. Its cover was embossed with a triangle. In its center, written in red, were the words Piper's Bible.

CHAPTER 17

The afternoon bell rang, and Roxanne charged into the hallway with the other teenagers. Swept along in the flow, she scanned faces, looking for Logan. Roxanne spotted him loitering at his locker with two of his football teammates.

"I need to talk to you!" she yelled over the noise.

"Have you seen April? She's not answering her cell phone or text messages," he said as his friends ambled away. "I heard about Mrs. Gilbert." Logan shook his head and his eyes grew soft with sadness. "Bad deal. I keep calling her house but no one's picking up."

"April's not there," Roxanne said.

"Then where is she?"

Roxanne shook her head. "I'm worried, Logan. I mean, she's been under a lot of stress lately and now this. . . ."

"What do you mean? Until this thing with her mother, I've been more stressed than April. The football team has a lot riding on the next game, and I need to keep my grades up."

At that moment, Roxanne felt nothing but contempt for April's boyfriend. "You're a real piece of work!"

"What did I do?" he bellowed. "April was mad at me last week, and now you. What is going on?"

She studied Logan's face, his handsome features perplexed.

"Look, I just want to tell April how sorry I am about her mom." He clamped his eyes shut and turned toward the lockers.

Roxanne's heart surged with unexpected compassion for the high school's star quarterback. Logan, with his dark wavy hair and muscular build, had always come off as being conceited; now he seemed lost and vulnerable.

The volume of noise in the hallway lowered to the laughter of a few stragglers and the sound of lockers slamming.

"Logan, there's something you need to know." Roxanne touched his shoulder. "April is pregnant."

Logan's face drained of color. His body slid down the locker to a squatting position. He clasped his face in his hands and stared at Roxanne through his fingers.

"I promised April that I wouldn't tell anyone, but things have changed."

Logan continued to stare.

"April has disappeared."

"What?" Logan scrambled to his feet.

Roxanne nodded. "No one has seen her since her mother's death. Not even her father. I'm really worried about her. I don't know where to look for her."

"She hasn't called you?"

Roxanne shook her head. "The services for her mom are tomorrow. I'm hoping she'll show up, but I don't know..."

"Why didn't April tell me?"

Roxanne heard men's voices from down the hall. She held a finger to her lips. "Someone's coming."

The principal rounded the corner with the town's chief of police, Art Patterson. The two were fully engaged in conversation, their voices lowered.

"Wonder why the cops are here?" Logan said.

The principal made eye contact with Roxanne and motioned to her. "Young lady, I'm glad you're here. Chief Patterson needs to inspect April Gilbert's locker, and I'm sure he would love to ask you a few questions, too." He turned to the chief. "Roxanne is a good friend of April's."

Patterson eyed the teenagers. "That's a good idea. I'd also like to talk to her teachers and her guidance counselor."

"Here it is," said the principal, stopping in front of April's locker. He checked a piece of paper and fiddled with the combination lock before turning his attention to Logan. "I've seen you hanging around with April. Are you two going out?"

"Yes, sir." The young man looked Chief Patterson in the eye. "My name is Logan Taylor."

"What if something's happened to April?" Roxanne blurted.

"Let's not think the worst," the chief said gently. He paused and cocked an eyebrow toward the principal. "Thanks, Mr. Albright. I'll let you know if you can be of further assistance."

The administrator lingered for a second or two as if he were trying to process the fact that he had been dismissed. "Well," he said, turning on his heels, "I'll be in my office if you need me."

In his absence, the hall was quiet.

Chief Patterson slid a little notebook and pen from his pocket. "Now, about those questions. . . ."

Roxanne folded her arms across her chest. "Not until you answer mine."

"Fair enough," Patterson said. "We haven't located April yet. But, hopefully, with some cooperation, we'll find her soon." He opened a small spiral notebook. "Can you tell me how things were going for April before her mom passed away?" He looked up at the kids. "How was she feeling lately? Cheerful? Depressed?"

Logan shrugged. "She'd been kind of moody."

Roxanne shot Logan a warning look.

"Do you know what was bothering her?" The chief poised his pen in anticipation of the answer.

Logan glanced at Roxanne, then ventured carefully. "Well, there was something bothering her."

"April had trouble at home," Roxanne blurted.

Chief Patterson raised an eyebrow. "Can you elaborate?"

April would die if I told her secret, Roxanne thought. "Things have been tough at home since her brother was killed in a car accident last year."

Art scribbled something on his tablet. "What about her father?"

"She didn't feel like her father cared about her either. He got drunk a lot after Benny died."

Patterson looked at Logan. "How long have you and April been dating?"

"We've been going out for about a year and a half."

"Any problems?"

"Well, we've had our fights, but nothing that ever split us up."

"Do you have any idea where April might be right now?"

"No. That's what's so strange," Logan said. "I can't believe she'd just take off."

Roxanne toyed with the idea of telling all she knew. *No,* she thought. *April would never forgive me.*

He pulled some business cards out of his pocket and gave one to each of the teenagers. "If you can think of anything else, no matter how small of a detail it might seem to you, please give me a call."

They both assured the chief that they would.

He flipped his notebook shut. "Cooperation is very important. If April is a runaway, every moment she's gone could take her further away. So time is our enemy. Understand?"

Roxanne and Logan accompanied Chief Patterson from the building and watched from the steps as he drove away.

Before Logan even had a chance to open his mouth, Roxanne said, "I don't see what April's pregnancy has to do with her disappearance. Besides, it's nobody's business."

Logan stared at her. "I would say her pregnancy is very much my business."

Roxanne nodded. "You're right," she said, feeling a bond of friendship form.

Jesse walked up the steps of the Hamlin Hotel. He entered through a rich, ebony-paneled entryway that gave way to an opulent lobby of velvet furnishings and gold tassels. In the center of the lobby, a large statue was poised in dance with a flute pressed to cold, iron lips. The plaque at its base read Pied Piper of Hamlin. Jesse felt a sudden surge of repulsion, but there was something else, something frightening. . . .

It's just a statue, he reminded himself.

At the front desk, a clerk watched him through lazy eyelids, his elbows resting on the counter. "Fabulous piece of artwork, don't you think?"

Jesse offered an awkward shrug. "It's not really my thing, I guess."

The smug smile vanished from the clerk's lips. "Really? Well, I suppose everyone is entitled to an opinion." The man stiffened and his demeanor turned officious. "Is there something I can do for you?"

"Yes. I would like to fill out a job application."

The clerk reached under the desk and pulled out a form. "We're not hiring right now, at least not in the hotel, but you might check with the restaurant." The switchboard lit up. The clerk picked up the receiver and waived Jesse toward the dining room.

The restaurant was empty. *Probably not unusual for 4:00 PM.* He noticed a waiter flirting with a cocktail waitress, but the hostess was nowhere in sight.

Jesse waited for a few minutes, then ventured through the swinging doors to the kitchen.

A teenager with a pronounced overbite stood near a

long butcher block. He was tearing up lettuce and tossing it into a large stainless-steel bowl. By the stove, a wiry man with his hair tied back in a ponytail was placing garnishes on some plates.

"Excuse me," Jesse said.

The teenager looked at Jesse out of the corner of his eye.

"Who would I talk to about work?"

The boy nodded in the direction of the stove.

The thin man fired a sharp glance over his shoulder. "I'll be with you in a minute." He adjusted the flame under a large copper pot, wiped his hands on a towel, and said, "I'm the day manager, Wallace Schatz. What can I do for you?"

"I'm looking for a job. It doesn't matter what kind. If it's an honest living, I'll do it."

Wallace tightened his ponytail. "I haven't seen you around. Is that some kind of eastern accent?"

"I'm new to town," Jesse said, "but I've got a lot of kitchen experience."

"Well, it so happens we need a dishwasher." The man ran his tongue over his teeth. "Guess we could try you out on the morning shift. Come in at 6:00 AM on Monday."

"I'll be here."

Wallace's small eyes narrowed. "Don't be late."

The mood had somehow shifted from business to personal. Jesse left, wondering what he'd done to land so quickly on this man's bad side.

CHAPTER 18

Ozmand pushed his skateboard down the side of the road, dodging snowdrifts as he went. A car approached from behind, and he hugged the side of the road, waiting for the vehicle to pass.

The car slowed to a crawl beside him. "Hey, Oz. Where were you after school?" Rudy hung his head out the window of his Cadillac Eldorado.

"I see you got your wheels working again." Ozmand said, stepping from his skateboard. He leaned against the vintage car and kicked a tire with the toe of his tennis shoe. "You've even got new rubber!"

"My old man helped out." Rudy revved the engine. "I need to blow out some cobwebs. She's been on blocks way too long. Let's go for a spin."

Oz tossed his skateboard into the backseat and climbed in.

They drove out toward the badlands and cut some fresh tracks over the desert flats. Up ahead, Bull's-Eye Hill came into view. Ozmand recalled how he and Rudy used to stuff their pockets with beef jerky and trudge up the hill with BB guns in tow. It was worth every step just to have the satisfaction of peppering a few tin cans with holes.

Rudy stopped the car on a high point and climbed out to look around. Oz chose to stay in the passenger seat. He rolled his window down and hung his arm out.

A rabbit darted past, this way and that, as if it couldn't decide which way to go.

"Remember when you got your .22 caliber rifle?" Rudy asked. He bent over and picked up a piece of rusty iron. It crumbled in his hand.

Oz laughed. "I'll never forget how my mom freaked when I brought home that dead cottontail and asked her to clean it for me." He drummed his fingers on the side of the car. "Listen, I have to get home."

"What's the rush?"

"I have things to do, that's all." Ozmand chewed his lip.

Rudy checked his watch. "It's about time for dinner. You want to eat at my house?"

"No, thanks." Ozmand avoided eye contact. "I've got plans."

"Yeah, sure," Rudy said as he returned to the car. He started the engine and drove in silence.

The Eldorado crested the hill, where bare trees cast shadows like sinister fingers. "Hey, man." Oz bit his lip.

"What?"

"Never mind."

Tires crunched on gravel as the car rolled to a stop in front of Ozmand's house.

Rudy's mood turned conciliatory. "I see your mom's home early." He gestured toward the light in the window. "Is she sick or something?"

"Cute!" Ozmand laughed and swung open the car door.

"Oh, just a minute." Rudy fumbled in the pocket of his denim coat. He produced two tickets and waved them in the air. "It wasn't easy, but I got tickets for the Ram's Fire concert in Kingston this weekend!"

"You should have checked with me first!" Oz felt a surge of guilt and tried to soften his tone. "I'm sorry, but I'm already going with some other people."

"Let me guess?" Rudy intoned sarcastically. "Get out," he said, and burned a patch of new rubber on the street.

Things have changed, Oz thought. There was nothing he could do. The secrets of the Piper's Guild now spread like a gulf between them.

April had not combed her hair or washed her face all day. She wasn't even sure if it was Monday or Tuesday. *What does it matter?* April strolled through the farmyard, leaving a trail of footprints in the freshly fallen snow. The field was a glistening white wonderland. Even the wire fence around the chicken coop was frosted with dainty white crystals that winked in the morning sunlight.

The air felt clean and crisp in her lungs. For a brief moment, April imagined that everything was fine, but her thoughts turned to her boyfriend and she ached for his arms. She felt movement and rested her hand across her womb, but there was no burst of wonder, no celebration of life—only resignation. "You wouldn't want me for a mother," she whispered.

April's toe caught on something in the snow and she nearly tripped. The partially decomposed carcass of a lamb lay at her feet. She stared at the lifeless form. April thought of her brother and now her mother, their faces fading into dust. The smell of death was all around. April clamped her hand over her mouth and hurried from the scene as if she could outrun her past.

Just outside the farmhouse, she paused to pull herself together. With shoulders squared, April went inside.

Sylvia was sitting at the kitchen table painting her nails. "How was your little stroll?" she asked without looking up.

"There's a dead lamb out there," April responded.

"Oh?" Sylvia looked up as she blew on the wet lacquer. "Poor thing probably got out of the barn and those awful dogs got it. People around here think they can just let their pets run wild." She shrugged. "I'll have to tell Wallace to put out some arsenic."

"Hey, you're finally out among the living," issued a friendly voice from the doorway. April turned to see Melanie, her dark hair falling in a tangle upon her shoulders.

"Well," Sylvia said, standing, "I'll let you two get better acquainted. I need to get busy before the little rug rats get here." Sylvia screwed the cap back on the bottle of polish. "Do you like this color?" she asked, flashing her nails.

"It's nice," Melanie said, then discreetly winked at April. After the older woman left, Melanie leaned close and whispered, "Looks like dried blood to me." She walked to the cupboard and pulled out a box of Cheerios. "Lunch around here is whatever you can scrounge up. Want some?"

April felt a wave of nausea. "No, thanks. I'm not very hungry."

Melanie grabbed a carton of milk from the refrigerator and a bowl and spoon from the drainer in the sink. "I know it's weird to eat cereal for lunch, but so what?" She sat at the table. "Pull up a chair and keep me company." It was more an order than a request. April took a seat at the table.

"Whoa!" Melanie laid her hand upon her round stomach. "This kid can kick!" She grabbed the carton and poured milk on her cereal. "How far along are you? You gonna keep it?"

"What did Sylvia mean about rug rats?" April asked, dodging the question.

"Every so often, one of the local daycare centers brings the children over for part of the afternoon. A field trip to the farm and all that." Melanie took a bite. "At least, that's what Syl' says." Melanie glanced at her watch. "I'd better wolf this down. Those miniature humans will be here any minute." She picked up the bowl and slurped the milk. "Syl' doesn't like us around when the kids are here." Melanie walked to the sink, rinsed her bowl, and put it in the dishwasher.

"Why?" April asked.

Melanie laughed and patted her stomach. "We're not exactly good examples, you know."

April felt shame welling up within her. "I think I need to rest," she said, then bolted up the stairs to her room.

April shut her eyes tightly. "I'm not going to cry," she whispered. A little voice within her whispered, *That's right, don't cry. You're not worth the tears. It's all your fault! You should have been the one to die—not your brother—not your mother!* Guilt scraped against her shredded heart.

She closed the door and leaned against it. *I will never let anyone get close enough to hurt me again.*

The view from the window had changed. The snow that had fallen clean and white in the morning hours had turned to mud.

Somewhere in the house, a cell phone was ringing. The rings stopped for a few seconds, then came again. *Why isn't anyone answering?* April wondered. The third time it rang, she went to investigate.

April hurried down the stairs and located the cell phone on a small table in the parlor. With her hand poised to answer, she called Sylvia's name. There was no response, so she picked up the receiver. "Hello."

"Who is this?" a man's voice growled.

April's heart raced. What if the caller was someone looking for her? She gripped the receiver and considered hanging up.

"Is anyone there? Answer me!"

April took a deep breath. "Who are you trying to reach?"

"Sylvia. Where is she?"

"I-I don't know," April stammered.

"The phones are off limits! Understand?" The man's tone softened. "You don't recognize my voice, do you?"

April's response was guarded. "You're Wallace."

"That's right." His voice turned sugary.

"Do you want me to go find Sylvia?"

"No," he said. "Don't bother. But if you see her, just tell her I'm on my way—should be there soon." With that, he hung up.

April replaced the receiver. Something about that man made her skin crawl. *But then, all guys are basically creeps,* she decided.

Back in the kitchen, Melanie was gone. Everything was quiet. April switched on the radio and made herself a peanut butter and jelly sandwich. She listened to the weather forecast as she ate. Another snowstorm was on the way.

April's thoughts turned to her best friend, who was probably beside herself with worry. *Roxie doesn't deserve this. If only I could call and let her know that I'm okay.* The farm had no landline, and Sylvia and Wallace would not allow the girls to use the couple's personal cell phones.

She brushed crumbs off her hands, switched off the radio, and was about to head back upstairs when a noise stopped her. Someone was crying. A child?

It was coming from the utility room next to the back porch. A load of clothes was spinning off balance in the washing machine. *Maybe that's it.* The cycle wound down with a whine, and April bent to pick up an old mop that had fallen over. That's when she noticed the cellar door and the unlatched padlock dangling from the hasp.

April pushed the door open. The smell of dust and perspiration tickled April's nose. "Sylvia?" There was a light on down below. She took a step down and the dry wood creaked.

Suddenly, she felt a hand grasp her shoulder. April whirled around to face Wallace.

"Where do you think you're going?" he demanded.

His pupils shrunk to laser dots, and the look on his face

frightened April. "I-I was looking for Sylvia. I heard a sound and I thought—"

"Hey, relax, Autumn." Wallace's thin lips curved into an exaggerated grin. He took her arm and tugged her back up the stairs.

"My name is April." Her skin crawled at his touch. She was relieved when he let go.

Wallace burst into laughter. "Of course it is. I was just messin' with ya." He closed the cellar door behind them. "You shouldn't be poking around these stairs. We don't want you to have an accident or anything." Wallace grinned, showing tiny teeth and gray-pink gums. "The basement is off limits—you hear?"

April's mouth felt dry. She nodded.

"Are you afraid of me?" Wallace looked down his thin, grease-slicked nose. "I'm a little rough around the edges, but I ain't that bad."

"I'm sorry," April muttered as she backed from the kitchen. April heard the faint sound of Wallace laughing as she went up to her bedroom.

CHAPTER 19

From the intersection, Roxanne watched the police officer directing traffic for the funeral procession. It didn't take long. Besides a few acquaintances and out-of-town family, the funeral was poorly attended and unceremonious. If it was anything like Roxanne's brother's service, there would be no preachers and no mention of God.

Roxanne looked at Rudy. He had grown two inches since the school year began. His jaw was strong and square just like their father's, and his build was as lean and sinewy as most of the Volcovich clan.

"Thanks for taking me," she said.

Rudy nodded and thrummed his fingers on the steering wheel of his car.

Feeling a rush of sadness, Roxanne slipped on a pair of sunglasses. She could feel her brother watching the tears roll down her cheeks.

"Are you sure you want to go to the cemetery?" Rudy asked, then reached over and patted his little sister's arm.

Roxanne nodded and wiped her nose with a tissue. "But I just want to sit in the car, okay?"

"All right, Roxie. Whatever you want."

With headlights on, the small procession of cars rolled through town to the cemetery. Rudy parked just inside the cemetery gate and switched off the ignition.

They waited for the mourners to spill from their cars and huddle around the casket. Words were said, and as the people stood somberly, the casket was lowered into the ground.

Roxanne scanned faces for her best friend, to no avail.

When the last car drove away, Roxanne was still searching.

"She's a no-show," Rudy said, starting the car against his sister's protests. "First her brother and now her mother. Maybe it was all just too much for April."

Roxanne dropped her face into her hands.

"You should take your mind off things." Rudy turned onto the road. "Hey, why don't you go to the concert with me this weekend? It just so happens that I have an extra ticket. What do you say?"

"It's not exactly cool to be seen with your younger sister." Roxanne mustered a half-hearted smile. "Wouldn't you be embarrassed?"

"Probably," he said.

"Okay, then, I'll go!"

"You're a real piece of work."

"Yeah, it runs in the family," Roxanne said, glancing back over her shoulder as the gravediggers shoveled dirt into the hole.

Jesse punched his pillow and rolled over again but still could not get comfortable. He had been tossing and turning since 1:00 AM, when he'd been awakened by another dream. The details eluded him, but the mood left behind was oppressive. He lay there awhile, starring at the ceiling.

He finally rose in resignation. The clock beside his bed indicated that he had been fighting insomnia for two hours now.

After slipping on his bathrobe, Jesse grabbed his sketch pad and sharpened a pencil. From the comfort of an overstuffed chair, he began to work on a rough sketch of Cali—her haunted eyes peeking out from under a fringe of bangs. When that was done, he flipped the page and sketched the old Subaru that had carried him to this town.

If only it could carry me back home again. Jesse missed the life he'd known in Pittsburgh. Most of all, he missed Mavis. There was something about this town that made him ill at ease.

Jesse crumpled the page in his hand and tossed it aside. If Mavis were around, she'd have rescued it from the floor just like she'd done when he was a child. He still couldn't believe that Mavis had saved all of his old art. The thought made him smile.

Jesse located the folder in the dresser beneath his clothes. He tucked it under his arm, stopped to light the flame under the teakettle, and returned to the chair to reminisce. There were silly, primitive pictures of toothy, grinning stick figures and cartoon animals. Some weren't bad for a kid. Jesse lingered on the drawing of a dove resting on a stone ledge. He remembered working hard on that one. The next sketch—a building five stories high—showed detailed brickwork. The structure's windows were capped with arched headers, and the stair-step roofline rose upward to a pointed crest.

I've seen this building. Where? The feeling was overwhelming. Jesse rubbed his tired eyes and tried to think, and then it came to him. It was the old Hamlin Brewery!

Jesse scattered the rest of the drawings on the floor in front of him and studied them with renewed interest. Most were simple subjects that would have been of interest to a small boy: a dump truck, a jet, a stray dog. As Jesse grew older, his art progressed to portraits of people, some crude, others finely detailed. Mavis had used to say he had a gift for capturing the moods of those who crossed his path.

One picture in particular caught Jesse's eye. It was nothing more than a scribbled mess upon what was once a crumpled piece of paper. *Why did Mavis save this?* he wondered. Maybe because the marks across the page were angry and deliberate. Jesse lifted the paper, trying to discern the lines of the original drawing. He held the page to the lamp and was able to make out the image of a man who appeared to be dancing. Jesse leaned close, squinting against the backlight. *What is that in the man's hand?* Jesse's flesh crawled. *It can't be!*

The teakettle shrieked, and the page dropped from Jesse's fingers. The dancing man was holding a flute to his mouth. It was a drawing of the Pied Piper, just like the one in the lobby of the Hamlin Hotel.

Cali opened a can of tuna and fished around the sink for a moderately dirty dish. She scraped her fingernail across its rough surface and shrugged. *Hard and crusties don't count,* she told herself, and loaded the plate with soda crackers and tuna. Cali grabbed a fork from a drawer and went into the living room.

Cyrus had not yet returned from wherever it was he went. It was just as well. Cali hated living under the skateboard king's roof, but these were the arrangements that had been made for her. Orders from the Guild's top were that Cyrus was to keep a close eye on her. She loathed every last one of them.

Cali plopped down on the couch and put her feet up on the coffee table. She picked up the TV remote and flipped through the stations. There was nothing on but a *Cosby Show* rerun; Vanessa was having problems at school because someone called her a rich girl.

"Oh, poor baby," Cali mused as dark thoughts clouded her mind. *What if Dr. Huxtable turned out to be a serial killer? Then those spoiled brats would understand that people can't be trusted.* She ate a forkful of tuna and stuffed a soda cracker in her mouth.

Cyrus walked in, slamming the door behind him. A cesspool of foul words spilled from his mouth. He threw his jacket onto the ottoman and muttered something about Mr. Pratt next door. "That old geezer is gonna get what's coming to him!" He peered through the window toward his neighbor's house.

Over his shoulder, Cali could see Mr. Pratt sweeping his sidewalk. "I think he's buff."

Cyrus whirled around, stomped over to the couch, and jerked the remote from Cali's hand.

"Hey! What are you doing?"

He turned off the television, then kicked her legs off the coffee table.

She glared up at him. "You'd better watch it! If you lay your slimy hands on me, I'll tell!" Cali noticed Cyrus cradling his hand, and she caught sight of a splint on his index finger. "Who knows?" she smirked. "Maybe the fingers on your other hand might wind up broken, too."

"I fell off my skateboard," he snapped.

"Sure you did." Cali took another bite of tuna and wiped a dribble of oil from her chin. "You might be able to pass that one off on one of those poor fools you bring in, but don't waste your breath on me."

Cyrus held out his hand and studied the splints.

Cali giggled. "Wow, two fingers, eh? You must have been a really bad boy."

"Shut up! If you were a gnat, I'd squash you."

"But I'm not," Cali taunted. "I'm a spider and I bite!"

Cyrus ignored her. He turned back to the window and his gaze grew cloudy. "It will be dark soon," he mumbled, "And I love the darkness."

—◦◦◦—

Chief Patterson sat at his desk, elbow deep in files. He had given his secretary strict instructions not to disturb him, but after hours of pouring over old cases his mind was muddled and tired. At this stage, Patterson would have welcomed a distraction. *Unlikely,* he thought. The corridor outside his office was quiet. Most of the officers were either home or cruising the streets until their shift was over.

Art thumbed through the stack of papers on his desk and tried to make sense of the information.

Ten years ago, a fourteen-year-old girl had hung herself from the swing set in one of the city's parks. Less than three months later, her best friend was found comatose, brain-dead from a massive overdose of sedatives.

Three years later, a hunting accident took the life of a fifteen-year-old boy. Before the year's end, two other boys fell to their deaths in what was classified as a rock-climbing accident. A third drank straight grain alcohol at a party and died. Early the following year, a car loaded with teenagers plunged into a canal on the outskirts of town.

And then there was the Gilbert boy, who drove his car from the rims.

Chief Patterson's thoughts turned to Leland Gilbert. *Poor son of a gun. His son, his wife, and now his missing daughter.* Patterson made a silent vow to find April. Alive, he hoped.

From the computer database, Patterson located the number for the Uniform Crime Reporting Division in Helena. He dialed. After the fourth ring, a prerecorded message gave the business hours at the state capitol.

Art hung up and reached into his shirt pocket for a nitroglycerin tablet. The familiar dull throbbing was back with a vengeance. He slipped a pill under his tongue and closed his eyes. The pain traveled to his shoulder and down his arm before it began to ease.

Art's thoughts turned to his late wife. If Bea were alive today, would he tell her about his deep sense of failure? How he had let the people of Hamlin down while their children fell like casualties of war around them? No. Art knew he would not have troubled Bea. But, now more than ever, he longed for the comfort of her presence.

Patterson stood and gathered the files on his desk. There was another stack to look at, but he decided to take them home. He shuffled out the door and locked it behind him. For the first time in all his years, he felt old.

———

With a scouring pad, Roxanne scrubbed furiously at a stain in Mrs. Crabtree's deep porcelain sink.

"You've been working so hard, dear. It's past 5:00 PM. Why don't you call it a day?" Theda Mae called out from the pantry. The old woman emerged with two jars. "Last summer's homemade chokecherry jelly," she announced. "I thought your mom would like some."

Roxanne gathered the cleaning supplies into a plastic caddy and placed it under the sink.

"Before you go, dear, let's take your troubles to the Lord in prayer."

The teenager's mouth fell open. "You are incredible, Mrs. Crabtree. You always seem to know when something is wrong."

The old woman looked over her bifocals. "I talk to the Lord, and he knows all about your problems." She smiled and pulled a chair from the table. "Come, sit down."

"How can God take the time to care about my problems?" Roxanne tossed the sponge into the sink and joined Theda Mae at the table. "I mean, let's face it, with all the troubles on this messed-up planet, he's got his hands full."

Theda Mae gently touched Roxanne's hand. "Our God is amazing, dear. No problem is beyond His reach, big or small."

"Why does he let people suffer?"

The old woman's face grew somber. "Did you know God cries? It says so right here." She tapped the Bible that was lying on the table. "This world is fallen, and it makes God sad. So sad, in fact, that he was willing to give His own Son to make things right. The rest is up to us."

Roxanne leaned back and crossed her arms. "But couldn't God just say the word and make everything perfect?"

"Sure, he could do that. Yet, God decided to bless mankind with the ability to choose. Without free will, we would all be like slaves. The decision to love and serve God was the best one I ever made. I feel for all the nice folks who think they're free when all the while they're just dragging the Devil's chains around."

"You have an interesting way of saying things." Roxanne watched her elderly friend picking through her cookie jar.

"Goodness, I better do some baking."

"Mrs. Crabtree," Roxanne pressed, "do you think God has a plan for me?"

"No doubt about it!" Mrs. Crabtree handed her Bible to Roxanne. "That's why I want you to have this. It will help you discover just what the good Lord's got in mind."

Roxanne tried to recall the old woman ever having been without her Bible. "Mrs. Crabtree! I can't accept. . . ."

"Of course you can, dear." Theda Mae held an aged hand over her heart. "The words are written here."

Roxanne opened the book's cracked leather binding as if it might turn to dust in her hands. Inside, among dog-eared pages and personal notations, Roxanne read the words aloud, "Don't be afraid, for I am with you."

CHAPTER 20

In the alley behind the Hamlin Hotel, Jesse took his first paycheck out of the envelope and looked at it. The amount was sparse, but at least it was a start toward helping with expenses. He put it back in his pocket and drew in a sharp breath. The frosty night air was heavy with chimney smoke. Jesse pulled the collar of his jacket around his neck and started toward home. The snow was a couple-three inches deep and still falling. The first layer had melted on the warm pavement and then frozen again, forming sheet ice.

An SUV slid past a stop sign into the empty intersection, missing Jesse by inches. Wheels spun and the vehicle fishtailed on toward the heart of town.

Jesse turned up the hill and carefully made his way along the side of the road.

Off in the distance the brittle air carried Lars's rich singing voice. "God is my refuge and God is my strength, a very present help in trouble; therefore I will not fear, though the earth be removed, and though the mountains be carried into the midst of the sea."

Beneath the glow of a yard light, Jesse spotted Lars

rustling through a stack of crates. "What are you doing?" he called.

"I need to plug the truck in so it'll start up in the morning."

"What's wrong with Emma's minivan?"

"Needs a new battery. Aha, here it is!" Lars plucked an orange extension cord from the bottom of a pile of junk. "I swear, some days I just want to hop in this old beater and keep on driving south until someone asks, 'Hey mister, what's that little plug hanging from your engine?'"

Jesse laughed. "Cheer up. I bring my rent offering!" He pulled out his first paycheck and waved it like a flag.

"This calls for a celebration!" Lars bellowed. "Come warm yourself by the stove and we'll make a toast with some decaf."

Just inside the door, Jesse took his shoes off and hung his coat on a hook.

Lars grabbed two cups of coffee and headed for the living room, with Jesse trailing behind. "Fire's good 'n stoked." The big man set the cups on the coffee table and rubbed his hands together near the old potbellied stove.

Emma appeared, looking unusually subdued. Her brow was creased with sorrow.

"What's wrong, Mama?" Lars moved to her side.

Emma lowered herself onto the piano bench. "Theda Mae called. Mr. Pratt's house burned to the ground a few hours ago."

"Oh, Lord! Is he. . . ?"

"Alive, but in a coma. The firemen pulled him out before he was burned badly, but his lungs suffered. On top of everything else, the poor man may have had a stroke."

"Maybe that's why the air was so smoky tonight," Jesse said without thinking.

Lars rubbed his bald head. "That shack was a firetrap. I should have gone over years ago and offered to help him rewire the place."

"Don't be too hard on yourself, honey." Emma reached up and squeezed Lars's hand. "They found a can of gasoline next to the building."

"Why in the world. . . ? Who would want to hurt an old man like that?"

Emma shook her head. "Poor Theda Mae. We should go comfort her."

"Mr. Pratt and Mrs. Crabtree, are they family?" Jesse asked.

"In a way," Emma said. "Mr. Pratt has always. . . , well, let's just say he's a loner. Theda Mae has looked in on him for years."

Lars chuckled. "Remember when Mr. Pratt had to have a gallbladder operation? Theda Mae went over to his house and cleaned it from top to bottom, then she stocked his refrigerator and pantry. She's a saint, I tell ya. That place was so filthy most people wouldn't have set foot in it."

"Would you two help me make sandwiches to take with us?" Emma asked.

Jesse and Lars followed her into the kitchen. She took some mustard and mayonnaise from the refrigerator and set them on the counter. "Lars, would you slice some meat and cheese?" Emma tossed Jesse a loaf of bread.

They formed an assembly line and prepared the meal in

record time. Emma threw everything into a grocery bag and set it down by the back door as Lars went outside to warm up the truck.

Jesse helped Emma straighten the kitchen until they were summoned by a quick honk of the horn.

"All aboard!" Lars yelled.

"Once a railroad man, always a railroad man." Emma sighed and grabbed her coat.

With his arms loaded with bags, Jesse slipped and nearly lost his footing.

"Good thing I got four-wheel drive," Lars said, stepping from the truck to offer a steady hand. He took the bags and arranged them beneath a tarp in the back of the truck.

Jesse opened the passenger door for Emma, but she paused and tilted her head. "You hear the phone? I'll be right back." She hurried back to the house.

Lars climbed into the cab of the truck and laced his fingers behind his head. "Might as well make yourself comfortable," he said. "I've spent half my life waiting on that woman." Lars winked at Jesse. "But she's worth it." He waved a finger at Jesse. "If you tell her I said that, I'll deny it."

"Your secret's safe with me."

"I'll be darned," Lars said as his wife emerged from the house and carefully picked her way across the icy ground.

Emma squeezed into the passenger seat beside Jesse. "Be careful!" she barked as her husband dropped the stick shift into first gear and spun the wheels.

"You want to drive?" Lars grumbled. "I'll pull over right now if you do."

"Don't be bull-headed!"

Jesse sank back into the seat between the couple as they bickered all the way across town, finally making peace when they rolled to a stop at Mrs. Crabtree's house.

Theda Mae was standing at her picture window, watching. She waved at the trio and hurried to greet them at the door.

"Any word on Mr. Pratt?" Emma asked after they'd been ushered inside.

"Not so good." Theda Mae sighed. "I was at the hospital, but they only let me peek in on him. I felt so helpless seeing Bernard lying in a coma. If I didn't have the Lord to lean on . . . ." Her aged eyes blinked back tears.

Prayer rose spontaneously right there in the entryway, not only for Mr. Pratt but also for each other. They exchanged hugs.

"I've made a fresh pot of coffee, and the water is on for tea, but I'm afraid I haven't been to the grocery store lately. My cupboards are beginning to look like Old Mother Hubbard's."

Lars jovially patted his wife's back. "Ma here brought enough sandwiches to take the wrinkle out of a big man's belly." He unloaded the bag and wasted no time in opening up the Ziploc and digging in.

After eating, Emma brushed crumbs from the kitchen counter and tidied up. "Would you like me to run you over to the grocery store so you can pick up a few things?" she asked Theda Mae.

"Oh, bless you, dear." The old woman's eyes expressed a depth of gratitude. "I haven't told this to anyone, but a few days ago I received a notice from the state. They are not renewing my driver's license."

"Now, why in blue blazes. . . ?" Lars yelped.

"Don't get all worked up," Theda Mae said with a matronly tone. "It's for the better, really. Last year I had a little fender bender, and recently I was asked to take an eye exam. Well, you can probably figure out the rest."

"It must be terrible for you," Jesse sympathized.

"Yes, but I have to face facts. I am getting on in age, and I certainly don't ever want to be a danger. The way I see it, this is all just part of God's plan."

Emma smiled at her old friend. "Don't worry about it. I'll just swing by and pick you up on the days that I run errands. We can do them together." Emma leaned forward, searching Theda Mae's face. "There's something else, isn't there? What is it?"

"The hospital is transferring Bernard to a nursing facility in Kingston this weekend, and I had my heart set on driving up there to be with him."

"Saturday, by any chance?" Emma asked.

"Why, yes."

Emma broke into laughter and looked heavenward. "Thank You, sweet Jesus. You are so good!" She turned to her husband and Jesse. "Remember the phone call?"

"When you went back into the house?" Lars asked.

She nodded. "It was Pastor Mathews. He said that a heavy metal band is playing this weekend at the Black Rock Events Center and he wants us all to come to Kingston for some street ministry. Guess which day?"

"Saturday?" Jesse asked. "That's perfect, because I

don't have to work this weekend. I'd love to tag along, if that's okay?"

Lars stood and stretched. "It's settled." He scratched his belly. "Saturday morning, I'll kick the tires on the minivan, knock some dust off its seats, and we'll swing by and pick up Theda Mae."

Jesse couldn't help but feel that God's hand was in motion. Something big was in the works.

CHAPTER 21

Ozmand walked past the blackened remains of Old Man Pratt's house. A police car was parked out front. An officer and a man wearing an outdated pinstripe suit were engaged in conversation. The men made animated gestures and pointed at the far corner of the building.

He sunk his hands into the pockets of his jeans and tried not to stare as he strolled by. The smell of Gasoline wafted to his nose, and from the corner of his eye, he saw shapes in the burnt rubble: warped metal cabinets and a glob of dark plastic and shattered glass that used to be a television set.

Ozmand quickly crossed the street, loped up the steps to Cyrus's house, and knocked.

Cyrus opened the door, a marijuana joint dangling from his lip.

"Wow, bad deal about Mr. Pratt's house burning down."

"You think so?" Cyrus smirked. He took a toke from his joint and inhaled deeply. Cyrus blew smoke toward the window and said, "Personally, I think the view has improved." He offered the joint to Oz.

"No, thanks." A string of smoke curled around

Ozmand's head, and he suddenly felt nauseated.

Cyrus finished the last pull of his joint. "What's on your mind, Ozzy boy?"

He shrugged. "I had a fight with Rudy. He got us tickets to the Ram's Fire concert, and I just blew him off. I feel like a jerk."

Cyrus pushed out his bottom lip. "Oh, you poor baby. Listen, man, I'm beginning to think I misjudged you. It's about time you grow some teeth, 'cause you're running with the wolf pack now." He walked over to Ozmand and stared directly into his eyes. "You and I are going to that concert. This music ain't just ear candy—it's a powerful form of worship. Think about it. Hundreds of people all mouthing words that glorify Satan." He laughed. "And most of them don't even realize it!"

"Guess I never really thought of it like that." Ozmand tried not to appear shocked.

Cyrus's eyes glistened. "The energy that comes off is totally unrighteous!" He dropped his hand on Ozmand's shoulder. "I know you've been to concerts before, but this time your eyes will be opened. You're gonna love it!"

This kid was beginning to spook Ozmand. He wanted to shake loose of Cyrus's grip, but instinct told him it wouldn't be that easy. "Sounds cool, man."

"After the concert we'll go to a party with the band."

Ozmand's mouth dropped open. "Ram's Fire is famous—*Inferno Alley* is topping the charts right now. Why would they let us hang with them?"

"Hey, man, they're our brothers." Cyrus puffed. "You're part of something big now, and it's growing bigger all the time. Just remember what I told you—there's no turning back."

All of Ozmand's earlier reservations vanished. "Don't worry, I'm not going anywhere."

———

April cleared the table, and Melanie washed the lunch dishes.

"Did you watch Looney Tunes this morning?" Melanie asked. "It was a riot!"

"Excuse me?" April raised an eyebrow. "You really watch that stuff?"

"It's a habit I picked up as kid." Melanie looked over her shoulder at April and winked. "I had you pegged as a Bugs Bunny fan."

April giggled.

"Wow, did I see a smile?" Melanie dried her hands and walked over to April. "So, why are you here, anyway? Did your folks go ballistic on you when they found out about your pregnancy?"

April dropped her head and brushed strands of hair behind her ears. "Something like that," she said weakly.

"Look, I'm not the bad guy here. I want to be your friend."

"I'm sorry. I just can't talk about things right now."

"Hey, that's cool."

April paused at a closed door near the kitchen's utility room. "Can I ask you something?"

"Sure."

"What's in the basement?"

"Oh, just your run-of-the-mill assortment of man-eating sharks, crocodiles, and World War II vintage land mines."

"I'm serious."

"I don't know. It's always locked unless Sylvia or Wallace are down there."

April touched her fingertip to the doorknob. "Aren't you curious?"

Melanie shrugged. "Guess I just figured it's none of my business. After all, these people took me into their home, no questions asked, so I ain't sticking my nose where it don't belong."

They quieted at the sound of Sylvia's spiked heels clicking across the wood floor in the parlor.

The girls turned expectantly toward the dining room. Sylvia appeared.

"How do I look?" She held her arms out and spun around. Sylvia wore a see-through black top with a satin camisole underneath and a pair of shiny spandex pants. She shook the bangles on her arm and tossed her head to show off the matching hoop earrings.

Melanie let out a wolf whistle. "You're gonna knock 'em dead, Syl'!"

"Are you going out?" April asked.

"Yes, doll, I'm steppin' out with my man." She took a mirror out of her clutch purse and examined her makeup. "We're going to Kingston. I think we might take in an afternoon movie and dinner, and after that"—she snapped her purse shut—"who knows?"

Wallace sauntered into the kitchen, scraping his long,

loose hair into a ponytail. He slid his arms around Sylvia. "Ready, babe?"

"What if I go into labor?" Melanie asked.

"Relax." Sylvia said. "Many of my girls have thought they were going into labor when it turned out to be nothin' but some Braxton-Hicks. Even if labor does begin, I'll be back in time."

"Okay," Mel grinned. "Go have a good time!"

Wallace turned to Sylvia. "You go warm up the car, babe. I forgot something." Wallace watched her leave, then went to the basement door. He pulled a key from his pocket and shot a warning look at the girls.

April looked away, but she could hear Wallace clomping down the stairs. A moment later, he was back, with a satchel beneath his arm. "Don't wait up," he said, securing the lock. "And don't let anyone in this house. Do you hear me?"

April blinked and swallowed hard. "Yes," she said meekly. It wasn't his words that were unnerving; it was the threatening way that Wallace looked at her.

Jesse grabbed his coat and joined Lars by the car. "I see you got the station wagon running."

"New battery and the minivan is raring to go." Lars closed the hood and gave it a pat. "We've logged a lot of miles in this thing, me and Em. Wonderful memories." A sublime smile spread across his face, and Lars drifted away with this thoughts.

The affection between this couple was genuine. Jesse tried to imagine his own parents. *Did they love each other? Did they love me?*

Lars pulled a pair of Handy Andy gloves from his back pocket and used them to buff a smudge from the hood of the van.

Emma backed through the kitchen door, her arms loaded with bags. "I could use a hand."

Jesse hurried over to help as Lars opened the back hatch of the minivan.

"Are you warm enough, Jesse?" Emma asked. "I've got an extra pair of gloves in the house."

"Not a bad idea." Lars loaded the last package and looked up at the cloudy, gray sky. "There's a storm forecast. Biggest one of the season so far."

"Oh, my!" Emma gasped. "Maybe we shouldn't go to Kingston."

"Now, don't worry, Mama," Lars said. "I'm sure the sun will be back out before you know it."

Emma closed her eyes. "Please increase my faith, Lord." She looked at Jesse. "I never liked traveling in bad weather, but we're in God's hands."

Soon they were across town and Lars maneuvered the automobile up to the curb in front of Theda Mae's house. She was waiting near the curb, and within minutes, they had her settled in the backseat. Mrs. Crabtree opened her tapestry bag and the aroma of pastries filled the air. "I made fresh doughnuts," she announced.

There was a sense of excitement among the small group, as if they were embarking on some great adventure.

They laughed and bantered over the drafty hum of less-than-airtight windows.

Up on the flats, the wind blew hard, rearranging the snowdrifts and carving swirling patterns on their icy surface. Every so often, a gust of wind would hit the side of the van with a rocking force.

About thirty miles out of town, Lars braked over a patch of black ice and the car slid on the road. "Hang on!" he said. He clutched the steering wheel. Wind pelted the side of the car, sending it into a full spin.

Emma clutched the dash in panic.

As if in slow motion, the minivan turned completely around and slid in the opposite direction. The car reeled sideways toward a reflector pole.

"Lord, help!" Jesse called out.

The old car missed the pole by a fraction of an inch and came to rest in a snow-filled ditch.

Lars stared straight ahead. His knuckles, curled tightly around the wheel, were white. "Is everyone okay?"

"I'm fine," Theda Mae offered.

"Me, too," Jesse said, though his knees shook.

Emma leaned her head back on the seat and offered a prayer of thanks.

Jesse and Lars got out of the car to survey the damage. The back wheels were sunk deep in the snow, but there was not a scratch on the vehicle.

"She's stuck," Lars said with resignation. "We'll have to get some help." He stepped onto the highway to scan the empty road for travelers.

"Over there." Jesse pointed to a small pillar of smoke

beyond a grouping of hills. "There's got to be a house over there. I'll go see if I can use the phone."

"That's a great idea. Call Reilly's Garage and have them send out a tow truck." Lars opened the trunk and lifted out a piece of plywood he had propped under the spare tire. "In the meantime, I'll see if I can dig her out and put something under the wheels for traction."

Jesse found a little dirt road and briskly followed it. Fifteen minutes later, he reached his destination: a two-story white farmhouse. There was no response when he knocked on the door, so he tried again. This time, Jesse caught a glimpse of movement behind the curtains. He was about to knock a third time when the door opened and a pretty blonde girl stood before him. He figured her to be sixteen, maybe seventeen years old.

"Yes?"

"I hate to bother you, but our car slid off the road and I was wondering if I could make a call."

The girl studied Jesse as if she were sizing him up. "We don't have a landline." She started to swing the door shut.

"Wait," Jesse pleaded. "What about a cell phone?"

"Sorry, I can't help you," she blurted. The door slammed shut.

Jesse understood the teenager's caution. It was a dangerous world and growing worse all the time. He looked around. There were no other farmhouses in sight, but Jesse knew it would be futile to knock again.

Frustrated, Jesse walked back to the car. Just over the rise, he saw a pickup breaking to a stop in front of the old station wagon. Jesse watched as a man wearing a cowboy hat rolled down the window and spoke with Lars. The Good Samaritan pulled to the side of the road, got out, and fished a large chain from the pickup bed. Lars helped him hook it to the van's bumper.

Jesse arrived in time to help push. The truck spun its wheels and grabbed just enough traction to free the old car.

The group showered the cowboy with gratitude and homemade doughnuts, then continued on their way.

—⁓—

Jesse and the others arrived in Kingston around 6:00 PM and headed straight to the nursing home. The facility, a sprawling brick institution, stood out in the older section of town.

"Ladies first," Lars said, holding open the door.

Inside, elderly residents loitered in the hallway, passing the time until dinner. Jesse detected a heavy sadness in their eyes as they studied each visitor for a familiar face.

Theda Mae approached the main desk to inquire about Bernard Pratt.

"He's in the special care wing. Still unresponsive." The nurse looked sympathetic. "You're his only visitor, so I'm going to bend the rules and allow you to see him, but only for a moment."

"Bless you, dear," Theda Mae said. Then, with the nurse's directions, she and her companions set off to locate the room.

Jesse stood to the side and prayed quietly as Theda Mae took the old man's hand.

"God is with you, Bernard. So don't give up." She took out a tissue from her tapestry bag and wiped a dribble of saliva from the corner of the elderly man's mouth. Mr. Pratt's eyes were half-open but vacant. Air wheezed through open lips that smacked rhythmically, yet no words formed.

"I'd like to stay for awhile." Mrs. Crabtree pulled a chair close to his bedside and slipped a brand new Bible from the tapestry bag.

Emma, Lars, and Jesse left quietly and fell in among an exodus of residents who were making a slow pilgrimage to the dining room.

Lars spotted a sitting area on the way, and they all settled in to wait for Theda Mae.

A mournful moan carried down the hallway, and Emma pitched forward in her chair. "Did you hear that? It sounds like someone needs help!"

"Now, Mama, I'm sure the staff is on top of things around here," Lars reasoned, but his wife had already gone to investigate.

They followed the sounds to a room that housed an ancient woman. She looked as frail as a foundling bird. She was slumped forward in her wheelchair, held in place by nylon straps.

The patient moaned as Emma rushed over to lift her back into place. "There now, that's better."

The old woman's wispy gray hair was worn completely bald in the back. Her thin legs quivered.

A nurse's aide appeared in the doorway. "Marie! Are you making a pest of yourself again?" From a metal closet, the aide produced a blanket, snapped it open, and laid it across the resident's lap. "Now, be a dear and don't bother these nice folks anymore. We'll bring your dinner as soon as we get everyone settled in the dining room." Before leaving, the aide cast a long-suffering look at the visitors. "She can be such a burden. I'm sorry if it upset you."

Emma touched the lady's shoulder. "I really don't mind."

The tiny, birdlike creature began to shake violently, and Jesse wondered if she might be going into some kind of convulsion. Her head bobbed precariously. Her languid eyes widened, and she opened her mouth to speak.

"Help me." The words issued forth like silk threads. Her gaze shifted to Jesse, and she gasped. "You're here! You came back." The old woman's eyes flooded with tears, and her chest heaved for air. Her bony fingers clutched at Jesse's shirt. "I always believed you'd come back."

Jesse cast a sideways look at Lars and Emma as he gracefully extricated himself from the old woman's grasp.

"No!" The resident's agitation grew. "Don't leave me."

"We'll pray for you," Lars offered.

"Wait!" The lady mustered strength and strained against the belts that tied her to the chair. "Please, push me over to my bed."

Jesse figured it was the least he could do after upsetting the poor woman. As they neared her bedside table, she lifted her hand and pointed a shaking finger at the drawer. "In there."

It contained a Gideon Bible, a box of tissues, and a turquoise brooch with a coral cross in the center.

"The pin. Take it."

"Oh, no, I couldn't. Really, it's—"

"Please!" The old woman's voice was shrill. Tears streamed down her crepe-textured skin.

Jesse looked to Emma for advice. She nodded.

The woman leaned forward, clutching the arms of her wheelchair.

"If it means that much to you. . . I'm honored." Jesse took the piece of jewelry in hand, then leaned down and kissed her forehead. "I'll pray for you whenever I see it."

This seemed to calm the old woman. She settled back in her chair. "One more thing before you go. Would you open my music box?"

Emma, standing nearby, lifted the lid of the delicate porcelain box, and music filled the room—a hauntingly familiar tune that sent a chill down Jesse's spine.

CHAPTER 22

Wallace Schatz steered the car slowly through a tree-lined neighborhood in Kingston. An inch of snow had dusted the street. He pumped the brakes as he neared an intersection. The tires slid on a patch of ice but grabbed again where street crews had laid a layer of sand.

Wallace craned his neck and peered at signs, barely visible beneath the dim glow of a streetlight. "What's the address again?"

In the passenger seat, Sylvia flipped down the lighted vanity mirror and rubbed a spot of lipstick from her tooth. "The same as it was the last time you asked."

"There it is—across the street!" Wallace pointed to a building with stained glass windows that looked like a church. The only thing missing was a cross. He flipped a U-turn and parked.

Sylvia got out and stretched as Wallace grabbed his satchel from the backseat and joined her. "What time is it, babe?"

"I can't see in the dark," Sylvia snapped. Then her voice softened. "Relax. I'm sure we're on time."

Wallace wedged the satchel under an armpit and draped his free arm over Sylvia's shoulder. They walked up the steps.

A short man wearing an unconvincing toupee answered the door and led the couple into what had once been a church sanctuary. The pews and Christian symbols had been removed.

A shapely woman named Thea was lighting candles on wall sconces. From atop a small stepladder she waved a long-barreled lighter and said, "Hey, Wallace. Hi Syl'. Hope you're staying for the party tonight."

"We wouldn't miss it. I hear the band will be here after the concert." Wallace licked his lips as Thea pulled the trigger and held a flame to another candle.

"Need some help?" Sylvia asked.

Thea moved the stepladder to another sconce. "Would you bring me a candle?" She pointed to a box near the altar.

A pale man with a silver goatee appeared from a door near the back of the room. He beckoned Wallace with an arthritic finger.

"It was nice of you to meet with me, Mr. Smith," Wallace prattled nervously as he followed the man to a small office. "I'm sure you will like the product."

Behind a long, black lacquer table, Mr. Smith settled into a straight-backed chair. He folded his hands in front of him and stared with eyes that were as cold as dry ice.

Wallace tugged at the collar of his dingy polo and fumbled with his satchel's clasp. He opened the case and spread the contents on the table.

Mr. Smith leaned forward, but his face betrayed no feeling. With his crooked finger, he pushed through piles of photos of little children in various naked poses. He lingered longer over one particular cluster.

"That's my personal favorite," Wallace volunteered. "I really captured the fear in this child's eyes."

Mr. Smith's lip twitched with a hint of a smile. "I might be able to sell these on the Internet. I've got a couple of different websites in mind. You've developed quite a talent with the camera."

Wallace puffed with pride. *Recognition at last.*

———

"There's a spot!" Roxanne pointed to an empty space in the parking lot of the Kingston Events Center.

Rudy steered his Cadillac Eldorado into the narrow slot and shot his sister an I-told-you-so look. "We should have come earlier. We're going to have to walk a mile."

Roxanne opened the door and squeezed her body through the narrow gap. She grinned at her brother over the roof of the car. "The hike will do us good."

Rudy turned the collar of his coat up. "Yeah, if we don't miss the concert."

The snow that layered the pavement had been trampled into slush by the crowd. "This is so exciting," Roxanne said as they followed the muddy trail.

Rudy picked up the pace. Roxanne struggled to keep up. "Hey, I'm not a racehorse, you know."

Before long, they merged with the long line at the ticket counter.

Rudy cocked his head toward the booth. "They're

turning people away."

"Good thing you bought tickets early," Roxanne said.

A Suburban pulled up, and the line parted to let it through. A middle-aged woman waited behind the wheel while a half-dozen kids disembarked.

Barely out of grade school, Roxanne surmised.

The woman reached through the vehicle's open window, waved, and said, "Have fun!" as the children melded into the crowd.

Rudy shook his head. "That lady won't get my vote as mother of the year."

Roxanne laughed, but her focus was on the group ahead of them in line. One girl was shaved bald except for a hairy star with a circle around it. Another wore shorts, high-heeled shoes, and a sleeveless shirt that exposed her pierced navel. The girl's lips were blue from the cold—or was it lipstick?

"I feel overdressed," Roxanne whispered to her brother.

"If you looked like that, Dad would lock you in your bedroom. And if he didn't, I would!"

"I must be seeing things!" Roxanne pointed to a familiar face. "What's Mrs. Crabtree doing here?"

In her shin-length wool coat and slip-on plastic galoshes, the old, blue-haired woman mingled among a sea goths and emos, enduring teenaged taunts.

Roxanne bristled protectively. "Hold my place."

Rudy grabbed his sister's arm. "She's holding her own."

Her brother was right. The group now huddled about the old woman as she engaged them in a friendly chat. "This is too weird!" Roxanne said.

"You never mentioned that Mrs. Crabtree is a fan of Ram's Fire," Rudy teased. They reached the ticket booth. He handed over his tickets and escorted his sister into the concert hall. There were no chairs on the main floor, but it was packed with standing fans.

Roxanne followed her brother to the upper level, listening to him complain about having to sit in the nosebleed section.

"Look! There's some space down by the stage!" Roxanne pointed to the ground floor as the warm-up band began to play. "Let's go check it out," she called and headed for the stairs.

On the lower level, they inched their way through the masses. The smell of perspiration grew stronger as they neared the stage, and the temperature became unbelievably hot. Someone smoking a joint exhaled in Roxanne's face as she squeezed through an opening.

Rudy grabbed his sister's arm. "This was a bad idea."

Roxanne pressed through the crowd, then turned and offered her brother a sheepish grin. The spot in question was covered with vomit. A rancid stench hung in the air. "Whoops." She offered her brother a sheepish look.

"Ram's Fire, Ram's Fire!" The fans drowned out the warm-up band. "Ram's Fire, Ram's Fire!" Someone tossed a smoke bomb on stage. It was quickly contained and whisked away.

The warm-up band ended their last song and earned a ripple of handclaps along with a spattering of jeers. The crowd turned restless as the stage crew set up for then next show.

Rudy said something biting, but Roxanne could not hear over the noise.

The fans began to surge. Roxanne and Rudy were pushed near the stage as Ram's Fire pranced onto the platform. The crowd erupted in screams and thunderous applause.

The slick-haired lead singer jammed on the strings of his electric guitar and the group launched into a frenzied opening piece, the drummer pounding a primal beat.

Girls swooned and raised adoring hands to their icons, while the boys bobbed to the vibrations.

The lead guitarist made his electric instrument mimic the sounds of a woman wailing, while the cranked-up bass picked up the tempo.

At the base of the platform, a couple dropped to the floor and started groping each other. Roxanne looked away.

In every direction, faces swayed to the rhythm—lips moved in unison, singing lyrics about death. Some fans made devil horns with their fists and shook them to the beat.

Roxanne could feel the pulsing rhythm deep within her body. The crowd began to chant, "Satan, Satan, Satan." She turned to her brother, but he was bobbing his head to the music. A sense of foreboding grew in Roxanne and quickly turned to panic. *Calm down*, she told herself. *It's just a concert.* Fear tingled down her spine, and her heart thumped wildly in her chest. Roxanne searched frantically for an exit sign, and she tugged on her brother's shirt to get his attention. "I've got to get out of here!" She fought her way through the mass of people until she found the door.

Outside, the frigid air stung her flesh, but she didn't

care. Roxanne ran until the sound of the band grew muted by distance.

Rudy's car was locked. She kicked his fender and tried to think. *What am I going to do?*

Then, Roxanne heard an acoustic guitar playing softly. "Amazing Grace, how sweet the sound that saved a wretch like me. . . ."

Near an old minivan, Roxanne spotted Mrs. Crabtree.

The old woman's bright eyes met hers. "I've been expecting you, dear."

"Expecting me?" The night was growing stranger by the minute.

Theda Mae opened her arms to welcome the teenager. "I've been praying ever since I spotted you in the ticket line."

Roxanne collapsed in the old woman's embrace and told her through sobs about the fear that had gripped her.

CHAPTER 23

He huddled in a thicket under the midnight sky trying to quiet his breathing. An owl hooted in the rustling trees above as eerie shadows danced across the ground.

Someone called his name, softly at first. "Come out. You can't hide forever." Hideous laughter issued from the darkness. Twigs snapped.

Every fiber of his being told him to run, but his legs would only move in slow motion. He tried to flap his arms and fly away, but the enemy grabbed him. . . .

Jesse awoke gulping for air. The nightmare was always the same—a voice among the shadows, footsteps drawing closer. He tried to shake the impression, but it lingered like a bad taste.

The glow of sunrise radiated through the window shade. As he lay upon his disheveled bed, Jesse forced his thoughts to the previous night at the Kingston rock concert. Three people had given their lives to the Lord, a fact that brought a rush of joy to Jesse's heart. And, as icing on the cake, they had been able to minister to a Hamlin teenager named Roxanne. All in all, the trip to Kingston had been fruitful, yet Jesse's mind could not escape the image of the old woman at the nursing home, of her cloudy eyes and of those gnarled fingers reaching for him as she spoke the words that now played over and over in his thoughts: "I knew you'd come."

The alarm clock beeped. Jesse threw back the covers and turned it off. He went into the bathroom and splashed cold water on his face, wishing he could wash away the turmoil in his soul. Jesse stared at his image in the mirror and saw the same unruly chestnut hair, same square jaw and deepset blue eyes. Yet he still did not know who he was.

"Lord, help me," he whispered.

Jesse dressed quickly, ran a comb through his hair, and made a mental note to get a haircut after work.

The morning air felt sharp to his lungs as he stepped outside. The snow that had fallen yesterday was now reduced to pockets of packed ice on the streets. Jesse skirted the slick spots as he hurried to work.

In the alley behind the Hamlin Hotel, the kitchen door banged open, and Wallace backed out carrying a load.

"Need some help?" Jesse asked.

Wallace flipped a strand of stringy bangs from his eye. "I can manage." He tilted the tub and waited for the mound of lard to slide into the dumpster.

Inside, Jesse grabbed a large bowl of potatoes and settled down to peel them.

A moment later, Wallace brushed past mumbling something under his breath. He ran his hands under a dribble of water and went to work pressing patties of sausage.

"Are you originally from this area?" Jesse asked.

"I've been around."

Jesse detected a faint southern accent. "Hamlin's an interesting town. I'm looking forward to exploring when I get a chance—maybe catch the view from the top of those red cliffs."

His boss grabbed a knife. "Dangerous up there," Wallace said as his blade sliced through an onion head. He dropped the onions in a pot. "There's an ice machine in the utility room. Why don't you grab a bucket and fill the breakfast buffet table?"

Soon the dining room buzzed with the clatter of dishes and friendly banter, but in the kitchen, Jesse resigned himself to Wallace's stony silence. He tried not to take it personally but was more than happy to clock out at the end of his shift.

"I'll see you tomorrow."

Wallace responded with a grunt.

The sun was out now, and despite puddles of muddy water, it had turned into a beautiful October day. An occasional breeze stirred the air and coaxed the last of the fall leaves from the trees.

Jesse decided to stroll to the Christian Outreach and see if Lars and Emma were there.

The town was unusually active. A couple was out walking a little dog. They paused at the corner of a yard while their pet relieved himself, and they smiled self-consciously at Jesse as he passed by. Some children bounced a plastic ball into the road. Jesse scooped it up and tossed it back. A young mother leaned over the railing on her sagging porch.

"Teddy," she scolded, "get back in here and finish cleaning your room!"

"I want to stay outside and play!" the child whined.

Who could blame the kid? Jesse sympathized. There probably weren't going to be many more nice weekends left in the year.

Jesse strode briskly through the town. He passed the window of an office supply store where an employee was hanging decorations: paper witches and cute little skeletons with arms and legs that dangled freely. Halloween was only a few short weeks away.

Jesse had always disliked the holiday, even as a child. The dreams came more often as Halloween approached. "Night terrors," Mavis had called them. She'd chalked it up to spiritual sensitivity and taught Jesse how to overcome through prayer. Since coming to Hamlin, though, the nightmares had returned.

"Hi, Jesse." An old, green Volkswagen Beetle pulled alongside him. Roxanne hung her head out the window. "Sorry about the concert. I don't know what happened—I just lost it." She paused. "I'm glad I ran into your group, though."

Jesse smiled.

"Where you going?" Roxanne asked.

"Over to the Christian Outreach."

"Want a lift?"

"That's the best offer I've had all day!" He climbed in and fished for the seatbelt. "I'm glad to see you made it back from Kingston all right."

Roxanne made a U-turn. "Rudy, my brother, was pretty upset. Says he'll never waste another concert ticket on me."

"Well, look at the bright side," Jesse said. "At least you'll never have to turn him down."

A few blocks later, Roxanne steered her car to the curb in front of the Christian Outreach. "What goes on in there, anyway?" she asked, running her fingers through wispy red hair.

"Lars and Emma use the place as a base for their work as street evangelists. You'd be surprised how busy we get in there. Oh, and we also make the best coffee around!"

Roxanne laughed.

"Want to come in for a cup?"

She shook her head and said, "Maybe some other time. My dad's waiting for me."

Jesse watched her drive away, then unlocked the door and stepped inside. His heart skipped a beat. The place had been ransacked. Furniture had been overturned and slashed with a knife, and the stuffing was strewn around the room. The walls were painted with big, black smiley faces. Rubber cement covered the carpet. Lars's computer and printer had been smashed. In the corner near the ceiling, a Mylar balloon hovered. Printed on it were the words Surprise! Surprise!

———————

"Where were you last night?"

Ozmand opened his eyes and blinked. His mother's face leaned close to his. He knew the look—lips pursed, nose wrinkled in frustration.

"Well young man? I'm talking to you!" Nan reached out and jerked the covers off her son. "I've been frantic all weekend! Do you know how worried I was when you didn't come home until late last night? I had visions of you lying on the highway in some tangled wreck. I was terrified!"

He rolled from his mattress with his fists curled.

Nan stepped back and crossed her arms. "You're going to be late for school." Her words came out tight and nervous.

Was that fear in her eyes? Ozmand plucked a shirt from his dresser and stepped into a pair of sweats. "Blow it out your ear!" he snarled.

Nan lunged forward and slapped his face.

Ozmand touched his throbbing cheek. With a surge of adrenaline, he slammed her against the wall. The smell of her hair products made him nauseous. He loathed her.

"If you ever touch me again, you're dead." Rage pulsed through Ozmand like a current. *It would be so easy.* He released his mother and watched her scurry toward the door.

He quickly shoved his feet into a pair of tennis shoes, plucked his backpack from the dresser, and brushed past Nan in the hallway.

Tears rolled down his mother's cheeks. "What's happening to you? I don't even know you anymore."

Oz stomped from the house, but the words had met their mark. The truth was that he had become a stranger even to himself.

———

Jesse opened the door for Theda Mae, whose arms were loaded with cleaning supplies. He took the box from her and set it on the floor.

The old woman looked around at the overturned cartons, stained carpets, and ripped upholstery. Her brow wrinkled. "Oh, my!"

"It's a mess isn't it?" Lars strode across the room and gave her a squeeze.

Theda Mae shook her head in dismay.

"It's going to cost a small fortune to replace everything," Emma cried. "And hours to clean up this mess. Can you believe that they dumped copy machine toner all over the carpet?"

"Remember, all things work together for the good of those who love God." She waved her hand in a half-circle. "Even this!"

Jesse admired Theda Mae's faith, yet the task before them was still daunting.

Lars disappeared into the back room and promptly emerged with fragments of a printer in his hand. "The police think they may have been after this," he announced. "Said they've had some complaints about our Halloween pamphlets."

"Good heavens, why?" Mrs. Crabtree asked.

Jesse lifted one of the paper tracts from the mess on the floor and blew dirt from its cover page. It was entitled The Origins of Halloween. He opened it and began to read. "The celebration developed from an ancient Druid New Year Festival, the Festival of the Dead."

"We never meant to offend anyone," Emma said wearily. "We know that most people just think of Halloween as a fun time for the little ones."

"God knows your intentions were motivated by love," Theda Mae said.

"We didn't make this stuff up." Lars said, reaching for

the tract in Jesse's hand. He turned it over and read the credits. "Printed with the permissions of the Royce Encyclopedia Association!"

The subject made Jesse uncomfortable. He turned to the mess and began picking up debris.

"I wonder if anybody ever trashed an encyclopedia for documenting history?" Lars barked.

Emma's face reddened. She grabbed a broom and began sweeping furiously.

"Remember," Mrs. Crabtree intoned. "We're supposed to count it all joy, even when we fall into various trials."

"It'll take more than vandals to crush my spirit!" Lars blustered.

Mrs. Crabtree clapped her hands together. "Let's have a cleaning party!"

"Great idea. I'll order pizza," Jesse volunteered.

Emma's face softened. Lars rolled up his sleeves, whistled a happy tune, and sifted through the refuse for salvageable items.

The mood had lightened, yet one fact remained that worried Jesse. Someone was trying to shut them down.

CHAPTER 24

April followed Melanie's lead as they milled around the old barn in search of chicken eggs. The girls gently kicked at mounds of sweet timothy hay while a brood of nervous hens squawked and flapped their wings in protest.

"I found one." April reached behind a spool of bailing twine next to the stall. "A nest," she said. "This is kind of fun. It reminds me of an Easter egg hunt."

Melanie appeared with the wire egg basket in tow. She leaned over for a closer look and wrinkled her nose. "I don't know about that one."

"What's wrong with it?"

"No telling how long it's been there—it might be fertilized." Melanie set the basket down on a stack of hay and rubbed the muscles near the base of her spine. "I once cracked an egg and an underdeveloped chick slid out."

"Gross!" April promptly returned the egg to its nest. "I guess you can tell I'm no farm girl."

In the dusty, filtered light of the barn, Melanie stiffened and grimaced. She laid her hands across her swollen abdomen.

April thought her new friend looked puffy and frail. "Are you all right?"

"I'm not sure. Here, feel this." Melanie reached for April's hand and placed it on her stomach. It was as hard as a rock.

"You think it's time?" April asked.

"I'm not due for a couple more weeks."

April tugged on Melanie's arm. "Let's go tell Sylvia."

Inside the farmhouse, Sylvia directed Melanie to the parlor and ordered her to lie on the couch. "Just take a deep breath, doll. Relax." She held up a watch to time the contractions. The first two were eight minutes apart, and the third one came four minutes later. After that, they stopped.

Sylvia smiled. "Good news, hon. False labor."

"False labor?" Melanie repeated with a mixture of relief and disappointment. "How will I know when it's real?"

Sylvia laughed. "If the pain gets unbearable, the contractions get closer together, or your water breaks, give me a shout." She looked at the wall clock, stretched her short, compact frame, and yawned. "Think I'll grab another cup of coffee and watch the Morning Show."

"What if this happens again?" April called as the woman sauntered off toward the kitchen.

"Don't worry, doll. When it's time, you'll know." Sylvia disappeared through the swinging door.

Chief Patterson followed the state insurance investigator around the blackened remains of what used to be

Bernard Pratt's house. "What d'ya think, Hal?"

"There is no doubt that a crime has been committed here." The investigator crouched down by what used to be the back porch. He crushed a piece of charcoal between his thumb and forefinger and smelled it. "It's a cryin' shame." The two men stood quietly for a time, as if each was searching for a place in his thoughts to file this sort of human violation.

Hal brushed black dust from his fingers. "You think it was just a kid who wanted to see what'd happen if he lit a match?"

"My gut tells me this is more than that." Art sank his hands deep into his trousers and jingled some loose change. "I'm not looking for an arsonist anymore. It's murder now."

"You mean . . . ?"

"Old Mr. Pratt took a turn for the worse last night, and they moved him from the nursing home back to ICU. He passed away early this morning."

Hal whistled through his teeth. "I don't envy your job, Chief." He cleared his throat. "Guess I'd better get back and file my report."

Chief Patterson lingered among the ruins for a few minutes before heading back to the station. Anger festered beneath his calm, and he clenched his jaw in resolve. Before his tenure as chief of police was over, justice would be served.

Art's secretary motioned to him as he walked through the door. "The state crime division faxed the information you requested. It's in your office."

"Thanks, Betty." Art poured himself a cup of decaf and trudged to his desk. The report confirmed his fears. For the last five years, the per-capita crime rate for Hamlin was almost twice the national average. The state crime division had no statistics for suicides, but Patterson didn't need a piece of paper to tell him this small western community had a serious problem.

The chief struggled to come up with a rational explanation. *What would turn a quaint little town like Hamlin into a bad place to raise a family?*

Art leaned back in his chair and rubbed his chin. *It just doesn't make any sense!* He took a sip of coffee, then pulled a police report from the top of the stack of files. Hit and run. A sixteen-year-old named Mark Elliot killed. The coroner's report was paper-clipped to the front. It listed the cause of death as internal hemorrhaging caused by blunt trauma.

The young man's body had been found by a rancher named Kit Kragler. He'd been driving on the old Brand Creek Road when he'd found the boy. The case was written up as an accident, and there were no suspects.

However, Mark Elliot had been in some kind of trouble just before his death. His parents had filed a complaint against him and petitioned the courts to make him a ward of the state.

Art flipped to the second page. The form was blank. He turned back to the front page to see who had filed the report. Officer Ian Scott.

The chief pressed the button on his intercom. "Is Officer Scott out on patrol now?"

"No, he's off duty today."

Art stared at the photograph taken for the coroner. A deep sense of shame enveloped him. A boy had died, yet Art could barely even remember the case. How could he have been so apathetic?

"Chief?" Betty poked her head through the door to his office. "Do you want me to call Officer Scott at home?" She lifted her bifocals and rubbed the bridge of her wide nose.

"Yeah, that'd be great."

Within minutes, Ian Scott was on the phone. "I remember the incident, Chief. What's bothering you about it now?"

"Just details. Or should I say, the lack of details."

"The case was pretty cut and dry. There were no witnesses, suspects, or motives."

"Why wasn't I filled in on this case?"

"Remember, Chief? That was when you found out that Bea's cancer was back. As I recall, you took your wife on some kind of vacation."

That explained a lot. Losing his wife had been the hardest thing Art had ever faced.

"I figured the kid got drunk, went joyriding with a bunch of friends, and fell out the back of the pickup," Ian explained.

Chief Patterson thumbed through the autopsy report. "There was no alcohol found in his blood."

"Maybe the kid didn't die right away."

Art thought he detected a hint of irritation in Officer Scott's voice. "Did you question any of his friends?"

"Of course I did. Nobody knew anything. No one saw anything. You know how it is."

"What about the boy's parents?"

"They were out of town. I believe they were checking into some kind of boy's home in Wyoming. Anything else?"

"All right, sounds like you had it covered." Art hung up

SHADOW *of the* PIPER

and tossed the file back on the stack, wondering if he was slipping. He picked up his old police cap, knocked dust off it, and spun it around on his finger while brooding about his career.

Have I made any positive impact on this community during my tenure as police chief? I hope retirement won't be my most significant act of service. Art grabbed his jacket and pushed his weary frame from the desk.

"I'm going to grab a bite of lunch and head home," he announced to Betty. "If you need to reach me, that's where I'll be."

"Are you feeling okay, sir?" Betty's brow creased with concern. "You look pale."

"Just tired," he said, offering a half-hearted smile.

Art drove the four short blocks to the diner. He took his usual spot at the counter and ordered the daily special. A few seats down, a customer settled his bill and dropped two quarters on the counter next to a newspaper.

"Are you taking that paper with you?" the chief inquired.

"Nope, it's up for grabs."

"Thanks." Art slid the Hamlin Review across the counter, unfolded it, and scanned the front page. The local Kiwanis Club was offering a hunter safety course, and the BLM was considering cutting back leases. Volunteers were needed at the Crisis Intervention Service Center.

He turned the page and skimmed the headlines. His eyes fixed on a photograph at the bottom of the page. It was a picture of an attractive blonde teenager in a cheerleader's outfit. *Have You Seen This Girl?* was written in big, bold letters across the top, followed by an article stating the details of April Gilbert's disappearance and a plea for help in locating her.

The chief felt his blood pressure rise. Leland Gilbert had taken matters into his own hands. "Fool," he grumbled, a little louder than intended.

"Who you calling a fool?" A tall, lanky cowboy straddled the stool next to Art. His grin was nearly lost in the deep crevices of his weathered face.

"Kit Kragler! I haven't seen you in a month of Sundays. How is the ranching business treating you?"

"Oh, I can't complain as long as the beef prices stay put. So, what's got you so riled?"

Art thumped the page of the newspaper with the back of his hand. "Just another private citizen trying to take matters into his own hands." Chief Patterson folded the paper and laid it on the counter. "Can I buy you a cup of coffee?"

"Sure."

The waitress arrived with a menu.

"I don't need a menu, darlin'," the cowboy chortled. "Just fill this cup and tell the cook to round up the special for me." He tipped his hat to the young woman.

She poured the coffees and sauntered away.

"It's ironic that I should run into you today. I was just going through some old police reports and your name came up."

"Uh-oh—I plead the Fifth!" The rancher followed with a wry grin. "Besides, you ain't got nothin' on me."

"Don't get worked up," Art cautioned. "It's about that Elliot boy who was killed."

Kragler took off his hat and set it, brim up, on the counter. "Terrible what happened to that poor kid. Did you ever find out who done a thing like that?"

"It was determined to be an accidental death."

Kit nearly choked on his coffee. "Accidental?"

"My investigator's assessment was that the boy fell from a moving vehicle, probably a pickup truck."

"Well, I ain't gonna tell you lawboys how to do your job." He watched the waitress set the plate of food on the counter and grabbed his fork.

"Listen, Kit, if there was something we overlooked in the investigation, I want to hear about it."

The old rancher thought about the question, chewing slowly and deliberately. He wiped the side of his mouth with his sleeve. "I often think about that day. It was in early June, and I was out feeding. Got stuck in a mud hole as I was headin' back. When I finally got myself out o' that mess, I drove up the road apiece before stoppin' to knock some big chunks of mud off my tires. That's when I seen him. That poor kid was covered with mud from head to toe, and he was lying there all twisted."

"He must have fallen from a moving vehicle."

Kit Kragler shook his head. "I don't think so."

"Why not?"

"There weren't hardly a spot on that boy that didn't have a tire track. One, maybe two tracks, if he fell from the hood of a truck and was run over, but this kid had so many tire marks on him I gave up counting. If you ask me, that boy was run down—least that's what I told that investigator of yours." Kit picked at his food.

Art's thoughts turned to Officer Scott's report. It hadn't mentioned tire tracks on the boy's body and the photograph only showed the boys face. *Ian lied. But why?* Art was suddenly aware of his heart. It skipped a beat and fluttered in his chest. Then the pain arrived, radiating concentric waves of intensity from his shoulder to his chest. His nitroglycerin was in his jacket by the front door. Art stood. It seemed so far away, so out of reach. The pain became unbearable, crushing him. Light danced before his eyes and faded to gray.

The next thing Art saw as he drifted in and out of consciousness was the flashing lights of the ambulance.

———

In Theda Mae's antique-cluttered living room, Lars stood and cleared his throat. "I would like to say something." He waited as a hush fell over the small prayer group.

"We have been blessed. I know that may sound strange after the Christian Outreach was vandalized, but I mean it." The big man's lip quivered, and he rubbed his eyes.

Emma put her hand on her husband's shoulder and said to Theda Mae, "We appreciate all your help and encouragement."

"That's what Christian family is for." Theda Mae smiled, then passed out lyric sheets.

Jesse lifted his guitar from beside the couch and began to strum a worship song, and they all joined in.

Afterward, Theda Mae opened her Bible to the book of Ephesians and read aloud. "Put on all of God's armor so that you will be able to stand firm against all strategies of the

SHADOW *of the* PIPER

devil."

The words resonated in Jesse's heart. Since his first day in Hamlin, he'd sensed something dark and oppressive.

"We're all called to pray." Emma looked about the small gathering and added, "I just wish there were more than four of us."

"It only takes one man or woman of faith to move a mountain," Theda Mae admonished. "Remember what it says in the Bible, 'The earnest prayer of a righteous person has great power and produces wonderful results.'"

The telephone rang.

"Would you like me to get it?" Emma asked.

Theda Mae smiled. "That would be lovely, dear."

Emma hurried into the library to answer. When she returned, her face was grim.

"What's a matter, Mama?" Lars launched from his chair and went to his wife's side.

"It's Mr. Pratt," Emma said. "I'm afraid he's passed away."

Theda Mae's pale eyes filled with tears.

Jesse whispered a silent prayer, yet something warned him that the worst was yet to come.

CHAPTER 25

Ozmand lifted his battery-powered lantern, but the walls of the old mining tunnel seemed to absorb the light and cast angular shadows upon his associates. They looked like hooded drones as they snaked single-file through the narrow passage.

Beneath the streets of Hamlin, the sound of swishing robes and shuffling feet marked the progression of the Piper's followers. No one spoke.

Ozmand felt excited—and maybe a little scared—about what lay ahead. If Hollywood movies were any indication, he was convinced that his first dark ritual would be a rush. He looked around for Cyrus, wishing he was close by. Somehow, they'd become separated.

Water dripped from the rock formations overhead and drizzled down his chin. He paused to wipe it away, and someone shoved him from behind. Dutifully, Ozmand kept the pace. Deeper into the pit, murky pools of water swallowed his feet. *What's that smell?* he wondered, as they neared their destination.

They came to a cinder-block wall and followed it to a

crude opening. Light spilled from a chiseled hole, four feet in diameter. The line slowed as each member passed through the narrow opening. Finally, Ozmand emerged into a large, windowless room, where he was directed to join a circle of associates.

The people of the Piper's Guild seemed to be following an invisible choreographer. They swayed to the left, chanting as the human circle turned. The circumference grew as more and more joined in.

From beneath the cowl of his hood, Ozmand tried to take it all in. *Those voices—those eyes! They look like zombies.* He spotted Cyrus among those gathered and gave him a little wave. Cy did not respond. The expression on his face was flat, his gaze hollow and distant.

Suddenly, two torches sprang to life, illuminating a small platform. An altar had been erected between the flames. To the left of the altar, an ornate armchair enthroned a figure whose features were obscured by the blackness of his hood. A large silver medallion hung from his neck.

A flicker from the torch flame glinted in the figure's eye, and Ozmand shuddered.

The tempo of the chanting built until it reached a fever pitch, and then something strange began to happen. An odd, narcotic sensation came over Ozmand.

The high priest stood abruptly and stretched out fingers decorated with long silver talons. His shrill voice sliced through the room like a Skilsaw. "Bring forth the offering."

From a table on the right side of the room, one of the associates retrieved a covered platter and obediently delivered it to his leader, who slowly removed the lid.

Ozmand gasped and hoped he'd not been heard. On the tray was a severed hand.

"Remains of a traitor!" the priest shrieked as he placed the tray upon the altar. "An offering of appeasement to the one we serve."

What did this man do to deserve this? Ozmand remembered Cyrus's words: "There's no turning back." Light danced in front of the teenager's eyes, and he forced himself to breathe.

The crowd's chanting became louder and more insistent. Ozmand mouthed the words, watching in awe as the offering began to smoke. The sour stench of sulfur curled through the air. Flames erupted with a throaty roar, devouring the hand.

Ozmand thought he saw a figure in the flames. Instinct told him to run, but he could not seem to move. He tried not to think about the upcoming Black Mass that would mark Halloween. Ozmand no longer wanted to know its secrets. *Be cool.* He wiped away beads of sweat and noticed that his hands were trembling—hands now chained by secrets.

The midnight hour passed and both the apparition and the high priest disappeared in a plume of smoke. Excitement rippled through the room, but a reverent mood remained.

It was over. Ozmand felt a rush of relief. He fell in line as the Piper's Guild began their somber ascent from the pit of hell. Mute and chilled by the damp, he wished he could turn back time.

—∽∿∽—

Cali sat alone in Cyrus's living room. The changing light of the television flickered across her face, ensconcing her in red, blue, and green. She hadn't moved in hours, barely aware of the evening shadows creeping across the room and morphing the world to darkness.

Outside, footsteps clomped across the porch, followed by the sound of a key scratching at the lock. Cali stiffened, then rested her hand upon the handle of the knife she'd slipped between the sofa cushions.

The lock turned, and Cyrus stepped inside and greeted Cali with an obscenity. "You still here?" He peeled off his jacket, tossed it on the couch beside her, and sneered. "Lazy cow! The least you can do is pay rent!"

"I don't have any money."

Cyrus swung his leg over the arm of the couch and perched there. "Maybe we can work something out."

Cali drew the butcher knife and held it to Cy's temple. "Maybe I could kill you." She gripped the knife handle so tight her fingers went numb.

"Hey, calm down," Cyrus said.

One quick jab, she thought, but changed her mind. "I'm going to bed."

Cyrus rolled to the floor and scrambled for distance. "You're insane, you know that?" he yelled as she slammed her bedroom door.

Cali placed the butcher knife upon her pillow and stared at the space that used to be a window. She had nailed plywood over it and then applied a layer of tarpaper she had stolen from a neighbor's garage. Still, despite the precautions, Cali knew they were watching, tracing her steps and burrowing into her mind.

Cali felt the pocket of her jeans and pulled out a plain white envelope that had been folded several times. She opened it carefully and retrieved the contents—a lock of fine baby hair. The envelope had come in the morning mail along with a message, which Cali had promptly burned.

She raised the wispy sprig of hair to her nose, searching for a lost memory. Cali realized that she could not even recall what her baby looked like. Her name was Brenna. She would be six weeks old by now. "Time stolen," she hissed. Cali slipped the hair back into the envelope, slid it into her pocket, and turned off the light. In the darkness of her tiny room, Cali drifted off to sleep with her fingers resting on the handle of the knife.

———

At the Hamlin Hotel and Restaurant, breakfast came and went. Now, in the clean kitchen, Jesse stared at the stacked dishes on the shelf, still warm from the dishwasher. Most of the crew slipped out the back door to the alley. Jesse had not been invited to join them on their break. It was just as well; judging from the cigarette butts scattered near the dumpster, they did more smoking than talking anyway.

Across the room, Wallace worked silently at the butcher block, turning the breakfast leftovers into gourmet delights for the lunchtime crowd.

"Need some help?" Jesse asked.

Wallace scratched his ear and said, "I can handle it."

Jesse spotted a smudge on a spoon and went to work

225

polishing the dinnerware. "Are you married?" he asked, trying to break the ice.

"Nope, but that don't mean I'm single." Wallace threw a handful of chopped carrots into a pot of chicken stock. He grabbed a stalk of celery and began to dice. "You ask a lot of questions. Any particular reason?"

"I'm just trying to be friendly."

Wallace carried the pot to the stove, then went to the back door and yelled, "Break's over! Get back to work!" He turned back to Jesse. "Tell you what, we're overstaffed today, so you can cut out early."

"You sure?" Jesse checked his watch. It was almost an hour 'till noon. "I don't mind staying."

The rest of the kitchen crew shuffled through the door smelling like cigarettes, and Wallace barked orders at them. He shot an impatient look at Jesse. "Like I said, we don't need you here."

Jesse hung up his apron by the back door and punched the time clock.

Outside, a gust of wind blew hard, and Jesse turned up his collar. The sun had done little to warm the air since his predawn walk, but the crisp blue sky was host to brushstroke clouds. It was a beautiful day.

With time to kill, Jesse wandered down a side street and, to his delight, discovered an ice cream parlor. Jesse dropped fifty cents into a newspaper vending machine, grabbed a paper, and went inside.

The parlor, a popular hangout, was decorated with pink stripes like an old-fashioned malt shop. Wire chairs and tables were littered with sprawling teenagers.

In the corner, a young boy plunked some change into a faux-vintage jukebox. He drummed the air to the blast of a hard rock tune.

Jesse ordered a double scoop of rocky road and sat down.

"Hi, Jesse!"

He looked up to see Roxanne standing next to an athletic-looking teenage boy, who she introduced as Logan.

Jesse smiled and rose from his chair. "Would you like to sit down?"

"No, that's okay. I have to get home and study for a test. I just wanted to say hello."

Logan pulled a hand from his varsity letter jacket and pointed at the newspaper that was lying open on Jesse's table. "Hey, Roxanne, look," he exclaimed. "It's April!" He snatched up the newspaper for a closer look. "I remember when that picture was taken. It was right before the homecoming game." Logan dropped the paper back on the table and dug in his jeans pocket but came up empty. "Roxie, do you have some quarters? I want to buy one of those papers."

"You can have this copy if you want," Jesse offered.

"Thanks."

Jesse glanced at the photo. "Wait, can I see that for a minute?" He looked closer. "I've seen this girl somewhere."

"Where?" Logan gripped the table.

Jesse rubbed his forehead. "I can't remember. But I know I've seen her recently."

"Recently?" Roxanne exclaimed.

"I'm sure of it." Jesse shook his head. "Still, I can't

think of where."

Roxanne's face dropped with disappointment as she rifled through her backpack for a pen. "If you remember, give me a call." She scribbled her phone number on a napkin.

Logan nudged Roxanne. "Let's go?"

After they left, Jesse turned his attention back to his melting ice cream and ambled through the backstreets. That's when he spotted Cali ducking into an alleyway.

Jesse called her name and hurried to catch up. He found her crouching next to a dumpster like a cornered animal. "Cali, are you all right?"

She cowered, looking confused.

Jesse's heart was moved. He held out his hand in an effort to coax her from the spot.

Without warning, Cali grabbed his fingers, jerked him toward her, and bit his arm.

Jesse yelled as he felt her legs twist about his feet. He fell to the ground on top of her and she wrung the collar of his shirt to pull him closer.

"Cali! What are you doing?"

Suddenly, the back door of a café opened and a waitress stepped outside for a smoke.

"Help me," Cali shrieked. "I'm being attacked!" She raked her jagged fingernails across Jesse's face.

The waitress bolted back inside.

Jesse scrambled to his feet as Cali released her grip. "Why?"

As if some invisible switch had been flipped, she stood, calmly wiped her mouth, and skipped away like a carefree little girl.

Blood trickled down Jesse's face. He ripped a piece of his shirt and put it over his wound, then turned toward home, wondering about the deranged girl who had brought him to Hamlin.

There's no telling what Cali will try next.

CHAPTER 26

Jesse cringed as Emma pressed a warm washcloth on his face.

"You might need stitches for that." Her brow furrowed with concern. "It's pretty deep."

Jesse drew back.

"Hold still," Emma said sternly. She poured hydrogen peroxide onto a cotton ball and pressed it to his wound. It stung. Emma pulled down his shirt collar. "Those marks on your neck are turning a nasty shade of purple." She frowned. "It's hard for me to understand why anyone would do something like this. I don't think that girl is playing with a full deck."

"Cali's a troubled kid," Jesse said. "There's a lot of pain and rage behind that shell of hers." He squeezed Emma's hand. "She needs our prayers."

Emma closed her eyes. "Forgive me, Lord," she whispered. "You came to heal the brokenhearted, to preach deliverance to the captives."

Jesse picked up the hand mirror that Emma had brought out and inspected his cheek. "The bleeding has stopped."

"I still think you should get stitches."

"I'll be fine."

She pursed her lips. "You think I'm being a mother hen, don't you?"

Jesse gave Emma a hug. "You're wonderful. Don't change a thing!"

A knock on the door broke the awkward sweetness of the moment. "I'll get it." Jesse strode across the room and opened the door.

"Jesse Berry?" a uniformed police officer asked, flipping open a leather-bound badge.

"Yes?"

"I have a warrant for your arrest." He told Jesse to face the wall and frisked him.

Thoughts raced through Jesse's mind. There was no need to wonder about Cali's next move any longer—her destructive intentions were crystal clear. *But what did I do to deserve this?*

"You have the right to remain silent. Anything you say can be used against you in a court of law. You have the right to speak to an attorney and to have an attorney present during any questioning. If you cannot afford an attorney, one will be provided for you. . . ."

The words jumbled together. "What is all this about?" Jesse asked.

The officer secured the handcuffs and turned him toward the door, but Emma blocked the exit.

"The young man asked you a question," she said. Her face was flushed with indignation.

The officer sidestepped Emma and without a reply

whisked his prisoner outside, where they were joined by two other policemen. Three patrol cars with lights flashing had parked haphazardly across the yard. It seemed ridiculous to Jesse that so much fuss was being made about nothing.

"You can't do this," Emma objected as she hurried along behind.

Jesse's stomach was in knots as the officer shoved him into the backseat of the squad car. He felt as though he'd awakened from a bad dream only to be confronted by a nightmare.

———

The nurse pulled the curtain around the hospital bed and put a blood pressure cuff on Art Patterson's arm. "You gave everyone quite a scare," she said. "We tried to contact your son, but he couldn't be reached. We'll try again." She pumped air into the cuff and listened through the stethoscope as it deflated. "That's a little better than it was yesterday."

The chief sat up. His body felt as though it had been hit by a cruise missile.

"I don't want you calling my son," Art barked. "He's got better things to do than worry about his old man." The nurse raised a hypodermic needle to the tube of the IV bottle hanging to his left.

"What's that for?" Art demanded.

"Just a little sedative. You need your rest."

"I don't want it," he snapped.

"Doctor's orders." She injected the fluid into the tube.

Art reached over with his free hand and pinched off the tube.

"Really, Chief Patterson! You're a little old to act so childish."

Ignoring the remark, he pulled the tape off his arm and removed the needle.

"What are you doing?" the nurse said. "We're just going to have to put that back in again."

Art climbed out of bed and stood. When the dizziness passed, he shuffled to the closet, found his clothes, and glanced sideways at the nurse. "You want to give me a little privacy, or are you waiting for a show?"

"You've had a heart attack. You can't leave."

"Watch me."

"If you leave without a physician's consent, your insurance might not pay." She crossed her arms across her chest and pursed her lips disapprovingly.

Art looked the nurse square in the eyes, then dropped his hospital gown to the floor. He chuckled as she hurried from the room.

He dressed slowly. The effort was so exhausting that he had to lean against the wall to catch his breath. Art wasn't sure if he had the strength to walk home, so he dialed his office from the telephone beside his bed. "Betty, it's Art."

"Chief! How are you feeling?"

"I'll be fine after a good night's sleep," he said. "Listen, I need a ride. Would you send one of the boys over to the hospital?"

Two orderlies appeared in the doorway, followed by the nurse.

"Looks like I've got to do some battle with the hospital staff. Tell my ride to hurry." Before hanging up, he added,

"I'll be waiting out front."

———

Ozmand slipped into his house and made a beeline for his room. He was grateful that his mother had not been there to greet him.

She's becoming a real drag, Ozmand thought as he pushed open his bedroom door.

Nan was hunched over an open dresser drawer rifling through his things.

"What are you doing?" he roared.

Nan straightened and faced her son. "I was looking for drugs." There was no apology in her tone.

Ozmand's mouth fell open. "All you had to do was ask. I'd be glad to share." He took a joint out of his shirt pocket, lit it, and then offered it to her.

"That's it!" Nan shrieked. She plucked the weed from his hand and dropped it into an empty Coke can that was sitting on the dresser. "You're heading for rehab!"

The teenager stared at his mother. She was trembling, and her face was pinched in a ridiculous attempt to look authoritative.

Nan sank to the edge of Ozmand's bed and drew in a deep breath. "This is a major problem, but now that it's out in the open, we can tackle it together." She reached out to him. "I love you, son, and I'll always be there for you."

Too little, too late, Ozmand thought, feeling a resurgence of the now familiar rage. The pressure rose in him swiftly like a geyser. Without warning, Oz balled his fist and hit his mother on the side of her head. The force of the blow slammed her to the floor.

Lying at his feet, Nan looked up, dazed. Quivering, she crawled toward the bedroom door. Her fear was palpable.

Ozmand felt a strange, emotionless detachment as he watched his mother squirm. It was as though she meant no more to him than a spider under his foot. Deep inside his heart an alarm sounded. Something was wrong, but he was powerless to stop it.

CHAPTER 27

Art Patterson woke up feeling tired. He lay in bed with a nagging fear dancing through his mind. The memory of the crushing pain of his recent heart attack was still fresh, a reminder of his own mortality. With stubborn resolve, Art threw off the covers and climbed out of bed. Someone had once said that work is the best medicine. "It's worth a try," he muttered, shuffling into the bathroom to shower and shave.

In the kitchen, against the advice of his doctor, he started a pot of stout coffee. Art sat down at the table to wait for it to brew.

A fly buzzed across the room in a waltz. Art's thoughts drifted over his career, and remorse rose in his gullet like a bad meal. When had suspicious deaths, violent crimes, and vandalism become so routine?

Art grabbed a swatter from the counter and smacked the fly with a single stroke. The coffee gurgled, and he poured some into a thermal cup and drove to work.

As he steered through the sleepy streets of Hamlin, Art felt a rush of excitement, almost as if he were seeing his hometown for the first time. Quaint, charming—words his late wife had used when describing their town to outsiders. When had Hamlin changed?

Without knowing why, Art took a hard left at an intersection and started for the Gilberts' house.

Leland answered the door wearing a pair of sweatpants and a dirty t-shirt. "Did you find April?" His voice raised an octave with hope.

"No. I'm sorry."

Mr. Gilbert rubbed dry, cracked lips. He looked terrible. The odor of alcohol billowed from his pores, and a scraggly beard had sprouted on his face.

"May I come in?"

"Sure."

The house was a mess, with newspapers scattered among empty beer cans and full ashtrays. Mr. Gilbert switched off the television.

"How are you doing, Leland?"

He dropped onto a plastic-covered chair and lit a cigarette. "How do you think I'm doing?"

"I didn't know you smoked."

Leland inhaled and shrugged indifferently. "Maybe it'll kill me," he laughed. "Guess I'm just too much of a coward to put a bullet in my head."

Art lost patience. "We will find that little girl of yours. But when we do, what kind of home are you going to provide for her?"

Leland glared at the chief and ground out his cigarette in the ashtray. "Did you come over to lecture me?"

Art softened. After all, the man had lost a son and wife, and now his daughter was missing. "I'm sorry, Leland. If anyone has a right to be bitter, you do. But. . . ."

"But what?"

"You shouldn't give up hope. How long has it been since you've gone to work?"

"I've been sick."

"I don't think hangovers count."

Mr. Gilbert stood. "Look, Art, you're welcome here any time you've got news about April, but save the social calls for someone who cares."

"Fair enough." Art drummed his fingers on a decorative table and let his eyes sweep across the room. "I'd like to look around if you don't mind. Maybe I'll turn up something that will help us find April."

Leland turned on the television and settled down to watch a rerun of Magnum P. I. "Do whatever you have to."

Art walked down the hallway. He stopped at the first door on the right and pushed it open. The room had blue plaid wallpaper covered with rock 'n' roll posters. A pile of clothing and sports equipment sat near the closet, and he realized it had been the boy's room. He continued down the hallway to the next room on the right.

April's room had a canopy bed covered in pink gingham. Art folded his arms and looked about with interest. There was nothing in the room that revealed April's age—no posters or makeup. No teenage trinkets. It was as if someone was trying to keep her a little girl.

He searched under the mattress and in the drawers, hoping to find a diary, but found nothing. He gazed at a row of school pictures taped to the dresser mirror. Instinct told him that April's friends knew more than they'd let on. He pulled his notebook from his shirt pocket, jotted a reminder to have another visit with the kids, and then slipped it back in his pocket.

Art's hand remained at his breast pocket. A dull pain surfaced with each beat of his heart but quickly faded. Art's chest heaved with a slow and steady breathing. He forced himself to concentrate on the case. April had apparently run away, distraught over her mother's suicide. If so, the chances of finding her alive were good. Art needed this success; maybe it would dispel his terrible sense of failure.

Art's arm shook slightly as he checked his watch. It was mid-morning, and already he felt physically drained.

"Find anything?" Mr. Gilbert leaned against the door.

Art shook his head and stepped out into the hallway, where the two men fell silent.

Leland spoke first. "I'm sorry about being so cynical. I know you're trying to help. Sometimes this house gets too quiet and I start to feel like I'm cracking up." He paused at the next door. "This was Benny's room. Darlene was going through some of Benny's things the day she died. Guess it was just too much for her." Leland's lip quivered as he bent over a mound of clothes next to the closet. "Maybe if I'd been around more, spent more time with her. . . ." He turned away and wept.

Art walked up to Leland and put a sympathetic hand on his shoulder. "You can't blame yourself. It wasn't your fault." He searched for words of comfort but found none, so he turned his attention back to the task at hand. The chief poked his toe at a collection of things that had once belonged to a living, breathing boy. He noticed a small book lying among

Benny's personal effects. Art bent down, picked it up, and read the black lettering on the front. "Leland, were you aware that your son was involved in the occult?" He held up the Piper's Bible.

"What?" The distraught father grabbed the book and stared at it. "Where would he have gotten a thing like this?"

"Good question, Leland. A very good question."

—⁂—

Jesse hardly noticed when the squeaky meal cart stopped outside his jail cell.

"Dinner," the guard croaked. He plucked a covered tray from the stack and fumbled with the little meal hatch.

Jesse offered a feeble smile. "Thanks, but I'm not hungry."

The guard yawned. "Suit yourself." He slid the plate through the opening and onto a little iron shelf. "I'll be back in an hour to collect it, and it don't matter to me if it's been touched or not."

The cart's wheels squeaked to the next cell, then onward to the next.

Jesse tried to make sense of the whole situation. He had been so sure that God had directed his steps to Montana. But, now, discouragement plagued him.

"How are you doing, son?" Lars appeared in the cell's corridor with Emma. "We had to do some fast talking," the big man whispered. "They don't usually let folks come back here, but we used to do some ministry at this jail, and I guess they felt they could trust us."

"We can only stay a few minutes," Emma added, forcing a smile.

Jesse climbed to his feet and clutched the bars. "I didn't know you used to do a jail ministry," he said. "How come you don't do that anymore? This place could stand some good news."

Emma sighed deeply. "One afternoon, when we showed up, the jail supervisor told us we weren't allowed to share the gospel anymore." Emma took hold of the bars as though she longed to pull them down.

"Could you do me a favor?"

"Anything, just name it," Lars said eagerly.

"Bring me my Bible from home."

Emma dug through her shoulder bag and pulled out the well-used book. "I thought you'd want it."

"Read Acts," Lars suggested, his voice resonating with compassion. "The Apostle Paul went through a lot, but in the midst of it all, God was right beside him."

Jesse offered a half-hearted smile, for, deep down, he knew his faith was being tested.

CHAPTER 28

April awoke with a start. A faint tingling of fear nagged her, but she didn't know why. She fluffed her pillow and settled back, waiting for the feeling to pass. Deep within her womb, a tiny, persistent thumping began. Her hand moved across her swollen abdomen and she felt movement. April imagined the little stranger trying to kick his or her way out. "Don't be in too much of a hurry to come into this world," she said, wondering what kind of mother she would be.

An agonizing scream pierced the quiet, sitting April bolt upright. She threw off the covers and listened, but all was still. Guided by a patch of moonlight on the wooden floor, she slid her feet inside her slippers and found her robe. The crying sound had come from somewhere in the house, she was sure of it.

April hurried down the hallway to her friend's bedroom. Melanie was gone! She knocked on Sylvia and Wallace's door. No answer. The sound arose again, deep and mournful. It faded to a moan, and April followed the sound down the stairs. It seemed to come from the bowels of the dark house.

In the kitchen, a sliver of light illuminated the basement door. It was closed but the padlock was gone!

April shuddered as a prickly sensation passed over her flesh. "Sylvia?" She pushed the door open and rubbed the goose bumps on her arms.

The house was silent now, and April's knees shook from the cold draft that was coming from below. *Maybe the noise came from outside. Maybe it's nothing to worry about.* But she knew better. *Where is Melanie?* And then she heard her voice—barely audible—pleading.

April carefully opened the door to the cellar, pausing when the old hinge threatened to give her away. She stepped onto the stairway and began her descent. The next step creaked beneath her feet. She cringed and shifted her weight, and the dry wood groaned. The palms of April's hands were moist with sweat as she clutched the railing. Things went better when she kept to the edge of the stairs where the wood was stouter.

A new wave of cries propelled her swiftly down the steps, and she found herself standing in a room devoid of windows and dark as coal. A strip of light outlined a door. She moved closer, summoned her courage, and knocked.

She heard hushed voices and the sound of heels clicking across the floor.

The door opened just wide enough for Sylvia to peek out. "What are you doing down here, hon? You'll catch a cold."

"But I heard Melanie and. . . ."

"April!" her friend screamed. "Help me!"

Sylvia blocked the teenager from entering. "Nothing to

worry about. She's in labor, but everything is going just fine."

"Can I just. . . ?"

"You'd only be in the way." There was an edge to Sylvia's sugary words. "You poor little thing. I'm sure this is upsetting to you. Wallace, why don't you go upstairs and make April a nice, soothing cup of tea?"

"No, really. . . ."

"Wallace doesn't mind." Sylvia's lips spread into smile, but her eyes were flat. "It's going to be a long night, hon."

———

Roxanne parked her Volkswagen in front of Mrs. Crabtree's house. The old woman met her at the screen door and ushered her inside.

Roxanne glanced at her watch. "Am I late?"

Mrs. Crabtree seemed anxious. "The housework can keep today. I was hoping you would drive me over to the jail."

"Is this about Jesse?" Roxanne said. "Everybody's talking about how he attacked that strange girl. I don't believe it's true."

Theda Mae raised an eyebrow. "I'm glad to hear that." She slipped on her heavy wool coat, grabbed her purse, and followed Roxanne to her car.

Mrs. Crabtree settled into the Volkswagen and laid her purse on her lap. She pointed her pensive face straight ahead and sighed. "That young man can use your prayers."

Roxanne turned the key and steered onto the street. "I'm not very good at that."

"Nonsense," the old woman retorted. "Just talk to Jesus

like you would a friend. It's as simple as that."

Roxanne navigated a turn, dropped the car into another gear, and gave it some gas.

"Careful, dear, you don't want a speeding ticket." Theda Mae clutched her purse as Roxanne took a hard turn into the jail parking lot and lurched to a stop.

"Here we are."

The old woman hopped from the Volkswagen and was already at the station door when Roxanne caught up with her.

Minutes later, the heavy steel door opened, and a fat little guard escorted Theda Mae and Roxanne down a long corridor. Near the end of the hallway, the man slipped a key into a metal door and pushed it open. The room looked sterile, with a series of benches positioned beneath glass windows laced with wire mesh.

"You got fifteen minutes," the jailer said.

Theda Mae balked. "That's all?"

"Space is limited, lady. We've got other visitors."

On the far side, a pregnant woman sat engaged in a hushed conversation with a man on the other side. She spoke quietly into a small, grated opening.

"Wait here and I'll go get the inmate." The guard left the room.

Roxanne sat beside Mrs. Crabtree and looked around nervously. "I've never been in a jail before."

Theda Mae started to respond, but rose instead as Jesse entered the room. His cheeks turned red when he saw Roxanne.

"What's a nice girl like you doing in a place like this?" he asked.

Roxanne laughed. "I'm just along for the ride!" When he lowered his gaze, she added, "That came out wrong. What I meant was, I figured you could probably use an extra friend right now."

"You're right." Jesse smiled. "I'm glad you both came."

Theda Mae leaned forward and studied the young man through her bifocals. "That's a nasty cut on your face."

Jesse's hand rose to his cheek. "It's nothing. I'm more concerned about why Cali lied. I never touched her."

Roxanne could see the pain in Jesse's eyes as Theda Mae tried to make pleasant small talk with him. After awhile, the conversation dwindled to silence that was shattered by the chubby guard. "Time's up!"

The other visitors began to trickle from the room.

"Is there anything you need?" Theda Mae asked.

"Yes, there's one thing. I wonder if you would get a hold of Mavis Berry and let her know what happened?"

"Of course! Do you have her number?"

"It's back at the apartment. The door is unlocked. You'll find my address book in the top drawer of the dresser. I'll pay you back for the long distance charges just as soon as I can."

"You don't need to worry about that, dear."

"Clear out, folks," the guard said, herding the visitors toward the door.

"Roxanne!" Jesse called as she turned to go. "I remembered where I saw that missing girlfriend of yours!"

Roxanne hurried back to the window "Where?"

"About a half-hour drive on the way to Kingston." Jesse stood. "It's off a dirt road on the right, but you can't see the farm from the road because of a small hill. The farmhouse is a white two-story—"

On the other side of the window, the guard said, "Okay, lover boy, let's go," and took him by the arm.

Roxanne was stunned. "Mrs. Crabtree was right," she whispered. "God does hear our prayers."

Theda Mae was waiting in the lobby.

"Jesse's house next?" Roxanne asked.

"I was hoping you wouldn't mind." Mrs. Crabtree squeezed the girl's hand. "You are such a dear."

Roxanne backed out of the parking space feeling almost giddy with excitement. *Jesse actually saw April!*

She knew where Lars and Emma Willis lived, but nodded politely as Theda Mae offered directions. All the while, her mind was fixed on Jesse's disclosure. She couldn't wait to tell Logan. Roxanne pressed on the throttle and blew through town.

"My goodness," Theda Mae said as Roxanne's wheels screeched to a stop at the end of the Willis driveway. "That was certainly an exhilarating ride!" The old woman smoothed a wild strand of hair and unbuckled her seatbelt.

"So, this is where Jesse lives," Roxanne said as they strolled toward the little guest cottage.

The door was unlocked, just as Jesse had said it would be. Roxanne followed Mrs. Crabtree inside. The place was a tiny one-room apartment, but it was tidy. Theda Mae headed straight for the dresser and opened the top drawer. Among some loose change and other odds and ends, she found the address book. "Here it is!" Theda Mae held the little book in her hand. A strange expression formed on her aged face and she stared into the drawer.

"Are you feeling okay?" Roxanne rushed to her side as the old woman lifted a piece of jewelry and closely studied it through her bifocals.

"Mrs. Crabtree?" Roxanne said.

"I'm fine, dear." She quickly closed the drawer, shoved her hands into the pockets of her tweed coat, and headed for the door.

Roxanne looked back at the drawer. It was crazy, but it had almost looked as if the old woman had stolen a piece of jewelry. *Naw,* she thought. *Anybody but Theda Mae Crabtree...*

CHAPTER 29

Logan slipped into the school's vacant auditorium feeling a slight tinge of guilt for skipping class. But he had to cram for a math test and needed a quiet place to study. With his backpack in tow, Logan climbed the ladder to the lighting platform where he had once worked as a theater technician. It was exhilarating to be up so high. There, Logan felt detached from his troubles.

Except for the occasional settling of the building's steel frame, all was quiet. Since no one knew that Logan came here he could count on being uninterrupted.

He opened his book to Chapter 3. Calculus was normally his best subject, but in the past few weeks, his grades had been slipping and his parents had voiced concern. Logan sighed. In light of April's pregnancy, a math test seemed like a small worry.

The idea that he was to become a father seemed surreal. He longed to hold April and tell her that everything would be okay. Logan balled his frustration into a fist and slammed it on the floor of the platform. The sound echoed aimlessly around the auditorium, then faded.

Logan settled back against a steel beam and tried to concentrate on something he could control—his calculus grade. He worked out the problems on his calculator. The hour passed quickly.

He forged a note from his mother, hoping it would fool the high school office staff, and quickly descended the steep metal ladder with barely enough time to make it to his next class.

The main building ebbed and flowed with high school traffic. Vain chatter resonated among the halls as Logan rushed to his locker to grab another book. From behind him, someone grabbed a fistful of his shirt. He spun around to face Roxanne.

"I've been looking for you everywhere!" Roxanne said breathlessly, her face flushed. "Did your mom tell you I came by last night?"

"No." Logan's voice betrayed his irritation.

"It's about April. I know where she is!"

———

The sun sank behind the bluff as Roxanne's Volkswagen rolled up in front of Logan's house. *At least the wind has died down*, she thought, buttoning up her jacket. Roxanne cranked up the car's heater and watched big flakes of snow melt as soon as they touched the windshield.

A minute later, Logan catapulted from his front porch, ran across his yard, and hopped in. "Let's go!"

Roxanne slipped her car into first gear. "What did you tell your mom?"

"It's none of your business."

"Sorry I asked."

Logan laughed. "No, that's what I told my mother!"

They stopped at a gas station on the edge of town and pooled their money for half a tank, then headed down the highway toward Kingston.

"Jesse said the farm is about a half-hour drive, right?" Logan said, checking his watch. "It's a quarter to seven now, so. . . ."

"Just to be on the safe side," Roxanne interjected, "I think we should start looking in about twenty minutes."

Logan stared out the window and drummed his fingers on the armrest. "Don't drive faster than the speed limit," he said.

"Aye, aye, captain!" Roxanne saluted.

About fifteen miles out of town, the sky darkened with storm clouds, and dry flakes of snow began to fall.

"I hope it doesn't get slick." Logan said. "You have good tires?"

"You worry too much." Roxanne flipped on her headlights and wondered what April would say when she found out her best friend had betrayed her trust. *Logan had a right to know about the pregnancy,* Roxanne told herself; yet guilt needled her. She gripped the wheel and strained to see past the flakes reflecting in the headlights. Roxanne felt like she had a bone to pick with April, too, though. *How could she just take off like she did?*

"Roxie," Logan asked, still gazing out the window. "How does April feel about me?"

"What do you mean?"

"Did she ever talk to you about her feelings? You know, like love or anything?"

"April said you could be a real pain in the you know what!" Roxanne laughed before catching a glimpse of Logan's pain. "Listen," she continued, "April didn't tell you about the baby because she didn't want to ruin your plans for college. I took her to Kingston for an abortion, but she couldn't go through with it. That tells me she really does care about you and the baby."

"I never told her that I love her," he said. "I guess I figured she'd just know."

Roxanne didn't respond. There was nothing to say.

"All right, slow down," Logan said, checking his watch. "Let's start looking for dirt roads." He leaned close to the window. "There's one!"

"I don't see a hill." Roxanne said. "It's going to be too dark to tell soon."

"I don't care if we have to drive every dirt road between here and Kingston," Logan barked.

"Calm down, we'll find her." Roxanne slowed the Volkswagen to a crawl. "Is that a road?"

"Yeah. Pull over." Logan rolled down his window to get a better look. "It looks like someone's been on it recently, too. I can see tire tracks in the snow. Let's go for it!"

In her excitement, Roxanne popped the clutch. The car lurched forward and died. "Oh, great," she whined. She pumped the gas pedal and turned the key. The engine wouldn't start.

"You want me to try?"

"Right, like you can get it started 'cause you're a male

or something?"

"You're going to flood it if you haven't already."

"Okay, I give up. I'm walking." Roxanne got out of the car. She sank her hands into her baggy khaki pants and trudged up the road. The only light was a large moon partially hidden by clouds.

"Wait up!" Logan ran after Roxanne, slipping on a patch of ice.

She waited for him to catch up, then walked silently beside him. The temperature was falling and Roxanne's feet were cold. "I hope this is the right road," she said.

Roxanne's worries were forgotten when Logan pointed to a two-story house illuminated by yard lights. She gave him a high five. "I can't believe our luck!"

They hurried toward their mark, but at the corner of the barn, Roxanne stopped and motioned Logan back. "Wait a minute. Let's stop and think about what we're gonna say. Like—do we just knock on the door and say, 'Hi, we came to take April back home'?"

The porch light came on and the teenagers drew back into the shadow of the barn. "I feel like I'm in a James Bond movie," Roxanne whispered.

Logan crouched down and peered around the edge of the building. He motioned to Roxanne and said, "There's a police car over there."

Roxanne peered around the building and saw it parked just on the other side of the farmhouse porch.

"Look at the snow on the windshield," Logan said. "It's been there a while."

"You think a cop lives here?"

Logan shot her a look. "How do I know?"

The front door opened and an elfish woman with short black hair stepped onto the porch. Roxanne watched her prop open the screen door and kick a mat out of the way. Two men emerged, carrying something heavy in a rolled up, stained blanket. They were talking, but Roxanne could not make out the words.

Suddenly, the elf woman turned toward the barn and strode briskly on her short legs.

Roxanne held her breath and clutched Logan's arm so hard he cringed. "Oh, man, we're so busted."

"Bring her in here," the woman called.

They heard the barn door slide open just around the corner.

Roxanne's heart thumped wildly. She heard talking through the flimsy wooden wall.

"Hey, Syl', where do you want me to put the body?" one of the men asked.

Logan's eyes widened in disbelief.

"In the stall," the woman called out with a steady voice. "Just toss a little hay over it for now. We'll get rid of the body tomorrow." There was a brief pause. "Thanks for helping out, Ian. We owe you."

"All in a day's work." Laughter passed among the trio.

"How about a cup of coffee before heading back to town?" the woman offered.

"Naw, I'd better get back on patrol."

"You're going to hurt Sylvia's feelings," the other man insisted. "It's a new espresso maker, and she's dying to try it out."

"I guess a quick cup wouldn't hurt."

At the corner of the barn, the officer stood so close that Roxanne could have touched his jacket. She held her breath, hoping he would not turn their way.

"It's stuck again!" The elf woman named Sylvia called out. "Wallace, hon, can you give me a hand?"

The officer stepped out of view and the teenagers could hear the trio pulling on the barn door.

"That's good enough," Wallace finally said. "That girl's not going anywhere."

Roxanne and Logan stood as stiff as boards along the barn wall, listening carefully as the voices trailed toward the farmhouse. "I'd like to discuss a little problem we're having with our other house guest," the woman said. The door of the farmhouse closed.

"I'm scared," Roxanne squeaked. "What are we going to do?"

"I have to know if that was April," Logan said, and dashed around the corner.

Roxanne followed and slipped through the barn door right behind him.

Inside, the darkness felt eternal. Roxanne whispered a prayer as she strained to see. "Logan? Where are you?" There was no answer. She was shaking now, more from fear than from the cold.

One minute passed like ten before Logan appeared. He grabbed Roxanne's coat and tugged her toward the door.

Outside, they skirted the barn, avoiding any patches illuminated by the farm light. Logan hurried Roxanne along. His face was as pale as the falling snowflakes.

They fled, propelled by adrenaline, not stopping until they reached the Volkswagen.

Logan leaned against the car to catch his breath. He bent down, grabbed his ankles, and blew hard a couple of times, then jumped in the passenger seat. "Move it," he hollered as Roxanne climbed in. She looked at Logan, her heart pounding in fear.

"W. . . , was it April?" she stammered.

His breath came fast. "No. It was some girl, but I don't know who. Listen, we'll talk about it as soon as we get out of here, okay? Let's go!"

"Please, God, let it start." Roxanne put the clutch in and turned the key. The cold engine refused to turn over.

"Put it in neutral," Logan directed. "I'm going to get out and roll it back onto the highway." He went to the front of the car and pushed it backward. As soon as Roxanne put the car in neutral, Logan tapped on her window. "Put it in second gear and keep the clutch in. When I yell now, pop the clutch."

"Look!" Roxanne pointed to the dirt road as the high beams of the squad car swung around the hill like a beacon.

Logan locked eyes with Roxanne and said through clenched teeth, "Let me do the talking."

As the cruiser drew near, Logan turned and waved his arms in the air.

The officer flipped on his spotlight and shined it on the teenager's face. The squad car rolled to a stop, and the man climbed out. The officer swaggered over to the Volkswagen, jingling a set of keys that hung from his belt. "What's the problem here?"

"Man, am I glad to see you." Logan's smile showed

more teeth than usual. "I was teaching my girlfriend to drive stick and she flooded the engine. We were just about ready to try a pop start."

"Some night to give driving lessons," the officer said, raising his eyebrow. "How long have you been stuck out here?"

"Oh, just a couple of minutes." Logan's voice cracked.

Roxanne remained behind the wheel as the officer helped push the car to the road. "Please, God." She mouthed the words silently. The clutch popped, and the car started on the first try.

"Well, I guess this is your lucky night." The policeman leaned down and peered at Roxanne through the window.

"Yeah, you can say that again." The words came out lame. Roxanne felt flushed and hoped it wasn't obvious.

"Yes, sir!" Logan gave a little wave as he opened the car door. "Thanks, Officer."

They headed back to Hamlin with the squad car behind them the whole way. In town, the cruiser turned toward the station, and Roxanne continued toward Elm Street.

In front of Logan's house, Roxanne pried her white-knuckled fingers from the steering wheel. "April needs our help."

Logan rubbed his worried brow. "I don't know who to trust. We obviously can't go to the police."

The reality of the situation was settling in. "We'll just have to come up with a plan ourselves." Roxanne tried to sound confident, but inside she was terrified.

CHAPTER 30

Chief Patterson pressed the intercom button and searched the top of his cluttered desk for a file. "Betty, would you do me a favor and bring in a cup of coffee?"

A few minutes later, his secretary walked through the door with a steaming mug in her hand. "I shouldn't be doing this," she said. "It's bad for your heart."

The chief took the cup in hand. "If I'm gonna die, it might as well be from your coffee."

"Okay—that settles it! I'm not going to be an enabler." Betty perched one hand on her hip and with the other wagged a finger. "Next time you want coffee you can just get it yourself. Besides, the exercise will do you good."

"You don't have to get nasty about it!" Art took a defiant slurp of coffee. He set his mug down hard, spilling some on the desk. "This isn't real coffee! It's decaf!" He sopped up the mess with a tissue. "Have you heard anything about Jesse Berry's fingerprints?"

"No word yet from the Department of Criminal Investigation."

"Would you check on it for me?"

Betty nodded and turned toward the door.

"Oh, and one more thing." Art flipped through a file. "There was a teenager killed a few years back. The kid's name was Mark Elliot. His folks moved away, but I'd like to get in touch with them."

"I'll check with the DMV. What are their names?" Betty asked.

"Ron and Mitzi Elliot. If I remember right, he worked for the county."

Art turned his attention back to the file spread out before him. He read and reread every detail, not quite sure what he was searching for.

The school guidance counselor had stated that Mark Elliot had been withdrawn, but the boy's parents described him as defiant and combative. They were on record as saying their son willfully stayed out until all hours of the night, exploding into a rage when challenged. The couple felt so threatened by Mark's erratic behavior that they'd been looking into placing him in a boy's shelter in Billings, Montana. That's where they were the night he died.

Art tapped a pen on the desk. "Loose ends," he said under his breath, while his thoughts turned angles. *If Kit Kragler accurately described the scene, then one thing is certain: Elliot didn't run over himself. So why weren't his friends questioned? Or, for that matter, even mentioned in the police report? Why wasn't a statement taken from Kit when he's the man who found the body?*

The case had never officially been closed. The sheriff's department had the jurisdiction to do so, but it always sought the cooperation of the Hamlin PD in joint investigations.

Art leaned back in his chair and rubbed his face. "This is not going to be easy," he sighed. For a moment, he considered slipping the file back into the cabinet and forgetting the whole business, but something nagged at him. At the bottom of the page, a hasty note had been scribbled: Probable cause of death—accident.

Art forced himself to look at the eight-by-ten glossy print included in the coroner's report. Unlike the photo taken by Officer Scott, these showed definite tire tracks across the kid's back. *What that poor boy must have gone through.*

Sympathy quickly turned to anger. Chief Patterson slammed the file on his desk and returned the photograph to the file. His eyes fell on something he had overlooked. There was a marking on Elliot's arm, nearly obliterated by bruises. Art turned on his desk lamp and leaned closer for a better look. A tattoo! The design was a circle with a man in the middle. The figure looked like the Pied Piper.

Betty rapped on the door and poked her head into the office. "I got the contact information for the boy's parents. I hope it's current." She set a piece of paper in front of him. "The Elliots have moved around a lot, but the latest address is in Bingham, Idaho."

"Thanks. You're a doll!" Art dialed the number and doodled on a piece of paper as it rang. He was just about to hang up when someone answered.

"Hello." It was the sleepy voice of a woman.

"Mrs. Elliot?"

"Yes."

"This is Art Patterson with the Hamlin Police Department. How are you today, ma'am?" The question was met with silence. "I'm calling in regard to your son Mark's case. I hate to bring up something that must be painful to you, Mrs. Elliot, but I'm doing a follow-up on the investigation and tying up a few loose ends. I was hoping you might answer some questions." There was still no reply. "Mrs. Elliot?"

"Why are you calling me after all this time?" she asked.

"I'm just going over some details, and I noticed the police report failed to list any of your son's friends."

"He didn't have any friends."

Art could detect bitterness in the mother's voice. "What about acquaintances? Any names would be helpful."

"I don't remember," Mrs. Elliot snapped.

"Do you know of anyone who might have had a reason to harm Mark?"

"It was an accident. That's what your report said. Why are you asking me this?"

"Mark had a tattoo on his arm," Art pressed. "It was a circle with an image of the Pied Piper in the center. What can you tell me about that?"

"How long are you people going to torment us? It was an accident! That's all I've ever told anyone. Please, just leave us alone!"

Suddenly, a man's voice cut in. "Who is this?"

"Art Patterson, Hamlin Chief of Police. Are you Mr. Elliot?"

"I am!" the man barked.

"I wonder if you might shed some light on a—"

"My wife is under a doctor's care, and she's easily upset," Mr. Elliot said. "We can't help you, and I don't want you to call here again."

The chief sat listening to dead air. A familiar pain rose in his chest, then ebbed. Art pushed himself up from his chair and walked out to the receptionist's desk where Betty sat typing.

"I'm going to take off a few hours early today and see if I can't clear the old gray matter of some clutter."

"I hear the fishin' has been pretty good lately on Silver Creek," she said without looking up.

He stopped to thumb through a stack of mail. "Has an ID come back yet on our inmate?"

"Don't worry." She shooed him toward the door. "I'll contact you on the radio as soon as I hear anything."

Art ambled out to his car. The pain in his chest was gone. Relieved, he opened the trunk to survey his tackle box and fly rod, stored neatly beside the standard emergency equipment. Bea used to tease him, saying, "I married a man who's always ready for action, whether it's catching criminals or rainbow trout!"

The chief made a quick detour up Main Street and stopped in front of J. D.'s Fly and Tackle Shop.

"It's about time you wet a line, Patterson." J. D. put a drop of head cement on the fly he was tying and looked up.

Art nodded. "Guess I've been busy lately."

"A man should never be too busy for fishin'." The shop owner stuck a pipe in his mouth, fired a lighter, and puffed until smoke encircled his head. "How are you feeling?"

"Word travels fast in this town," Art mumbled. "I'm moving a bit slower, but I'm doing fine."

"Well, you can't keep a good man down. What can I get for you today?"

"I need a half-dozen Royal Humpies." Art leaned over the display case to inspect an exotic assortment of bait.

"I've had some luck lately with Blue Duns. How 'bout I toss in a few? My treat."

"Thanks." Art slid his wallet from his hip pocket. Music blasted next door, and the dull beat of the drums and bass thumped through the wall.

"There they go again!" J. D. took the five-dollar bill Art handed him. "I can't believe they call that stuff music. They blast it out o' those speakers every day when school is out. It draws those kids like flies—no pun intended."

"Well," Art said, "look on the bright side. Maybe it'll bring in some potential customers."

"When was the last time you saw a kid out fishin'?"

"Let me think." Art rubbed his hands. "My boy used to wet a line every chance he could."

"Yeah, but it's a different world now. Here you go." J. D. dropped some change into Art's hand. "Let me know if the fishin's any good."

"Sure thing. Take 'er easy." Art stepped outside and looked around. It was a beautiful afternoon, with a mild breeze and a clear sky. Most of the earlier snowfall had already melted into the thirsty ground. The weatherman had forecast weekend storms.

Art took in a long, deep breath and let his mind wander over all his unfinished business. He had been putting off telling the officers to gear up for Halloween patrol—"ghost busting" as they called it. In recent years, vandalism had become a growing problem, and the childish pranks of yesteryear had given birth to malicious mischief. The PD had come to view this holiday in much the same way that the fire department looked upon the 4th of July. *We all have our own kind of brush fires to put out,* he mused. *Maybe a blizzard will blow in and put a damper on things.*

He made a mental note to post an overtime schedule, then pushed all thoughts of work aside and dug in his pocket for the keys to the trunk. He blew dust off his tackle box and made room for his new purchases. From the corner of his eye, he caught sight of a small group of high school kids straggling into the music store.

Art closed the trunk and walked around the car to the driver's side. Something in the music store's window caught his eye. Displayed on a black satin backdrop was a selection of CDs. One in particular interested him. On the cover was a hazy picture of the bleached white skull of what appeared to be a goat lying on a gray marble slab. On its forehead, a five-pointed star with a circle around it was drawn in dripping blood. The name of the group was Ram's Fire.

Art went inside and approached the clerk. "Excuse me, I'd like to ask a question."

The pimple-faced young man stretched his mouth in an ear-to-ear grin. "Hey, whatever it is, I didn't do it!" A cluster of teenage girls giggled.

"There's a CD in the window with the skull of a goat on it," Art said without betraying his irritation.

"Yeah, that's Ram's Fire's new album." The clerk pointed to a promotional poster on the wall. "Don't tell me you're into them!"

Art leveled a sobering look at the smart-mouthed young man. "You got a copy of their lyrics?"

The clerk looked surprised. "What'cha wanna know?"

"Satanic symbolism and content."

The young man laughed. "Doesn't mean anything. It's just style—sells CDs." The clerk flashed his tiny teeth and rolled his shoulders. "Look, I'd love to stand around and chat, but I'm a highly motivated business type." He turned his back on Art and called to a kid who was digging through a pile of discount discs. "Can I help you find anything?"

"Just looking." The young customer lifted a ball cap and ran his hand through straight brown hair and left.

Art shook his head and headed outside.

The young man who had been browsing through the bargains was leaning against the building. He looked like he had something on his mind.

Art nodded and said, "How ya doing?"

"Hey, man, Marty was messin' with you about Ram's Fire. They're hardcore."

Chief Patterson took a good look at this teenager. "What do you mean when you say hardcore?"

"Death metal—some call it satanic." The kid shrugged. "It's just music if you ask me."

"What's your name, son?"

"Rudy Volcovich."

"Thanks," Art called as the teenager strolled down the sidewalk.

Chief Patterson climbed into his cruiser and once again tried to clear his head. The turnoff to Silver Creek was only a few miles outside of town, but the dirt road was long and rustic. He parked near his favorite fishing hole and wet his line. The fish were hitting on Royal Humpies—mostly brook trout too small to keep. It didn't matter. For a little while, Art forgot everything except the challenge of fooling the fish. Over the years, he had perfected the sport until he could finesse the bait with a flick of his wrist and gracefully drop a fly down where the current changed. He made it look as natural as if the insect had fallen from the sky.

Just as the sport's golden hour approached, the chief's cell phone beckoned from his car. Reluctantly, Art reeled in his line and walked up the hill to retrieve his voicemail.

It was Betty, asking him to call her.

Chief Patterson punched the office number. "Yeah, what's up?"

"I just heard from the DCI, Chief. They've completed the fingerprint check on that Jesse Berry assault case. The boys at the DCI would like you to give them a call."

"Okay. I'm on my way back to the office. I'll phone from there." He gathered his gear, tossed it in the trunk, and headed back to Hamlin.

Back at the station, Art found the number on his desk. He closed the office door behind him, sat down, and dialed the number.

"Division of Criminal Investigation, Officer Kenny Robbins speaking."

The chief identified himself. "I hear you have some information on one of our inmates—Jesse Berry?"

"Let me see. . . ."

Art listened as Officer Robbins rattled his fingers over a keyboard. "The satanic porno ring? Oh, no, that's the one I'm working on for the Kingston PD. Here's your file. This one's pretty interesting."

"Wait a minute. Did you say satanic?" the chief asked.

"They've been having some problems over in Kingston. You know, ritual abuse and things like that. We hosted a seminar on the subject last summer." Officer Robbins paused. "Didn't your agency get the notice?"

Chief Patterson scratched his chin and tried to recall.

"The local bookstores up our way can't keep occult books on their shelves. We're also finding all kinds of suspicious graffiti and some animal mutilations. Every once in a while we hear about a case of ritual abuse, but it's pretty hard to prove anything. Most folks think of the Devil as the product of someone's neurotic imagination."

"I've always thought along those lines, too," Art agreed.

"Satanists take their beliefs very seriously. These people are extremely secretive and quite adept at covering their tracks." The man paused. "Say, are you having a problem down your way?"

"I don't know, but it doesn't hurt to stay informed." Chief Patterson rolled a pencil on his desk. "So, what do you have on our inmate?"

"Let me see. . . oh, yes, this one was very interesting. We sent Jesse Berry's prints to the Western ID Network. At first, they didn't come up with anything, but then we got lucky. Our tech up there ran it through a separate area in her database for missing child identification and she got a hit. You ready for this?" Mr. Robbins paused for affect. "It seems Jesse Berry is an alias! His real name is Nathaniel Ellington . The family had friends in high places. Apparently, his grandmother pushed this investigation clear through to the governor."

Art leaned forward in his chair. "I remember the case! The Ellington boy disappeared after a car accident. We always assumed that he and his parents drowned in the river where their car went off. Two bodies were recovered but not the boy's." The chief scribbled a hasty note to himself. "Are you absolutely sure about this ID?"

"Positive. The kid's grandmother provided a great set of fingerprints she had gotten from a law enforcement booth at the county fair. The algorithm scores and minutia points were extremely high."

Chief Patterson's mind wandered back to the time of the Ellington boy's disappearance. Marie Ellington had been a regular at the station, always stopping by to demand updates on the investigation. She'd been dismissed as a grief-stricken grandmother.

The pain in Art's chest came back with a vengeance. He fished for a nitroglycerin pill from his shirt pocket and slid it under his tongue.

"Patterson?" the voice on the phone asked.

Art wiped sweat from his lip. "Sorry. I'm going to need a copy of the state investigation."

"Sure thing. I'll fax it over in the morning. Let us know how this whole thing turns out."

"Yes, I'll do that. Thanks for your time." Chief Patterson leaned over his desk and ran his hands over his crew cut. He pressed the intercom on his desk. "Betty, I need another old file." He gave her the details of his request and instructed her to leave whatever she found on his desk. "I'm going to go visit one of our inmates."

Art made his way down the long corridor—the same hall where Marie Ellington had once stood demanding justice. Now, nearly twenty years later, her pleas had finally come home to roost.

CHAPTER 31

The front door of the high school sprang open and Ozmand stampeded down the steps with the other students. He spotted Cyrus in the park near the band shell with one foot resting on his skateboard.

Cyrus locked eyes with Ozmand, and his lip curled into a half-smile. "Been waitin' for you," he said. He dug a piece of food from one of his back teeth with his pinkie.

A group of middle-school boys gathered. "Future converts," Cyrus sneered, then launched his skateboard onto the band shell's slab and did a few tricks to wow his young fans.

He circled back around to bask in their praises, but it wasn't enough. Cyrus zeroed in on a shy kid and said, "Why is this geek hanging out with you guys?"

The color drained from the boy's face.

Ozmand empathized. As a child, he had also been shy and the focus of bullies. He stood mute as Cyrus continued his humiliation.

"What are you, some kind of freak of nature?"

The boy hurried off.

"What's a matter—heard your mama calling?" Cyrus laughed and shoved his skateboard toward Ozmand. "Show our hatchling friends some tricks while I slip on my rollerblades."

Ozmand obeyed and was pleasantly surprised when the kids watched reverently. A few minutes later, Cyrus stole the show with his blades, then settled back to mine the group for talent. "Show me what you're made of," he said, picking on subjects deemed worthy of his attention.

One boy tried to walk the board, but the wheels shot out from under his feet and his head slammed to the concrete.

Cyrus roared with glee. "What are you trying to do? Crack the slab?"

Rudy Volcovich appeared from nowhere and knelt beside the boy. "You okay?" The crimson-cheeked kid rubbed a growing goose egg and blinked back tears. "You'd better put some ice on that."

Ozmand braced himself as his old friend walked over to Cyrus and stood inches from his face. "I see right through you."

"Whoa, man, you could use some mouthwash." Cyrus held his nose. "Have you been eating trash?" He kicked off the rollerblades, jammed his feet into street shoes, and sauntered away with his new fans trailing close behind.

"What's the matter?" Rudy yelled after him. "You afraid somebody will mess up that skunk-tail hairdo of yours?"

Cyrus halted abruptly and slowly turned around. "You may think you're something special, but you're nothing but a cockroach."

Rudy clutched his breast. "I'm hurt!"

"You know what I do to cockroaches? I step on them—real slow—applying just enough pressure to make 'em squirm. Then I—"

Rudy laughed. "Don't you kids have anything better to do than hang out with a guy who entertains himself by messing with people?"

No one cracked a smile. As if bewitched, they followed their skateboard guru as he marched across the park.

"Aren't you going to follow the great and mighty Cyrus?" Rudy asked his old friend.

Sudden anger arose in Ozmand. He squared his shoulders and turned away, but Rudy grabbed his sleeve. "Let go of me!" Oz snarled with a viciousness that surprised him. "Don't ever do that!"

Rudy's eyes widened. "What's with you, man?"

Ozmand crossed the street and, without looking back, took a shortcut through a residential area, cutting across a lawn as he went.

The Woodruffs, as usual, had spared no expense for Halloween. Fiberglass spider webs hung from their front porch corners, and lightning strobes flashed in their front window, accompanied by a spooky soundtrack of screams, moans, and creaking doors. Every year, Mrs. Woodruff dressed up like a witch and passed out candy to the kids while Mr. Woodruff, with a stocking over his face and a plastic hatchet in hand, would leap out and scare the children as they left. Ozmand had hated going when he was little, but Nan had dragged him there every year. "After all," she would say, "the Woodruffs were so sweet to go to all that trouble."

He tried to slip through the yard unnoticed.

"Hi, Oz," Mrs. Woodruff called. "Hope you drop by this weekend."

Who needs trick or treat? Ozmand thought as his mind turned to the Piper's Guild. He had graduated to the real thing.

—*∿*—

Roxanne reached for the ringing phone, but someone else in the house picked up first.

She grabbed her terrycloth bathrobe and hurried down the stairs, hoping that it was her mom and not her nosy brother who had answered the phone.

She found Rudy in the kitchen with the receiver pressed against his ear. "Roxanne can't come to the phone," he said. "Says she's sick. Who is this anyway?"

"Logan."

"I'll take that!" Roxanne flew across the room and tried to snatch the receiver from her brother's hand.

"You don't move like somebody who's ill." Rudy said. He lifted the receiver just out of her reach, then held it to his ear and said, "Hey, Logan, what are you doing calling my little sister anyway? I thought you and her best friend were going out."

"Mind your own business!" Roxanne yelled.

As if someone had flipped a switch, Rudy tossed her the phone, then jerked open the fridge door and began to rummage.

Roxanne cupped the receiver and said, "You think I could have a little privacy?"

Her brother emerged from the fridge with his arms loaded with sandwich material. "Don't mind me."

"Logan, I'll have to call you back." Roxanne hung up, fired a caustic look at Rudy, and bolted upstairs to her bedroom. She searched for her cell phone under stacks of clutter and finally found it beneath a pile of dirty laundry. The battery was spent.

Exasperated, Roxanne padded down the hall to her parents' room and used the phone on her mother's bedside table. She dialed Logan's number, and he answered on the first ring. "What's up?" she asked.

"I ran into some trouble with my parents," he said. "There's no way I can get out of the house until Friday night.

"But this is a matter of life and death!" Roxanne gasped. "Maybe your priorities are screwed up. I mean, come on! This is no time for the good boy routine."

"Shut up, Roxanne! Ever since I came home late the other night, my old lady has been making my life miserable. She's driving me to school in the morning and picking me up every afternoon."

"What are we going to do?"

"We've got to wait. If I ace the calculus test tomorrow, my folks will let me out for the Halloween Dance."

"What if something happens to April between now and then? Can you live with that?"

There was a long pause on the other end of the line, and Roxanne knew she'd struck a chord. "We need time to plan," Logan said. "These people aren't your run-of-the-mill farmers. They killed somebody."

Click.

"Did you hear that? We'd better continue this conversation tomorrow at school," Logan said and hung up.

Roxanne replaced the phone and raced down the stairs just in time to see her brother jogging toward the front door. She blocked his exit. "Were you eavesdropping?"

Rudy's eyebrows arched innocently. "Oh, were you on the phone?"

"I knew it!" Roxanne blurted. "Swear you won't say a word to anyone."

Her brother's expression grew serious. "On one condition," Rudy said. "I want to know what's going on."

CHAPTER 32

All morning the county attorney's office buzzed with activity. The reason for the hubbub was splashed across the front page of the newspaper on Nan Wright's desk:
MISSING LOCAL RESURFACES AFTER TWO DECADES

"It's hard to believe." Nan shook her head, folded the newspaper, and tossed it aside. The article's contents seemed unreal. All these years working for the county attorney and he had never mentioned a brother. Nan's heart went out to her boss. *What a shock it must be to him.* She imagined Brock consoling Nathaniel—a stranger. Nan's throat closed with a sudden rush of empathy. *No more a stranger than my own son.* Ozmand had not come home again last night, and her imagination had run wild with scenes of drugs and bloody accidents.

She picked nervously at a hangnail on her index finger, then bit at the loose skin. Nan had planned to ask her boss for the afternoon off so she could speak with her son's guidance counselor. *But now, with everything going on in the office . . . .*

Nan slid a compact from her purse and discretely

inspected her battered face. The makeup was holding up. The angry purple around her eye was barely visible, but some swelling remained. *Did Brock notice? If he did, he made no mention of it.* Nan snapped the compact shut, wishing she could make the memories of that night go away as easily. Her hand shook at the thought of Ozmand's twisted face and those hate-filled eyes.

The conference room door opened, and a portly man in a business suit emerged, followed by the county attorney.

Nan recognized William Platte, a Kingston lawyer with a reputation for theatrics.

Brock thrust out his hand. "Thanks, Bill."

"First thing tomorrow, I will sit down with your brother and prepare a defense."

"My brother. . . ." Brock rubbed his chin reflectively. "I still find the whole thing incredible."

The door opened, and a reporter from the Hamlin Review filled the room with questions. "Mr. Ellington , how will this affect the inmate's legal counsel?" the woman asked, pencil and pad in hand.

"A special prosecutor will be called in from another county," Brock said. "I'm sure you'd agree that it would not be ethical for me to prosecute my own brother."

Platte's bushy eyebrows kissed in a frown. "I hope this won't hinder Friday's arraignment?"

"That will be up to the special prosecutor, but I don't foresee a problem with it going ahead as scheduled," Brock said.

"Do you really believe his amnesia story?" Platte asked.

"I haven't yet spoken with Nathaniel. As for his mental

state, I have no further comment." Brock turned to his secretary. "Nan, reschedule all my appointments. It's time I got reacquainted with my prodigal brother."

—⁓—

Emma Willis caught sight of her husband's reflection in the bathroom mirror. He shuffled past wearing his old plaid bathrobe and sheepskin slippers but stopped to loiter as she finished brushing her teeth.

"I can't find the morning paper," Lars complained. He tapped his foot impatiently as his wife rinsed. "Have you seen it?"

"Did you look under the bushes? Sometimes the paperboy—"

"I looked there!" he barked. "I was down on my hands and knees on that cold sidewalk."

"Oh, you poor thing." Emma grabbed her husband's cheeks and gave them a squeeze. "I'll pick up another one at the grocery store."

Lars shook his head. "No, it's the principle of the thing. I'm going to call the newspaper."

"Suit yourself." Emma glanced at her watch. "I'm late! I told Theda Mae I'd pick her up at nine."

She drove straight there and found Mrs. Crabtree bundled in a thick coat waiting on the porch.

Theda Mae settled herself in the passenger seat and smiled sweetly. "Bless you for taking me to the market, dear."

"I had to go shopping, anyway." Emma said pulling onto the street. "Besides, I'm glad for the company."

"You do so much I almost hate to ask for any more favors."

Emma shot the old woman a sideways glance. She seemed pensive. "What's on your mind?"

"I need a ride to Kingston. There's someone there I need to see."

Emma turned right at the stoplight and rolled slowly across the grocery store parking lot. "Actually, Lars and I have been planning a trip to the mission up there. We've got a big pile of old coats and blankets to drop off. How soon do you want to go?"

"Today," Theda Mae said.

"Oh, I don't think today. . . ." Emma stumbled over the words as her mind sorted through all her daily chores. Most of them could keep, she decided. "Jesse's expecting our visit this afternoon."

Theda Mae nodded. "I spoke with Jesse this morning. In fact, he's part of the reason I need to go to Kingston. Believe me, dear, if there were any other way, I would have found it." Her voice had a desperate ring. "The bus isn't running until Saturday."

Inside the store, Emma grabbed a shopping cart. "How about tomorrow?"

Theda Mae looked relieved. "Do you think we could get an early start?"

"Of course."

Emma filled the cart with goodies while Mrs. Crabtree picked up a few staples. In the checkout line, they waited behind a teenage girl buying a pack of cigarettes and a mother of two who was complaining about the expiration date on a coupon.

Mrs. Crabtree rooted around in her purse and pulled out some change. She offered to pay the difference. The woman refused and quickly settled her bill.

The conveyor rolled with Emma's groceries. "Oh, I almost forgot," she said, grabbing a newspaper from the rack and placing it with the other items.

Emma glanced at the Review's headline as the checker ran it through the scanner. She retrieved the paper, stuck it under her arm, and paid the cashier.

With their purchases securely in the trunk, Emma slid behind the wheel of her car and stole another look at the newspaper. "Unbelievable!"

"What, dear?" Theda Mae leaned close and squinted. "I'm afraid my glasses are at home. Would you read it to me?"

Emma cleared her throat and read.

In an unexpected turn of events, a sexual assault suspect turns out to be Nathaniel Ellington , brother of prominent Hamlin County Attorney Brock Ellington .

The mystery began to unfold when a man calling himself Jesse Berry was apprehended early last week on a sexual assault charge. The drifter's true identity was discovered through fingerprints taken shortly before his disappearance at the age of six. A routine fingerprint check turned over a fresh clue in the twenty-year-old case—the disappearance of six-year-old Nathaniel Ellington .

As a boy, Ellington was presumed drowned in an accident that also claimed the lives of his parents. Berry's fingerprints match those of the missing boy.

"There's no doubt in my mind," said Ken Robbins of the DCI. "This young man is Nathaniel Ellington ."

Theda Mae was unusually quiet.

"You don't seem surprised," Emma said.

"I had a feeling." The old woman twisted the handle of her tapestry handbag. "Please, continue."

Emma nodded, then found her place again.

County Attorney Ellington declined to interview, but stated that Nathaniel had been living among "street people" in his former home of Pittsburgh.

Arraignment is scheduled for October 31st at 9:00 AM.

"Street people?" Theda Mae bristled. "It makes the poor boy sound like a vagrant!"

"You knew Nathaniel Ellington when he was a boy, didn't you?"

"Yes. His grandmother and I were close friends and prayer partners." Theda Mae drifted off in thought, then added wistfully, "Marie adored her youngest grandchild. She never gave up hope that little Nat was alive."

"What about his brother?"

Theda Mae bit her lip and chose her words carefully. "She worried about Brock, but in a different way. Soon after the family tragedy, her elder grandson began to make noises about Marie's competence. She felt he wanted full control of the Ellington ' assets, so she changed her will, adding a provision demanding absolute proof of Nathaniel's death before any assets would be dispersed. Brock was furious to say the least."

Emma folded the newspaper and set it down on the car seat.

"Remind me to bring a copy of the newspaper when we go to Kingston," Mrs. Crabtree said. Then she added cryptically: "We may run into someone who'd be very interested in the article about Nathaniel Ellington ."

⎯⎯

Hamlin's modest jailhouse was quiet except for the periodic moans issuing from the next cell. Jesse lay upon his cot, awakened from an afternoon nap by another nightmare. It was still fresh in his mind. A dark figure moving swiftly through the trees, calling for Nathaniel. In the dream, he ran from the figure, but it made no difference. The fingers closed around his neck. . . .

"Mavis," Jesse whispered, "I hope you're praying now."

Jesse heard the door open at the end of the corridor. He listened to the jingling of keys. A few seconds later, a uniformed guard appeared in front of Jesse's cell and fiddled with the lock.

A man in a business suit hung back a few steps behind the guard, watching Jesse with dark eyes. He ran fingers through his short clipped hair and stepped forward when the bars swung open.

"Want me to stay?" the guard asked.

"No need. I'm sure my brother won't be a threat."

Jesse swung his legs from the cot and stood as Brock introduced himself. "It's been a long time, Nathaniel. Don't worry about a thing. Lucky for you, I'm the county attorney. I know people. I have engaged the finest counsel."

"Thanks." Jesse studied Brock as he pulled up a chair.

"We've got some catching up to do." Brock forced a smile. "So, I hear you remember nothing about your life here."

Jesse nodded. "That's right."

Brock folded his arms and leaned back until the metal chair squeaked. "You have Mother's eyes."

"What was she like?"

"Our mother was well-bred and spirited."

Are we discussing a thoroughbred horse? Jesse wondered. "Do you have a family album? Anything to help me remember?"

"I'll see what I can do." Brock laced his fingers

together. "All these years you were living in Pittsburgh?"

Jesse nodded.

"What made you come to Hamlin? We're not exactly on the beaten path."

"I came to Montana with a girl. Cali hinted that she had information about my past."

Brock pursed his lips. "Are you talking about the girl who is accusing you of assault?"

"That's right. She—"

Brock raised his hand to silence Jesse. "Don't say any more. I don't want to know anything, in case I'm called to testify." He shot to his feet and paced the cell. "This just doesn't make sense." He stopped abruptly and tapped his chin thoughtfully. "Who knew your real identity? That's what we need to find out."

"Cali is the only one who can shed light on that question," Jesse said. Yet, he knew from experience that getting a straight answer from the deranged girl wouldn't be so easy.

CHAPTER 33

Ozmand sat on an old, torn hassock in the corner of Cyrus's living room reading vintage Fabulous Furry Freak Brothers comic books. He looked over the top of the pages at Cali, who was sprawled across the filthy couch with her legs propped up on the TV stand.

Other than an occasional blink of her eyes, she hadn't moved in over an hour. Ozmand studied Cali as she stared at the music videos on the television screen. The girl appeared transfixed by the flashing lights and primal beat.

"Hey, do you know when Cy's gonna get here?" Ozmand asked.

Cali ignored him, scratching her tangled mat of hair. She aimed the remote and clicked manically through channels without stopping.

There's something off about this girl, Ozmand thought.

Her eyes sliced his way and narrowed into slits. "What are you staring at?"

Ozmand tossed the comic back onto the stack and raised his hands in the air. "I was just wondering if you get bedsores staying in the same position all the time."

The words that came out of her mouth would have made a Las Vegas comic blush. Oz felt a rush of amusement. *She finally noticed I'm alive!*

Cali rolled her bare legs off the couch and stood. Wearing an oversized pair of shorts held in place by a leather belt, she looked rather comical. Her t-shirt was knotted at her waist, exposing a belly button ring. Suddenly, she lifted a heavy glass ashtray from the coffee table and hurled it across the room at him. It clipped his elbow before knocking a large dent in the drywall behind him.

Ozmand cradled his elbow, let out a string of profanities, and chased Cali out the door.

"Leave me alone!" She whirled around, her eyes wild with rage, and then suddenly began to laugh. It began as a deep cackle and ended in a whimper. "I was nine months pregnant when they found me." Traces of foam formed in the corners of her mouth as a mournful sound escaped. "If they'd only come just two weeks later. . . ."

"So, where is your kid?" he asked.

The girl's eyes looked crazed.

Ozmand took a cautious step back and felt relieved when Cali wandered down the street, muttering to herself.

———

Jesse greeted Lars and Emma through the mesh-lined glass. "Have you heard from Mavis?"

"Theda Mae spoke with her this morning," Emma said, her forehead creased like a worried mother. "Have you seen this?" She held out a copy of the newspaper.

"My lawyer brought me a copy this morning."

"So you've already been appointed a public defender?" Lars asked.

"Brock Ellington —my brother—hired some big-time trial lawyer from Kingston." Jesse shifted in his chair, recalling the discomfort he'd felt during the recent reunion with Brock. There had been no memory, not even a stir of recognition—only a feeling of detached prudence.

Lars and Emma exchanged a quick look. "That's good, isn't it?"

Jesse mustered a smile. "I'm not sure. This lawyer acts as though I'm guilty. He tried to talk me into a plea bargain."

"That's ridiculous!" Emma huffed.

"They want to say that I'm mentally unstable." Jesse looked at the couple sitting across from him. "I have no childhood memories before I showed up in Pittsburgh. I'm sure that doesn't look good."

"Do you remember anything?" Lars pressed.

"Sometimes I have dreams about a train. I'm being chased." Jesse rubbed a kink in his neck.

"I can't imagine what you must have gone through as a child, losing your parents the way you did." Emma pressed her hand against the glass. "I wish I could break this down and give you a hug."

Jesse stared down at the table. "Sometimes it seems as though I'm just about to remember, but the images turn to sand and slip away."

"Maybe we can help," Lars said. "I'll head over to the library and see if I can find some old clippings about your family or the accident."

"That's a great idea!" Emma said. "I'm going to Kingston tomorrow with Theda Mae. She was a good friend of your grandmother's. Maybe she can offer some insight."

"It's worth a try," Jesse said with growing unease. *Maybe there are some things that were meant to be forgotten.*

—〰—

Cali could feel the owner of the bookstore watching her over the rim of her glasses. She had been in the store for nearly an hour, fingering the bindings but making no selections. Cali pulled another book from the shelf and casually flipped through the pages, glancing up at the proprietor every so often. She shoved the book into a random slot and sauntered to another display.

"May I suggest something?" the woman droned behind a terse smile.

"Yes," Cali responded with a straight face. "What would you recommend for an illiterate?" She raised her eyebrows in mocking expectation. "Like, what do you read?"

The woman came around the counter and grabbed Cali's arm. "Listen here, you smart-mouthed little—"

Just then, the bell on the door jingled and the store owner turned her attention to an older couple. "I'll be right with you," she crooned sweetly, waiting until they moved out of earshot before turning back to Cali.

"Loitering is a crime!" she said through clenched teeth.

Cali tried to break free from the owner's grip, but the woman pressed long, red nails into her flesh. Cali pinched her face into a defiant smirk. "Sharp nails," she said. "Do you shave your legs with those things?"

"Get out!" the proprietor ordered and shoved the girl toward the exit. She held the door open and pointed her finger. "Out!"

"Excuse me, ma'am." A UPS man struggled past with three large boxes. "I need you to sign for these packages."

"We must do lunch sometime," Cali said, batting her eyes at the older woman. "Let me know when you're feeling better."

Without responding, the proprietor ushered the deliveryman to the back room with the shipment.

Cali released the door and stepped back into the shadows of a little alcove reserved for children's books and old comics. She tiptoed to the corner of the room and squeezed her slight body between two bookcases. There, Cali crouched behind a mountain of smelly stuffed animals that Irene kept on hand in case a customer brought in a sticky-fingered kid. She checked her watch. It was almost five. *It won't be long now,* she thought.

"Have a nice day," the UPS man called as he left.

Irene engaged in shallow small talk with a patron and rang up a sale.

Cali passed the time by tearing at a piece of loose wallpaper. The store grew quiet, but every once in a while Cali thought she heard the proprietor turning book pages.

Finally, footsteps creaked on the wooden floor, and Cali visualized the old hag tidying up the place. From her burrow, the teenager thought about those who had hurt her. Rage simmered.

She had an overwhelming compulsion to leap up and

scare the wits out of the woman, but she steeled herself. The thought brought on a spasm of muffled giggles. Cali felt relieved when the lights went out and she heard the sound of the deadbolt sliding into place.

Cali lunged across the pile of stuffed animals and exploded into hysterical laughter, hooting so hard her ribs hurt.

A few moments later, Cali stood, stepped over the clutter, and felt her way through the darkness before locating the Oriental rug. She rolled it up until the trapdoor beneath was exposed, then threw open the wooden hatch as if it were cardboard. "Oh, man!" Cali gasped, covering her mouth with her hand. The pungent smell had worsened, like a rotten pile of wet garbage on a hot day. She took another deep breath of fresh air before descending into the putrid catacombs.

Along with the odor, the water level had risen. She grabbed a battered flashlight that she had stowed upon a little rock ledge and waded through shin-deep water. Cali worked her way under Hamlin's streets to the hidden entrance of the old brewery. She knew of an entrance that the others didn't. Wielding such knowledge felt like power.

Cali climbed a short distance up the iron girders of a concrete structure, then slid on her belly through an air vent that opened into the basement of the old building. She stepped down onto an archaic boiler that had not seen a fire in years and dimmed her flashlight.

Cali rubbed furiously at the goose bumps on her arms. She was chilled to the bone, and her toes were going numb. Bare feet were quieter, she decided, slipping off her tennis shoes and soggy crew socks. Cali stashed them under a pile of rags.

The wood flooring overhead alerted her to movement. With one hand on the ladder, Cali cocked her head to listen while the fingers of her free hand ran over the smooth edge of the kitchen knife she had secured to her waist with duct tape. An involuntary spasm snaked up her spine, and she sucked in a deep breath.

Without reason, Cali clutched a handful of her hair and pulled until each strand ripped from her scalp. The pain brought temporary relief but did nothing for her deeper issues. It was the violence done to her spirit and soul that festered within her now. If only the Piper's Guild had left her alone, maybe she could have gone on pretending.

"It doesn't matter," Cali said flatly. "Only one thing matters now."

With cat-like stealth, she made her way across the cold slab floor and crept up the dark stairwell. At the top, she paused to look through the keyhole. Satisfied that the coast was clear, Cali put her hand on the doorknob and turned it slowly. Her heart was pounding like a kettledrum as she stepped out into the corridor.

A door to the left flew open, spilling light into the hallway.

Cali jumped behind a stack of wooden beer-bottle crates. She held her breath, unsure if she was visible.

"Now look what you've done!" The woman raised her raspy voice over the shrill cry of an infant. She sounded vaguely familiar. Cali peeked around the crate to get a glimpse and recognized her immediately. The woman called herself Seraphina, and she belonged to the Guild. Cali's fist curled.

Seraphina, in her late forties, hid her graying hair beneath a black scarf with a dangle of beads sown randomly around the edges. A loose silk skirt billowed behind her as she moved down the hallway to a restroom a few yards from Cali. She flipped on the light and cranked the sink's faucet to full flow. Cali watched as she scrubbed a spot from her blouse.

The haunting cries of a baby echoed through the corridor, and Seraphina's lip stiffened. She crushed the paper towel into a tight ball and heaved it into the trashcan. "You can cry all night for all I care!"

From the dark hall, Cali exploded into a blind rage. She flew at the startled woman with the knife, shrieking like a banshee. A piece of duct tape that was stuck to the blade fluttered in the air like a silver flag.

Seraphina clutched her chest in shock and stumbled backward into the lavatory.

Cali stopped a few inches short of her and burst into staccato laughter. "I didn't scare ya, did I?"

The woman shrieked a profanity, then smoothed her skirt with nail-bitten fingers. "I knew you were trouble from the start," she sneered. "Brother Raven is going to hear about this."

"Sweet!" Cali grinned. "But who's gonna tell him?"

From the room to the left, the infant's cries began to wane.

"I want my baby." Cali pointed the knife at her captive's face. "And I'm warning you—I got nothing to lose." Cali pushed the woman through the doorway and into the room where the baby was. She pressed the blade against Seraphina's back. "Don't try anything!" Her heart skipped a beat, for she knew that her foe was capable of the stuff of nightmares.

Cali glanced at her surroundings, careful not to take her eyes off her prisoner for long. In the corner beside a radiator stood a portable crib with an infant in it, who alternated between exhausted sobs and little sucking noises.

On the opposite side of the room, a plaid couch sat cockeyed on three legs. Light from a naked bulb spilled across a cheap card table in the center of the room. Tarot cards were spread, ready to read.

"You're a pitiful little creature," Seraphina hissed. "I can feel your fear!"

Cali faltered for a moment. A rush of confusion rippled through her mind. "Shut up!" Her voice squeaked out like a cornered rodent.

Seraphina threw her chin up in laughter. "Shut up?" she mocked.

Cali clenched the knife in her fist so tight that all color drained from her fingers. She opened her mouth and a sound escaped like steam whistling through a tea kettle. She raised the knife and lunged forward.

Seraphina dodged to the right as the blade caught her blouse and ripped the fibers. "Don't hurt me!"

As a child, Cali had pleaded those very words herself. But there had been no mercy then; there would be none now.

"Don't do it," Seraphina cautioned, staring into the girl's eyes as she advanced again.

From the corner of the room, the baby began to softly coo and gurgle. Cali turned her head to look, just for a second; it was a deadly mistake. In the next instant, she felt the cold barrel of a small derringer at the base of her neck.

"Drop the knife," Seraphina ordered. "You empty-headed little fool! You thought this was your kid, didn't you?"

Cali's mind whirled.

"This isn't your baby!"

"I don't believe you! You're a liar!"

"See for yourself." With the pistol in hand, Seraphina motioned toward the crib. "This is a male child. If I remember right, yours was a girl."

"Was?" Cali cried. She hurried to the crib and unfastened the dirty disposable diaper. Seraphina was right. "What have you done with her?"

"She made a nice little offering." A wicked grin spread across Seraphina's face.

"No." The word rose as a deep lament, and Cali sank to the floor, sobbing. "My baby was the only thing I ever did right, and you took her from me."

"You're right about that. She was the only good thing to ever come from the likes of you."

"You won't get away with what you did."

"I beg to differ," Seraphina said smugly. "There is no record of a birth. Why would anyone believe you? Poor thing, you're really quite disturbed."

"Stop it!" Cali put her hands over her ears.

"You're weak and miserable, not even worthy of pity," Seraphina taunted. "Get up!" She kicked the teenager. "Did you hear me?"

Cali climbed to her feet and was ordered, at gunpoint, to walk down the hallway.

She considered running, but Seraphina stopped abruptly

and shoved her inside a utility closet. As the door was bolted and darkness closed in around her, Cali resigned herself to a fearful fate, for those in power were merciless beyond measure.

What does it matter? she thought. For Cali felt dead already.

———

Somewhere over the Midwest, the 737 encountered turbulence and Mavis Berry awoke to the *BING* of the Fasten Seatbelt indicator. She glanced out the window but saw only the reflection of her own face. Night had fallen.

Mavis checked her watch. It was almost 9:00 PM. She must have been asleep for a while.

A young flight attendant walked up the aisle making sure all the passengers were secured, and Mavis called out for her attention. "Can you tell me how long until we get to Kingston?"

"We should be landing in about forty minutes. We have a headwind this evening, so we're about fifteen minutes behind schedule."

"Thank you." Mavis lifted her winter coat from the empty seat beside her and covered her legs with it. From a vinyl travel bag at her feet, she pulled out her page-worn Bible and laid it on her lap.

Mavis had been praying faithfully for Jesse even before his troubles began. In her lifetime, she had shed many tears before her Lord; not once had he failed to encourage her with his Word. "Those who plant in tears will harvest with shouts of joy."

She ran her hands over her fleshy arms and settled back in her seat. Mavis felt a stirring deep within her heart, calling her to action. She opened her Bible to the eighteenth chapter of Proverbs and read, "The human spirit can endure a sick body, but who can bear a crushed spirit?"

Mavis closed the book and folded her hands. "Sweet Jesus, give me wisdom."

As the plane moved across the Montana sky, she awaited the Lord's reply. Thoughts of Jesse's suffering plagued her, but Mavis shook the faithless musings aside and adjusted the little airline pillow. Then, just when she found a comfortable spot, a vision illuminated her spirit, bringing with it the burden to pray. In her mind, Mavis saw Cali. The girl's face was buried in her skinny arms, and she was huddled in a dark and lonely place.

CHAPTER 35

At the Quick Mart on the edge of Hamlin, Theda Mae purchased two cups of coffee and wandered back out to the gas pump where Emma was topping off the tank. "I hope you know how much I appreciate this ride to Kingston. Lunch is on me," the old woman said and climbed into the van.

"I'm excited about our little road trip." Emma climbed behind the wheel and gave her friend a quizzical look. "My curiosity is killing me."

Theda Mae handed her a cup of coffee. "I don't mean to be so mysterious, it's just. . . . There's something I need to know before I say anything."

"I understand," Emma sighed, then changed the subject. "Nice weather for this time of year, don't you think?"

"Yes, dear," Theda Mae said, but her thoughts were elsewhere. She slipped her hand into the pocket of her wool coat and curled her fingers around the item hidden there.

"Isn't that Brock Ellington over there?" Emma pointed to a man hunched over a payphone, the receiver pressed to his mouth. "You'd think our county attorney would have a cell phone." She pulled away from the Quick Mart and merged onto the highway. "Did I tell you that Brock hired a lawyer for Jesse—I mean, for Nathaniel. It's going to take time to get used to the name thing."

"I know what you mean, dear," Theda Mae returned.

Time on the road passed as the women chatted about little joys like the fall colors, which they both agreed had never been more spectacular.

On the last leg of the hour-long trip, Theda Mae dozed off, but awoke with a start when Emma turned on the radio, searching for a Christian station. "Oh, I'm sorry, dear. I meant to be better company!"

"You only snored a little," Emma said with a wink.

The late morning sun fell across the mountains that cradled the city of Kingston. The van rolled into the city and headed straight to the nursing home.

Emma found a parking spot near the front entrance and cocked her head toward her elderly charge. "Ready?"

"I feel it's only fair to let you know why we're here," Theda Mae said as they walked toward the building. "I'm searching for a friend, and I have reason to believe she may be a resident."

"You don't mean Marie Ellington?" Emma said looking into the old woman's eyes.

"Yes, dear." Theda Mae spotted the front desk. "Do you recall the last time we were here a few weeks back? You and Jesse visited with a patient in a wheelchair."

Emma nodded.

"That woman gave Jesse a piece of jewelry."

"That's right—a brooch."

"It was no ordinary piece of jewelry." Theda Mae

pulled the brooch from her pocket. "This oval of turquoise with a corral cross in the middle was custom-made by my late husband. He was an amateur jewelry maker. I helped my husband design this particular piece for a birthday present."

"For Marie Ellington!" Emma's mouth dropped open. "If it was her, then she really did know Jesse."

"We'll soon find out." Theda Mae headed for the receptionist's desk and waited for someone to appear. An aide zipped past carrying a tray of medicine, but she never looked their way.

A nurse rounded the corner and skidded to a stop at the desk. "Can I help you?"

Theda Mae nodded. "I'm looking for a resident by the name of Marie Ellington."

"It doesn't sound familiar. Let me double check." She ran her finger down a list of names on a clipboard. "Sorry. There's no one here by that name." A buzzer sounded and the young nurse excused herself as she disappeared down the hallway.

"One day Marie just vanished—no phone call, not even a card," Theda Mae explained. "It wasn't like her at all. Brock said the death of her son, daughter-in-law, and grandson was just too much for her. He told me that she grew tired of living with the reminders of her loss and decided to start a new life at a retirement community in Florida. Brock refused to tell me where his grandmother had gone." Theda Mae pressed her lips together. "He said Marie was emotionally fragile and that I would only reopen old wounds."

"It does raise some red flags," Emma agreed.

"Especially given the fact that Marie felt certain that her

little grandson, Nat, was alive. We prayed for him often, and she was doing all she could to find him." Theda Mae rubbed her hands together. "I need to speak to the woman who had Marie's brooch. Maybe she can tell us where to find her."

"I don't recall the room number, but it's down this hallway." Emma led the way down the corridor, peeking into rooms as they went. A bald man was snoring on his bed while a radio played at full volume next to him. Another gentleman kicked back in an over-stuffed chair. There was a morbidly obese woman in a housecoat. In the next room, they found the sought-after patient.

The empty wheelchair was the first thing Theda Mae saw. Then her eyes fell upon a bird-thin lady strapped to the steel-framed bed. "Hello?"

The sound of whimpering began softly at first, then rose in pitch as if coming from a cornered animal. The patient looked up with pleading eyes.

Theda Mae's heart simultaneously rejoiced and broke. "Marie—it *is* you! Heaven help us! What have they done to you?" She leaned over the bed and cradled her friend in her arms as tenderly as one would comfort a child.

"What's going on here?"

A male nurse stood in the doorway, filling the frame with his bulk.

As he strode into the room, Theda Mae noted the syringe in his left hand. She tried to remain calm.

"What are you doing?" he scowled. "This patient has an NVP—that's No Visitor Policy."

"You talk about this poor woman as if she were a bottle of aspirin!" Emma blurted.

"What are your names?" he challenged.

When they didn't answer, the nurse set the syringe on the nightstand and picked up the telephone. He glared at the two women as if daring them to leave.

"No harm done," Theda Mae said smoothly. "We were just paying a visit next door and heard this poor dear calling out." *It was, after all, the truth*, she reasoned.

He put the phone down and folded his arms across his chest. "I have to ask you to leave."

The intercom suddenly came to life. "Code Three, stat!" The male nurse bolted for the door before skidding to a brief stop to wag his finger at the women. "I'll be back to check. You'd better not be here!" Then he rounded the corner and was gone.

Marie struggled to sit upright. "Please, help me," she whispered with a voice as weak as a frayed thread. "They were talking. I heard them." She stretched her cadaverous arm toward the bedside table.

"What is it, Marie?" Theda Mae leaned over her friend, who reached for her with claw-like fingers.

"Theda Mae?" She tugged on her wool coat, pulling her closer. "Is it really you?"

"Yes, dear. We're going to try and help you."

Emma peeked out the door. "He's coming back!" she called.

"Father God, send your angels to guard over Marie and keep her in your care, in Jesus's name, we pray." Theda Mae took a handkerchief from her bag and gently wiped saliva from the corner of Marie's mouth. "We'll be back—I promise."

"Party's over," the young man announced. He took Emma by the arm and roughly escorted her out into the hallway. Theda Mae followed.

Silently, the women left the nursing home. Theda Mae felt strangely calm. God was with them, of this, she was sure.

Outside, a brisk western wind blew around a fresh skiff of snow. Emma pulled her collar up around her neck and threw open the car door. "I've never been treated so rudely!" She rubbed her arms, climbed behind the wheel, and waited for Theda Mae to settle. "Did you see the way he grabbed me?"

"If only I had known Marie was this close." Theda Mae's face grew hot with anger. "All these years, Brock Ellington has lied to me! Why?"

"That's a good question," Emma said, pulling away. "But what can we do to help her?"

Theda Mae slid her hands into her coat pockets, seeking a bit of warmth. Her fingers touched something hard and round. She grasped it and pulled it out. "What in the world?" In her hand was a loaded syringe. "Marie must have hid this when I was praying for her!" Theda Mae turned the syringe over in her hand and smiled at Emma. "Would you be willing to spend the night in Kingston?"

"Will we be back in time for Jesse's arraignment?"

"Oh, yes. But first there's a little business to take care of." Theda Mae turned grateful eyes heavenward. "I believe the good Lord has given me a battle plan!"

CHAPTER 36

Jesse checked the time on the wall clock. He had been sitting in the little meeting room at the jail for over ten minutes now watching his lawyer shuffle through stacks of paper. Mr. Platte lingered over the police report, and Jesse's confidence waned.

The lawyer blew a puff of air through his fleshy jowls, touched the tips of his fingers together, and looked at Jesse through beefy eyelids. "Nathaniel, have you thought over my counsel?"

"I'd like to be called 'Jesse' if you don't mind." He stood and walked over to the window of the conference room. Outside, the wind was blowing through the trees. Mottled light flickered on the floor near his feet. "You know how I feel, Mr. Platte. It would be a lie to say that I wasn't in my right mind." Jesse frowned. "And more importantly, I'm innocent!"

The lawyer ran his tongue over his teeth, and it made a smacking sound. "I'm not sure that you fully comprehend the risk of offering a plea of innocence. A jury can be unpredictable at best. Your decision could mean the difference between a prison sentence or a relatively short stay in a mental facility."

Jesse's frustration grew. "I did not touch Cali."

William Platte folded his arms, exposing perspiration stains. "Very well. I'll see what I can put together, but you're not making my job easy." The attorney rose to his feet and slipped the papers into his briefcase. "Give me a call if you change your mind." He stabbed at the door buzzer with his finger and was escorted from the room.

Jesse prayed silently as he was ushered back to his cell. Just before the bars swung shut, the guard pulled a manila envelope from his jacket and said, "Lars Willis left this for you."

Jesse sank to his cot and opened the envelope. It was filled with photocopies of newspaper articles along with a few black-and-white snapshots. He switched on the little wall lamp and studied the first clipping, a photo of a gathering at the mouth of a mineshaft.

The caption read: Baldwin R. Ellington, owner and operator of Ellington, Inc., signs minerals contract with Mina-co.

Jesse studied his father's sharp features, but there was no more familiarity in that face than in a stranger passing on the street. Jesse felt nothing but sadness for this man who had lived and died leaving no trace of sentiment in the heart of his youngest son.

The next clipping added another dimension to Baldwin Ellington. Not only was he the largest employer in the area, he was a civic leader as well. Mr. Ellington served on the city council and was active in several clubs. His name was on the cornerstone of the Masonic Lodge as a charter member.

Jesse searched through the stack for a photo of his mother. He found only one. It had been taken at a chamber of commerce banquet three years before her death.

Growing up in Pennsylvania, Jesse had created a mental image of the woman who bore him, a kind woman with a round face. Once or twice, he'd indulged himself with fantasies of a woman driven by a broken heart to find her missing child.

Jesse fixed his eyes on her frozen features. Mrs. Ellington sat gracefully poised at the head table, gazing up at her husband as he accepted an award. She was a pale beauty, with ringlets of dark hair falling across her slender neck. At first glance, she appeared fragile; and yet, he thought he detected a hardened quality to her eyes.

The next snapshot was a picture of a woman in a cotton shirt and baggy jeans. She had an unruly head of hair with an obvious cowlick. *Just like mine!* The woman stood before a low picket fence corralling a generous flower garden. *I was there at the very moment this photo was taken,* Jesse told himself. Memories trickled through his thoughts. He envisioned the woman proudly holding up a fresh catch of fish or leading him on a nature walk, teaching him about milkweed, grasshoppers, and wild blackberries. Jesse could almost smell the sweet fragrance of wildflowers on her hand as she held his. "Grandma Marie," he heard himself say. Jesse actually remembered her soft lap and her ruddy, sun-kissed skin; most of all, he remembered the way she'd loved him. "My sweet little Nat," she used to say.

Warm tears rolled down his face. They weren't tears of

sadness but of overwhelming joy. He had found something that was lost—something precious. He felt as if God had turned on an attic light and opened a trunk. Memories wove through his senses like the threads of a tapestry.

He recalled walking down Main Street holding Grandma Marie's hand and playing in the city park as she spread out a picnic.

And then, a sinister fog rolled in to steal his joy. A deep sense of foreboding churned in the pit of Jesse's stomach, rolling and building like a deadly tidal wave.

"Even though I walk through the valley of the shadow of death," he whispered, "I will fear no evil, for You are with me."

In the heart of downtown Kingston, Emma hesitated at the door to a tall, slate-gray building. "Are you sure about this?" she asked. The brass plaque beside the revolving door read WKLJ, CBS Affiliate—Kingston's Only Local News Channel.

"There's no doubt in my mind, dear. This is the direction God is leading me." Theda Mae pushed her way through the revolving door one step ahead of Emma. They entered a spacious lobby with marble floors that echoed under the old woman's purposeful steps and led to the information desk. "I need to speak with someone about a story."

The beautiful young receptionist peered at the women from beneath a thick awning of lashes. "Most of the staff is in a meeting," she said politely and poised a pen in her hand.

"But if you give me your name and number. . . ."

"It can't wait!" Theda Mae said firmly. "Someone's life may be in danger."

The girl lowered the pencil and looked blankly at the switchboard as if trying to figure out where to direct this piece of information.

"I need to speak with a reporter." Theda Mae's words, ordinarily soft, carried a ring of authority.

"Of course." The receptionist punched a number on the switchboard and waited. "There's someone here who needs to see a reporter." She listened, pressing the telephone to her ear. "Yes, I realize, but. . . ." The girl's face reddened, and she blurted, "It's a matter of life and death!" Visibly relieved, she looked across the desk at Theda Mae. "If you'll take a seat, a reporter will be right down."

Emma watched the numbers on the elevator. Several people came and went before a man entered the room dressed in a white shirt and black slacks. He wore a tie that hung loosely from his neck. She nudged Theda Mae. "I bet that's our reporter."

The man made eye contact with the receptionist, who nodded toward the women. He lumbered slowly across the room. The stride suggested to Emma that the reporter was more than a little skeptical of their emergency. "Ladies, I'm Jimbo Griles." He held out his large hand and shook theirs as the introductions were made. "What can I do for you?"

Theda Mae got right to the point. "I believe someone is trying to kill a friend of mine."

The man directed the ladies to a small alcove near the window. "All right," he said settling into a seat across from them. "Pardon the cliché, but I'm all ears. Tell me why you think this friend is in danger."

"She's being held against her will at the Kingston Nursing Home," Emma interjected.

Jimbo Griles folded his arms across his chest.

"I know what you're thinking," Theda Mae said, "but this is different. Marie Ellington is being kept under a different name."

The reporter rubbed his face. "Sometimes families take measures to ensure privacy for their loved ones. Maybe she was in the beginning stages of Alzheimer's, or. . . ."

"No," Theda Mae insisted. "Marie knew who I was. She asked me to help her. I believe she was being drugged."

"Why?"

"The whole thing is very complicated, but the short answer to your question is greed," Theda Mae said. "There's a great deal of family money at stake."

Jimbo Griles's eyes met Emma's as if trying to assess her reaction to all this. He stood and looked down at Theda Mae. "I'm very sorry, Mrs. . . ."

"Crabtree."

"We just can't go around accusing nursing homes of misconduct, especially without proof." He flashed a smile. "I'm sure you understand."

Theda Mae launched from her seat. "I'm only asking you to look into it." She placed a loaded hypodermic in his hand. "We interrupted a nurse who was just about to administer this to Marie. If I'm right, this will prove my friend is being drugged, or worse."

"You took this from the nursing home? What if this is

an essential medication? Besides, people in nursing homes are sedated all the time."

"Marie herself slipped this into my pocket. If you could have seen her face—she was terrified." Theda Mae looked into the man's eyes. "Please, I beg you."

Griles's face contorted as though he were engaged in some kind of internal struggled. "Oh, for crying out loud," he rumbled. "My brother-in-law is a chemist. I'll see what he says, but that's as far as I'm going."

Theda Mae leapt for joy and kissed his cheek. "Bless you!" she said and settled down with Emma for a long wait.

—◈—

Lars awoke to the sound of a stray cat yowling for scraps. He reached for Emma, but her side of the bed was empty. Then Lars remembered his wife's phone call. "We need to stay in Kingston tonight," she'd informed him, mumbling something about a test that needed to be run.

"Is Theda Mae okay?" Lars had asked.

"She's fine. We're both fine," Emma said. "Oh, you think. . . . It's not a doctor test. Listen, I've got to go. I'll explain everything tomorrow."

"Impulsive woman," Lars grumbled as he threw back the covers. It was one his wife's little idiosyncrasies that he found attractive—except, of course, when it irritated him. He climbed out of bed and slid his feet into a pair of sheepskin slippers.

The stray cat yowled again, this time joined by another. "Okay, okay, just hang on to your whiskers. Leftovers are coming!" Lars threw on his worn plaid robe and shuffled to the kitchen. He got a pot of coffee brewing and rifled through the fridge for breakfast supplies. To his delight, Lars found the makings for huevos rancheros, a dish that Emma didn't care for. He whisked the eggs like a TV chef and grabbed for the jar of salsa. It slipped through his fingers, hit the edge of the egg pan, and sent the food flying.

Outside, the cats responded to the clatter by crying louder. Raw eggs and salsa were splattered across the floor. Glass shards were everywhere. Lars's face flushed. He clenched his teeth and said, "Lord, this is the day You have made—please help me rejoice and be glad in it!"

Lars scooped up the mess in a dustpan, ran a damp paper towel over the floor, then searched the fridge for a leftover tuna casserole to toss to the cats. "At least someone around here will get to eat." The strays devoured the offerings while Lars looked around for the morning paper. It was nowhere to be found.

"Last straw!" he stomped back inside like a willful child. In his bedroom, Lars dressed quickly, hoping his wife had a good excuse for leaving him alone like this. *Emma is going to get a piece of my mind, that's for sure.* His stomach growled as he checked his wristwatch. Jesse's arraignment wasn't until 11:00 AM. There was still time for a peaceful breakfast downtown.

The Greyhound bus slowed and signaled for a turn. Mavis checked her watch—almost 9:00 AM. Because of a weather delay at the Salt Lake airport, Mavis had been up all night, traveling for more hours than she cared to count. At least the bus ride from Kingston to Hamlin had been pleasant enough for a nap. Mavis felt a rush of excitement. Soon, she could look Jesse in the eye and tell him everything would be all right.

The driver turned onto a winding hillside road, dropped the gears, and snaked slowly upward. Just over the mountain crest, the town of Hamlin came into view. Nestled in the cradle of a rust-colored canyon, the town resembled pictures Mavis had seen of European villages. The houses were adorned with bric-a-brac and colorful trim, like gingerbread homes, cheerful and sweet. *Appearances can be deceiving*, Mavis reminded herself. Righteous indignation rose within Mavis when she thought of Jesse languishing behind bars in Hamlin's jail.

The bus slowed and then turned into a Greyhound station. Mavis looked out the window and spotted a man in a gray uniform sweeping leaves into a neat pile. As the driver approached, the man propped his rake against the building and used hand signals to direct the bus to a parking spot. Air brakes squealed. "Okay, folks," the driver called out. "If Hamlin is your destination, you need to give your luggage ticket to the station manager. For those who are continuing on, you've got an hour for breakfast. We'll be pulling out of here at exactly 10:15 AM."

The bus door sprang open, and the uniformed man stepped forward. "Right on time."

Mavis was the last person to exit the bus and fell in line at the baggage counter behind an elderly man with a marked limp.

"When are you gonna buy some real luggage, Earl?" the station manager asked as he placed a paper grocery bag secured with duct tape on the counter. "Next."

Mavis stepped forward and pointed to the luggage cart. "That small blue suitcase is mine."

The manager snatched the suitcase from the cart and pushed it across the counter to Mavis.

She thanked him. "Is there a phone I could use?"

"Local call?" Mavis nodded. "Right behind the desk."

She pulled a slip of paper from her wallet and dialed. There was no answer. "Should have told someone I was comin'," she muttered.

The manager cocked an eyebrow. "Did you say something?"

"Could you give me directions to the courthouse?"

"I hope you're not going to file some kind of complaint against us," the man said cautiously.

"Oh, heavens, no!"

His face relaxed. "You just go straight up this road for about three-quarters of a mile. Turn left and you will be on Main Street. The courthouse is on the last block."

"Thanks for your help." Mavis started for the door.

"Hey, lady," he called, "you forgot your piece of paper."

She returned to the counter, grateful not to have lost Lars and Emma Willis' number.

The manager grinned sheepishly. "I couldn't help reading the note. If you're lookin' for Lars Willis, he's across the street havin' some breakfast. That's his old green pickup truck." The man folded the paper and handed it back to Mavis.

"Oh, bless you!" she called, then hurried from the building and crossed the street.

The café was buzzing with customers. Mavis scanned the counter and the vinyl-covered booths for an older man. "Lars Willis?" she called. "Is there anyone here by the name of Willis?"

"Right here." Seated at the far end of the lunch counter, a big man with a balding head waved a beefy hand in the air.

"Am I glad to see you!" She bustled across the room. "My name is Mavis Berry."

"Mavis!" Lars bellowed. He stood and embraced her like an old friend. "Emma and I have heard so much about you. We didn't know you were coming."

"I knew Jesse would try and talk me out of it. How is he?"

"Hangin' in there," Lars said. He offered to buy Mavis some breakfast.

"I understand the arraignment is scheduled to begin in about an hour," she said. "Let's try to grab a good seat."

Lars dropped a generous tip on the counter and escorted Mavis out to his truck. "Jesse talks about you all the time. I feel like I've known you forever." He bounced the old pickup over some ruts, rattled around a few corners, and pulled into the courthouse parking lot.

"That was a short drive!"

"Welcome to Hamlin, Montana!" Lars held out his arm and escorted Mavis inside.

The windowless courtroom smelled of dust and lemon oil. There must have been two dozen spectators whispering in their seats. Mavis was glad they had come early.

They found seats in the third row, and Lars saved a couple extra. "My wife and a friend of ours should be here soon."

To the left of the judge's bench, a door opened. An officer escorted Jesse to one of the two rectangular tables in the center of the galley. A hush fell over the room.

Mavis resisted a swell of tears. She leaned toward Lars and whispered, "He looks so pale. And those dark circles under his eyes."

"It's been rough on the boy." Lars craned his neck to look at the door behind them. "I wonder what's keeping my wife?"

"All rise," the bailiff called. "Court is now in session, the Honorable Judge Gerald Webber presiding." The judge made his entrance from an ornately paneled door behind the bench, took his seat, and waited for the people to do the same. He flipped through a stack of legal papers, then studied the defendant. "Nathaniel Ellington."

Jesse rose respectfully. "Yes, your Honor." He ran a hand through his combed hair, giving rise to an unruly cowlick.

"You can remain seated. Are you under the influence of any substance that would impair your ability to understand these proceedings?"

"No, your Honor, I am not."

"In a few minutes, I'm going to ask for your plea. You may plead guilty, not guilty, not guilty by reason of mental illness, or no contest. If you plead not guilty, you have a right to legal representation and to a trial by a jury. To be convicted, all of the jurors must agree. During such trial, you have a right to face witnesses against you and to offer evidence on your own behalf, including your own testimony and the testimony of any witnesses you decide to call. Do you understand?"

"Yes, your Honor."

Judge Webber lifted his glasses and massaged the bridge of his bulbous nose. "If you enter a guilty plea or plead no contest, you give up your right to a jury trial and to offer any evidence of your guilt or innocence. You also give up the presumption of innocence and the right to remain silent, in which case you would be required to testify under oath regarding the events of the crime. Do you understand all that I have said?"

"Yes, your Honor."

The judge's head bobbed and he consulted the papers on his bench. "You have been charged with second-degree sexual assault of a minor, which is a felony that could bring a minimum of four years incarceration." He fingered the collar of his robe. "How do you plead?"

Jesse looked squarely at the magistrate. "Not guilty, your Honor."

"Very well," the judge said. "The court date will be set for November 28 at 9:00 AM. Because you are new to this area, I believe you pose a flight risk. Therefore, bail is denied." He slammed his gavel on the bench. "Court is in recess until 2:00 PM."

"All rise," the bailiff twanged.

Everyone did as instructed. As soon as the judge left the room, a rumbling erupted among the courtroom spectators.

Mavis maneuvered through the crowd of spectators and hurried up to the front. "Jesse," she called.

His eyes widened when he saw her. "Mavis?" Jesse reached over the banister and embraced her. "I can't believe you're here."

"I couldn't stay away," she said softly. "You listen to me. Everything is gonna be all right."

The court officer tugged on Jesse's arm. "I'm sorry you have to see me like this," he said as the officer led him from the courtroom.

Emma had never ridden in a police detective's car before, but she was too nervous to enjoy the ride.

"I don't want to be a pest," Theda Mae said to the officer, "but I'm still trying to process the whole thing. Could you repeat the story once more?"

"They found enough potassium chloride in that hypodermic to kill an elephant," he said somberly. "I'd say your friend was pretty lucky you happened along when you did."

"It was more than luck," Emma said from the backseat.

Theda Mae clutched her handbag. "I just hope we're not too late. What if they moved her, or worse?"

"That's why I'm breaking procedure by bringing you along. I'm counting on your help to identify this patient."

At the nursing home, they pulled up behind a police cruiser. "Wait here," the detective instructed the uniformed officer, then followed the women inside.

A round-faced nurse wagged her fleshy cheeks and said, "May I help you?"

Theda Mae smiled. "I don't recall seeing you here yesterday."

"It was my day off. What can I do for you?"

"I promised one of your residents that I'd look in on her. Poor dear seemed lonely, but I can't remember her name." Theda Mae rubbed her forehead. "Oh, dear, I must be getting forgetful."

"What room was the patient in?"

"My mind is like a sieve these days," Mrs. Crabtree said. "I'm sure that I can show you."

The nurse heaved herself from a padded chair and followed the visitors around the corner.

"This is it—third room on the right." Theda Mae pointed to a closed door.

"You must be mistaken." The nurse said. "This patient is not supposed to have any visitors."

"Oh my, is that so?" Theda Mae's eyes widened.

"Is there a reason for this restriction?" the detective inquired.

"It doesn't really matter anyway," the nurse added. "This patient isn't with us anymore."

Theda Mae gasped, and the detective stepped forward to steady her.

"The woman you're asking about didn't pass away— I'm sorry if that's the way it came out. She's just being transferred to another nursing home, that's all. I saw an orderly wheeling her to the parking garage a few minutes ago."

The detective flashed his badge. "Which way to the parking garage?"

SHADOW *of the* PIPER

The nurse's mouth dropped open, and she pointed to a set of metal doors. They were on their way.

The parking garage was quiet. Aside from a few dozen cars and a small stable of white vans, it was fairly empty. From somewhere in the bowels of the garage a faint whimper was heard. The detective slid his pistol from a holster inside his jacket and motioned for the ladies to stand aside.

With stealth, he approached the stable of white vans, stopping every so often to listen.

Emma and Theda Mae watched from behind a concrete pillar. The cry grew louder, and the detective threw open the back of a van. "Police! Come out with your hands where I can see them!"

"That's him!" Emma said when a man emerged. "He's the one who threw us out yesterday."

"Marie, dear, are you all right?" Theda Mae called out, but there was no answer.

CHAPTER 37

Roxanne did not look up from the ironing board when Rudy walked into the kitchen. She could feel him hovering behind her, almost breathing down her neck. Roxanne wished she'd never told her brother about April and the farm, but it was too late. The damage was done.

"Ironing?" Rudy said, grabbing an apple from a bowl on the counter. "Now, that's something I don't see every day." He took a bite and chewed loudly. Roxanne felt herself stiffen.

"Black shirt," Rudy mused. "Good Halloween color." He took another bite. "Going out tonight?"

She pressed the hot iron to her black cotton blouse and watched a puff of steam rise. "Are you my keeper?" Roxanne placed the iron on its stand and faced her brother. "You're really starting to get on my nerves."

"This apple is mushy!" Rudy lobbed it across the kitchen. It missed the garbage can. "Oops."

"I don't want you checking up on me!"

"What are ya gonna do about it—tell Mom?"

"Just leave me alone!" Roxanne hung her shirt on a

hanger and turned to go.

Rudy grabbed her elbow. "Are you and Logan planning something?"

Roxanne broke free of his grip. "I already told you too much."

Her brother stared at her with worried eyes. "I think you should let the cops deal with helping April."

"You know that's out of the question! At least one cop is involved. For all we know, they're all involved." Roxanne sighed. "Just pretend that I never opened my big mouth!"

"I'll think about it." Rudy walked across the kitchen, picked up the apple core from the floor, and dropped it in the garbage can.

Roxanne left with a nagging suspicion that, as far as her brother was concerned, this issue was far from settled.

⸻

Cali laid her ear against the closet wall. Somewhere behind the drywall, the old brewery's steam pipes groaned and creaked.

She stared into the darkness, her thoughts wandering aimlessly from one bitter memory to the next. Things had become mixed up, like paints that had blended to a repulsive shade of gray. That was how Cali felt inside. Her heart beat faster knowing what Brother Raven's people would do to her. They were probably gathering right now. Terror clutched at her throat, and she cried out, "Jesus—help me!" *Did those words actually come from my mouth?* She remembered the night in Pittsburgh when Jesse had said, "Jesus loves you,

Cali." She had been defiant then, but now, Cali desperately needed to believe. *Could it be true? How could God love someone like me?* All the shamefulness of her past entered her mind. "I'm sorry," she whispered. "Help me change."

Just outside the closet, Cali heard a floorboard creak. *They've come and it will all be over soon.* She felt a remarkable calm, and it surprised her. *No matter what they do,* Cali realized, *this peace will remain.*

The door swung open and the bright beam of a flashlight blinded her. She crouched in the corner like a small animal.

A voice whispered, "Cali! You don't have much time."

The light turned and she saw Ozmand, dressed in a brown ceremonial robe. He lifted his finger to his lips. "Shh!" He looked around. "You've got to be quick. If they find out, I'm dead." In his hand was an extra robe and a hideous Halloween mask. "Put these on."

"I don't understand—you're letting me go?"

He nodded. "I overheard Cy and one of the others talking about you. They'll be here soon." Ozmand pulled the hood over his head. "Look, all I can say is you'd better get as far away as you can."

Cali watched him hurry down the hallway. She couldn't believe it—Ozmand Wright had just risked his own life to save hers!

—◦◦◦—

Roxanne pulled up in the alley behind the school auditorium and gave the car horn a swift blast. A group of kids she knew from class turned and motioned to her. "Hey, Roxie, come on over!"

She rolled down the Volkswagen window. "Maybe later," she said, turning up the car heater. "Have you guys seen Logan?" They shrugged and shook their heads.

Roxanne rolled up the car windows and rubbed her arms.

Under the dim light of a streetlamp, she watched trick-or-treaters scamper down the alley. The beat of a rap band resonated from the back door of the auditorium, and a young couple giggled in the shadows.

Where is he? Roxanne drummed her fingers on the steering wheel.

Suddenly, the door opened and Logan slid into the passenger seat. "Sorry I'm late," he said, trying to catch his breath.

"Where have you been?" Roxanne yelled.

"Never mind. Let's just go."

As she put the car in gear, Roxanne saw Rudy's blue Eldorado cruise past on a side street. "Oh, no."

"What's wrong?"

She pointed. "That was my brother."

"Do you think he saw us?"

"No. Rudy would have stopped. But I'm sure he's trying to find me. We'd better keep a lookout."

By the time the little green Volkswagen turned onto the highway, Roxanne felt satisfied that Rudy hadn't followed them.

"Okay," Logan said, "let's go over the plan. First, we park just around that little hill. We'll take the flat tire out of the trunk and put it on your car. That will give us a reason to go to the farm." He drew in a deep breath and continued. "I'll hide behind the barn while you knock on the door and ask them for help."

"Right," Roxanne agreed. "I'll divert their attention by asking if I can borrow a jack for my flat tire. As soon as they come outside, you slip into the house and get April. I hope they have a jack!" Roxanne gripped the steering wheel and said a prayer out loud.

Logan snorted cynically. "When did you turn into a Jesus fish?"

"Don't you believe?"

"I go to church on Easter and Christmas, just like everybody else."

Roxanne steered down the highway, thinking of her own family's brand of holiday religion—it seemed like pomp and empty ritual now. "I just know that God cares."

"Maybe you should put in a good word for me."

Roxanne's headlights caught highway reflector lights as they streaked down the road, and they traveled in silence the rest of the way. Roxanne stopped just on the other side of the hill, where her car would be hidden from the highway.

Logan jumped out and changed the tire while Roxanne held a flashlight for him. When the jack was lowered, the tire went flat. Logan tossed the jack in some sagebrush.

By the light of the full moon, the teenagers made their way up the dirt road, listening to the sound of gravel and rocks crunch under their shoes.

They topped the hill, and the farmhouse came into full view.

"Get down," Logan whispered, and Roxanne crouched beside him, keeping to the ravine. As they neared, a yard light washed across the grounds. They tried to hug the shadows.

"I'm scared," Roxanne said.

"We're not turning back," Logan replied. He made a dash to the barn.

Roxanne swallowed hard, squared her shoulders, and approached the farmhouse. Standing on the whitewashed porch, her heart thumped furiously. Roxanne tried to calm her nerves and knocked. There were footsteps.

A smile froze on Roxanne's lips as a shadowy form darkened the door's oval window. Blood-red fingernails parted the lace curtain, and a woman's pale, round face appeared.

"What do you want?" the woman called through the glass.

"I have a flat tire!" Roxanne blurted.

The door opened a crack.

"Maybe I could borrow a jack?" Roxanne's voice sounded an octave higher than normal. She cleared her throat.

"Where is your car now?"

"It's on the side of the highway."

The door opened wide and the pixie-haired woman said, "Come on inside, doll. I wouldn't want you to get a chill."

"I took a chance on someone living up this road. Pretty good luck, huh?" Roxanne's cheeks hurt from smiling.

"Well, I should say so!" The woman studied Roxanne. "My husband, Wallace, is out in the barn, but he should be in any minute. I'm sure he'd be glad to change your tire."

Roxanne felt the color drain from her face. *The barn!* "I don't want to be a bother—I mean, if he's busy I can call someone from town." Perspiration sprouted on her palms and she rubbed them on her blue jeans.

"Call me Sylvia, hon." She grabbed a cigarette and tapped it on the coffee table before lighting it. Sylvia took a long pull, then tilted her head back and blew out a steady stream of smoke, watching Roxanne through the haze.

The front door flew open and a tall, greasy man shoved Logan into the living room. "Look who I found snooping around."

Sylvia's eyes sliced from across the room. She took another pull from her cigarette and her lips spread into a grin. "Well, well, well."

Roxanne tried to scream, but no sound came out. She stared at the woman in horror as cigarette smoke curled through her teeth. *Lord,* Roxanne prayed silently, *please help!*

CHAPTER 38

It had been a surprisingly quiet evening at the police station, especially for Halloween. By now all the trick-or-treaters where tucked safely into their beds having sugar dreams. *The night's still young,* Chief Patterson reminded himself. He checked his watch: 9:45 PM. *Not quite the witching hour.*

Art leaned back in his chair until it creaked, wishing that he too could lay his head on a pillow. He could not seem to catch his breath, and mild pain radiated in his chest. If Beatrice were alive, she would make a fuss; but as long as the boys at the station put in overtime, he would do the same. That's the way it had always been.

Chief Patterson leaned forward and tapped the eraser end of a pencil on his desk and watched it spring back up. He stood and stretched his weary body, then ambled out front to see if anything was happening there.

Officer Scott was leaning against the counter, visiting with the dispatcher.

"Any activity?"

"It's pretty quiet, Chief," Scott said. "Except for a little action down at the cafe."

"What kind of action?"

Officer Scott winked. "The boys are interrogating the new waitress."

Chief Patterson smiled. He wondered why Ian Scott never hung out with the other officers. *To each his own,* he figured.

Art poured himself a stout cup of coffee and wandered back to his office. He had just settled down to take his first sip when a commotion erupted in the lobby. The door to his office flew open with a bang. A wild-eyed girl bolted for his desk. Scott grabbed for the teenager, but she slapped the officer with a rubber Halloween mask.

Chief Patterson launched from his chair. "What's going on here?"

The girl jammed her heel into Officer Scott's instep. He yelped and twisted her arm until she fell to her knees in pain. "Sorry, Chief. This crazy kid just blew right past me." Scott slapped handcuffs on the girl—a little too rough in Patterson's estimation.

"Are you sure that's necessary?"

"Better to err on the side of caution," Officer Scott said. "I'll take her down for a blood test and let her cool off in jail for the night."

Art held up a hand. "Wait a minute." The girl looked familiar. "Aren't you the one who filed an assault charge against Jesse Berry?"

"Yeah, so what?"

"You're Cali Black."

The girl rolled her eyes. "Like, I don't know that?"

He motioned her closer. "What are you doing here?"

She glared up at Scott, then turned to Chief Patterson. "I'll tell you if you make this big Jethro go away."

Art nodded. "That will be all for now, Officer Scott."

"But, Chief," Scott protested, "this girl is violent. She's either crazy or on drugs."

Patterson's patience wore thin, and he shot his officer a warning look.

Officer Scott's lips pressed together. "I'll be right outside if you need me." He closed the door behind him.

"Have a seat."

Cali remained standing, shot him a caustic look, and struggled to free her hands now cuffed behind her back.

Art sat on the corner of his desk as the girl glanced around the room. "They probably have this place bugged."

"Who?"

"Take these handcuffs off and I'll tell you."

Art shook his head. "The other way around."

"They brought me here when I was nine months pregnant and then stole my baby." Cali began to pace. "I was drugged, but I remember everything! They tried to tell me that my baby died, but I know she was born alive. I saw her!"

"That should be easy enough to check," Art assured her. "The hospital has records."

"She wasn't born in a hospital!" Cali snapped. "These people aren't stupid!"

Chief Patterson was getting impatient. "Maybe you should tell me who 'these people' are."

Cali looked over her shoulder at the door and leaned close to Art. "The Piper's Guild."

"What, some kind of a club?"

The girl laughed. "A club that likes to party with the Devil."

"Are you talking about satanic ritual?" Art let the realization sink in. "Is there anyone who can confirm this?"

Cali fixed her eyes on Chief Patterson. "Not if they like breathing!"

"You're willing to talk to me."

She shrugged and said, "I'm as good as dead already."

Something in her eyes moved Chief Patterson. "I'll take a statement and we can go over the details."

Another ruckus blew up out front. "Halloween gets worse every year." Art pushed himself from the desk and said, "Excuse me, miss, I'll be right back."

"I need some help!" A teenage boy banged his palms on the front desk. "I've got an emergency!"

Art recognized the kid with whom he'd spoken outside the music store. He put his hand on the young man's shoulder. "Your name is Rudy, if I recall."

"That's right." The boy's face was crimson. "Listen, you've got to do something before my sister gets hurt!"

"Slow down, son. Why don't you start from the beginning?"

"Roxanne and a kid named Logan are trying to rescue her best friend." Rudy drew in a sharp breath and continued. "The people who have April are dangerous. I mean, they've already murdered someone!"

Chief Patterson was stunned. "Are you talking about April Gilbert?"

Rudy nodded. "April is at some farm outside of town."

Chief Patterson took hold of Rudy's arm. "Where is this farmhouse?"

"I only know it's somewhere between here and Kingston."

"Think! I need more details."

"Sounds like the Schatz place to me," Cali said from the doorway. "That April girl is probably pregnant. That's how they get them there. Sylvia and Wallace promise to take care of everything." She laughed cynically.

Art turned back to Rudy. "Do you know if April is pregnant?

"How would I know? Look, shouldn't you be hopping in your cruiser? My sister could be in serious trouble!"

"Remove these handcuffs and I'll show you where the farm is," Cali said.

Chief Patterson snapped his fingers at Officer Scott. "Give me the keys."

"But, Chief. . . ," Ian protested.

"Don't argue, just do it!" Art growled. "And call the rest of the boys—tell them I'll need some backup. Then get a statement from this young man." Chief Patterson grabbed his hat and asked Betty to get an address on the Wallace farm and call the judge for a warrant.

"I want to go with you," Rudy protested as Chief Patterson ushered Cali out the door.

"Sorry, son. I can't justify taking you along, too." Art offered a reassuring nod. "But I'll do everything I can to find your sister."

———

Chief Patterson checked his watch as he turned off the main highway. It was almost 10:30 PM. "You're positive this is the way?" He glanced at Cali.

"Yeah, I'm sure." Cali scowled. "I never thought I would be helping a cop."

Art steered his car up the primitive dirt road, dodging a large rock, and followed the long driveway around a small hillside.

"That's it!" Cali motioned toward a Victorian farmhouse.

Chief Patterson turned off his headlights and backed down the road until the car was hidden from view. He flipped the switch on his radio. "Betty, where's my backup?"

"On the way, Chief."

Art replaced the receiver and settled back to wait.

Cali slouched low in the seat and put her feet on the dashboard. "You know that guy who's in jail because of me?"

Chief Patterson nodded. "Nathaniel Ellington —aka Jesse Berry."

"Well, I lied," she announced. "Jesse didn't do anything."

Incredible, Art thought. Words of reprimand were forming on his lips when he caught sight of headlights in the rearview mirror. It was a police cruiser. Chief Patterson rolled down the window and waved Officer Scott on ahead. He followed close behind.

"Stay in the car," the chief said as the patrol car rolled to a stop in front of the house. Art glanced over and was surprised to find his young passenger huddled on the floorboard of the car. She was trembling. *Poor kid,* he thought as he lumbered up to the porch where Officer Scott was waiting.

Art rang the bell and pounded on the door. There was no response. "Police—open up!" He tried the door, but it was bolted. "Wait here, Ian. I'll go see if we can get in through the back."

"Don't you think we should wait for a search warrant?"

Chief Patterson ignored his officer and walked around the side of the house, sweeping the shadows with his flashlight beam. The back door was locked, but its flimsy frame gave easily against his weight. Inside the small utility porch next to the kitchen, Art called out again. "Police!" All was calm.

Quickly, he made his way through the house and unlocked the front door for Officer Scott. "It looks like nobody's home. Let's poke around." He switched on a ceiling light.

"If you ask me, I think we made a mistake listening to those crazy kids. The whole department could get sued over this."

Chief Patterson raised his hand. "Quiet," he said. "I'm going to have a look upstairs." His intuition paid off. In a small bedroom, April Gilbert lay as pale and still as a dead girl. He shook her, but she was unresponsive.

"Is that the Gilbert girl?" Officer Scott asked from the doorway.

Art nodded. "She's either very sick or drugged. In any case, we need an ambulance."

"Probably why the kid ran away," Officer Scott said. "Drugs."

"We're going to need some fingerprint kits. I want a forensic team to go over this place with a fine-tooth comb." A pain throbbed in Art's shoulder and radiated down his arm. He fished a nitroglycerin tablet from his shirt pocket and slid it under his tongue. "I'll call the station. You keep an eye on the Gilbert kid."

Art fished his cell phone from his jacket.

"Put the phone down, Chief."

Art turned to see the barrel of a pistol aimed right between his eyes.

"I said, put it down," Officer Scott repeated.

Chief Patterson slid it back into his pocket. "What's going on?"

"You couldn't leave well enough alone, could you, Chief?" He removed Art's pistol from his holster.

"I don't understand, Ian. Why?"

"Money," Officer Scott said smugly. "There's a photo lab in the basement."

"What kind of a lab?"

"You are so naive," Ian smirked.

"Pornography?"

"That's right. A lucrative little sideline." Officer Scott shoved Art toward the front door. "Where's the crazy girl?"

"I dropped her off in town," Art lied.

"Start walking out to the barn." Scott jabbed the barrel of his gun into the chief's ribs. "No heroics."

"Think about what you're doing," Chief Patterson reasoned.

"Oh, I've thought about it," Ian said. "You've been despondent for some time, Chief. Everybody knows how lonely you've been since your wife passed away."

"It will never work," Art said.

"And then," Ian continued, "there's your recent ill health."

Chief Patterson stopped just outside the barn and stared at Ian. "You have it all planned out, don't you?"

"It's simple, really," Officer Scott said. "This investigation turned out to be just another rabbit trail, and this was the last straw."

On the other side of the barn door, movement caught Art's eye. *Cali!* He quickly averted his eyes, hoping he hadn't given her away.

With a violent thrust, Ian shoved his boss to the barn floor and raised his pistol. Art thought of Beatrice, and a surreal calm fell over him.

From behind his attacker came a flicker of moonlight on metal, and the head of a shovel slammed down upon the officer.

Ian's eyes rolled back into his head. He dropped to his knees as Cali stepped from the shadows to unleash her fury upon him. The shovel came down once again on the back of his head.

Chief Patterson scrambled to his feet. "That's enough, Cali!" He retrieved the gun that had fallen from Ian's hand.

The girl dropped the shovel and stood by while Chief Patterson handcuffed him to a pole.

"You could have been killed," Art scolded. "Why in the blue blazes did you try something so stupid?"

"I watch a lot of television. Besides, do you think that creep would have given me a ride back to town?"

"You got a point." Patterson checked Ian's pulse. "At least you didn't kill him, but he needs medical care."

"Listen!" Cali cocked her head and made her way to the far side of the barn. "Over here!" Together they brushed straw from an opening on the barn floor and lifted a hatch. Two bodies lay in a musty potato cellar. Art recognized the kids as April Gilbert's friends.

"I think the girl is breathing," Cali said. "Not sure about the boy, though."

Chief Patterson retrieved his cell phone, punched the speed dial, and gave Betty the directions to the crime scene. "Get an ambulance here. Send two! Contact the state police and the sheriff's department and get them out here. Then round up the rest of the boys and have them meet me at the station. We've got some loose ends to tie up in town."

CHAPTER 39

From a hilltop bench, Rudy watched for Chief Patterson's return. A string of cruisers sped through Hamlin, but he saw no sign of the chief or Roxanne.

The town's streetlights cast crystal halos in the frosty air. Rudy shivered. His jaw hurt from clenching against the cold, but he dared not go home for his winter coat. His mother was uncanny. One look at her son's face would tell her that something was wrong. *No—going home is not an option. Not without my little sister.*

Rudy refused to budge until he saw the chief's car. He felt a tumult of emotions: fear, anxiety, helplessness, and, most of all, guilt. *If only I'd told someone sooner, Roxie wouldn't be in this mess.* Rudy had turned the whole thing over and over in his mind until his gut roiled. How could he tell his parents that Roxanne might be in serious trouble, or worse? Rudy smashed his fist onto the bench.

The sound of sirens met his ear. A squad car streaked through town, red lights flashing.

Rudy shot to his feet, watching as the cruiser screeched to a stop in front of the old brewery. Chief Patterson emerged—without Roxanne.

———

Jesse wasn't sure what time it was when he was roused from his slumber. He waited in the dark cell with a curious sense of expectation. Just beyond the walls, he heard muffled voices crackling over the dispatcher's radio. There was a rumble of rushed footsteps and hurried commands. Suddenly, the cell block door flew open, letting in a streak of light. The guard walked briskly toward him. "Mr. Ellington ," he said, tossing an overloaded key ring in the air. "I have orders to release you. We just need you to sign a few papers."

Jesse stood. "You mean I can go, just like that?"

"That's what I said. All charges have been dropped."

A wellspring of joy rose up in Jesse. He raised his hands in the air in thanksgiving. It was true: Nothing was too difficult for God!

———

"Spread out and surround the building," Chief Patterson ordered. For a second, his thoughts drifted back to the strange girl he had just dropped off at the police station. He hoped Cali had been telling the truth when she'd said the Piper's Guild met in the basement of the old brewery.

He had placed Cali in protective custody, but in the rush for justice had forgotten to thank her. It was a small detail, but it bothered Art. He adjusted the gun belt around his waist and motioned another squad car to the rear of the building. The backup team was nearly in place.

An officer with a pair of bolt cutters went to work on the lock. "I can't remember when there's been so much excitement around here," he said, cutting through steel. "I heard the state police are sending a high-powered forensic team out to that farm."

"Yeah, yeah, Bailey," the chief said impatiently. "Can you hurry it up?" Seconds later, they crashed through the rusty door. Patterson lifted his flashlight and peered into the dark building. "Come on."

"You think that's a good idea, Chief? I mean, shouldn't we wait for more back-up?"

Art stepped across the threshold. Broken glass and other debris crunched under his boots.

The officer followed cautiously as they moved through a small maze of rooms to the main brewery building.

Chief Patterson cocked his head to listen. From a large heating duct, sounds rose and fell in waves.

The officer pushed open a door and listened. "Sounds like an army."

Art slipped his pistol from the holster and moved down the stairwell ahead of Bailey. "Strange smell."

At the bottom of the stairs, they stood in front of a set of ornate double doors. The stench that hung in the cold basement air was the least of their worries. On the other side of the doors, the chanting grew to a frenzy.

"It's now or never," Art said, and burst into the room. "Police! Don't anybody move!"

People in brown gowns stood stunned. They were assembled around what appeared to be a makeshift altar constructed from straw bales. Flashlight lanterns with red bulbs burned on either side of the room. Startled eyes stared at him from beneath hoods. A baby lying on a black satin swag in the center of the altar began to fuss.

Just beyond the altar, a man and a woman stood in ornate red and gold robes. Chief Patterson pointed his gun at the couple and said, "Back away from that child."

The man, his face swallowed by the shadows of his deep hood, stepped aside, but the woman stumbled and the hood slipped from her head. "You must be Sylvia Schatz. I assume your husband Wallace is around her somewhere. We have a lot to talk about." Chief Patterson lifted the infant from the altar. "Whose child is this?" No one answered.

"Chief!" Officer Bailey called. "That smell—I just figured out what it is. Sewer gas! You know, methane!"

"This whole building could blow any minute!" Chief Patterson said. "Bailey, come get this kid and take him outside! Everybody evacuate the building!" Art tried to hurry the drones with a frantic wave of his pistol, but they reacted slowly, as if in a stupor. The exodus seemed to take forever.

The smell of gas assaulted Art's nostrils. "Come on, kick it into gear!" His neck began to throb and beads of sweat formed on his brow. A shooting pain traveled through Art's left shoulder and up into his jaw. Chief Patterson leaned against the basement wall, struggling to catch his breath. *Oh no,* Art thought, as the sensation moved past his shoulder and then exploded with crushing force inside his chest.

Rudy was knocked from his feet by the explosion. The ground beneath him rumbled as a blinding fireball burst into the night sky.

He scrambled for footing only to dodge a twisted hunk of metal that spun through the air along with a shower of debris. He ran toward the chaos. Up ahead, he could see smoke and fire and hear muffled screams. Flames shot from the ground as if they were coming from the pit of hell.

"What happened?" he yelled as people scurried past. There was no response—just faces frozen by shock.

The earth trembled beneath Rudy's feet and he lunged to the side as the road crumbled and dropped away. A timber groaned and snapped. Rudy spun around just in time to see the used bookstore collapse amidst a tangled gnarl of electrical wires.

In a matter of minutes, half of Brewery Lane was engulfed in flames.

"Rudy!" someone called.

"Who's there?" he said.

"It's me, Ozmand."

Rudy followed the voice to a pile of rubble and was horrified to see his best friend's charred face. A fire burned nearby, flickering in Ozmand's frightened eyes.

"Hang on, I'm coming." Rudy ran a wide berth around the sinkhole where the road had been. The rest of his best friend's body was buried beneath the rubble. Rudy began to fling away the bricks. There was a heavy beam across Ozmand's chest. Try as he might, Rudy couldn't budge it.

Ozmand grimaced in pain. He whispered something.

Rudy leaned closer.

"Satan's ain't worth dying for." Ozmand gasped for air and then closed his eyes.

"Oz!" Rudy cried, but his best friend was gone.

CHAPTER 40

Jesse couldn't believe his eyes. One minute he had been walking home from jail, praising God for his sudden release, and in the next instant, the earth beneath his feet rumbled and quaked. Fiery debris rained down upon the heart of Hamlin. Jesse's ears still rang as he turned back. Near the center of town, a series of explosions erupted from the ground.

Jesse prayed as he took a shortcut through an alley. Suddenly, a shadow sprang to life and he was slammed against a wall. Jesse strained in the dark to see the face of the attacker. The man was dressed in a colorful robe. "Who are you?"

"My friends call me Brother Raven. You can just all me brother." Brock Ellington slipped the hood from his head and stepped into a wash of moonlight. "It must have been fate that brought you down this alley tonight, Nathaniel. We have some unfinished business."

"What are you talking about?"

Brock's eyes fired with hatred. "You betrayed our family secrets—and traitors must die."

"Secrets?"

Brock stared into Jesse's face. "You really don't remember anything, do you?" He laughed. "You told our grandmother about the rituals, about the children. She threatened to tell our parents about me. I had to do something, so I tampered with their brakes." Brock's face contorted in rage. "You were supposed to be with them the day they crashed into the river."

"It was you!" Jesse blurted. "When I was just a boy, you tried to kill me!" Like Pandora's box opening, the painful memories came screaming back. "You came for me—I could see it in your eyes! I knew!"

Brock seemed pleased by his brother's revelation. "You ran, but I caught up with you down by the train yard."

"And tried to choke me!" Jesse felt sickened. "You wouldn't stop beating me."

"I thought you were dead when I threw you on that train." Brock spoke as if he had tossed out a bag of garbage. "Still, there was a seed of doubt." His eyes narrowed. "But then, Grandmother had a provision written into her will. She named you as her sole beneficiary until your death could be proven. You see my problem don't you, little brother? I had to find you and bring you back here." He smiled. "Cali was the bait."

"What happened to Grandma Marie?"

"That old hag was always shooting off her mouth—insisting that you were alive!" Brock shrugged. "I had her declared incompetent and squirreled her away in a nursing home. Nobody listens to senile old women."

Jesse grabbed Brock's sleeve. "Where is she? Tell me!"

"It's a shame you won't have time to get reacquainted."

Brock raised a dagger. "Neither of you will be around that long."

"Freeze!" In the mouth of the alley, a patrol officer stood gripping his pistol. His face registered recognition. "Drop your weapon! Brock Ellington, you are under arrest for the attempted murder of Marie Ellington."

Without warning, the county attorney wheeled around and lunged at the police officer. A gunshot echoed through the alleyway.

Brock dropped to the ground, his dark eyes riveted on his brother. "This is all your fault." Blood trickled from his mouth.

"You're wrong," Jesse said, feeling a deep sense of sadness as Brock's soul slipped away. "You had a choice, and you chose darkness."

CHAPTER 41

"Logan," his mother whispered. "You have visitors."

The young man opened his eyes in the hospital room and struggled to orient himself.

"Are you up to it?" she asked.

He nodded and pressed the controls to elevate the back of his bed. His mother left his side and walked to the door.

"He's going to be okay," Logan heard her say, "but he needs his rest."

"Don't worry, Mrs. Taylor," Roxanne assured her as she entered the room. "We won't stay long."

Mrs. Taylor's gaze fell upon April's swollen abdomen. "A-Are you. . . ?" she stammered.

April nodded.

"Is it. . . ?"

"Yes, it is my baby," Logan said, and watched the look of disappointment spread across his mother's face. She opened her mouth. "Mom," he cautioned. "We'll talk later."

Abruptly, Mrs. Taylor left the room. April hung her face in shame.

Roxanne reached out and squeezed her friend's hand,

leading her to the bedside. "Logan," Roxanne teased, "you're still as ugly as ever."

Logan smiled. "Brat," he said hoarsely.

"Yeah, and you're still just as rude," Roxanne retorted.

Logan stretched his hand toward April.

She moved to his side. "I'm sorry, Logan. I'm so sorry." She draped herself across his chest and wept.

"Hey, don't cry," Logan said, stroking her silky hair. "I would do it all again for you. I love you, April."

She lifted her head to look at his face.

"Will you marry me?"

"What about your hopes for MIT? What about your future?"

"I want you in my future. Please say yes."

"What are you waiting for?" Roxanne chided. "Can't you see the boy is hopelessly in love?"

April leaned close. "Yes," she whispered in his ear, "I will."

—∿—

The sun was barely yawning when Jesse loaded the suitcases in the back of the Willis' van. He helped Theda Mae and Mavis into the van.

"I've got great news," Emma announced from the front passenger seat. "Peter and Caroline Mathews are adopting a baby. Could be one of those little lambs rescued last weekend."

"Praise the Lord!" Theda Mae clapped her hands together. "It just goes to show—even what the Devil intends for harm can be turned around for God's glory."

"Everybody ready?" Lars glanced in the rearview

mirror as Jesse settled on the bench seat next to Mavis. "Off to the station!" He started the engine and turned in front of Theda Mae's house.

"There's still time to change your mind," Jesse said to Mavis. "My grandmother and I will be moving into the big house soon. There's plenty of room. I'm thinking about inviting Cali to stay there while she gets some counseling."

Mavis shook her head. "Wish I could stay, darlin', but I got my marching orders—Pittsburgh is where my battle is." She squeezed his hand. "Your fight is right here in Hamlin, Montana."

As the Dodge angled down the side-hill road that overlooked Brewery Gulch, Jesse considered Mavis's use of military metaphors. "Could we stop for a minute?"

Lars pulled the van to the side of the road and left it running as Jesse and Mavis climbed out.

They stood for a moment, taking in the view down below. In the misty dawn, they could barely make out the yellow police tape that marked the perimeters of the gulch. What once had been known as the heart of Hamlin was now reduced to a massive, smoldering sinkhole. *It looks like a war zone.* Jesse felt a rush of sorrow for the people who had perished.

"That would be a great place to build a church, don't you think?" Mavis asked as she cinched her wool coat.

Jesse was considering the idea when rays of sunlight broke through the clouds and fanned across the devastation, chasing shadows from the rubble. A scripture came to mind. "The light shines in the darkness, and the darkness can never extinguish it." Jesse smiled. "Yes, I believe it would."

ABOUT THE AUTHOR

From her Grandfather's tales about Buffalo Bill to the mystique of the West, L. P. Hoffman's imagination was primed at an early age. In her transient childhood, she experienced the dark side of Caribbean culture and survived war in the Middle East. As an adult, the author has traveled the world and moved among Washington insiders. L. P. Hoffman values unique perspectives and believes that culturally relevant stories born of experience are the ones best told.

Read more about
L.P. Hoffman

LPHoffman.com

Buy Books

HopeSpringsMedia.com

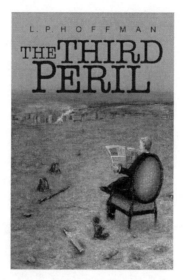

Is Coming!

In 1777, General George Washington experienced a divine visitation at Valley Forge. "Three great perils will come upon this nation." An angelic being describes the Revolutionary War and the Civil War, but warns, "The Third Peril will be the worst." Today, this message is revisited. Six-year-old Connor Hays, son of the Chief Economic Advisor to the President of the United States, insists that an angel told him, "War is coming to America!" But who will believe a child?

The Third Peril
L. P. Hoffman's Next Novel
Is Coming, April 1, 2013
www.TheThirdPeril.com
www.LPHoffman.com
For updates, "Like"
L. P. Hoffman, Author on Facebook

TheThirdPeril.com